ENCORE

ENCORE

ACADEMY OF STARDOM - BOOK FIVE

BEA PAIGE

"It's more important to try to surround yourself with people who can give you a little happiness, because you only pass through this life once. You don't come back for an encore."

~ **Elvis Presley.**

*To the characters within this book
that changed my life, and to my readers
who fell in love with them.
Encore is for you.*

Bea Paige xoxo

PLAYLIST

Like all of the Academy of Stardom books, I recommend that you listen to the suggested tracks for the dance scenes in particular.

At the start of each chapter there is a song title, in the ebook version you can click on this to take you to the track on my Spotify playlist.

Please note, that not every chapter has a dance scene, but every chapter has a song.

For those of you reading this in paperback, you can find the playlist for Encore listed on Spotify under Bea Paige author.

See you Again

PEN

WE NEARLY DIDN'T GET a chance to love again, the Breakers and I.

Circumstance, misunderstanding, distrust, and a past filled with the kind of pain that cut so deep, almost ruined everything. But in the end we found our way back to each other through the one thing each of our souls craved.

Dance.

Dance gave us a way to communicate when we couldn't find the words to speak.

Dance allowed us to express our deepest emotions and lay them bare.

Dance revealed our true selves, the person we hid from the world.

Dance brought us together.

It tore us apart.

It healed the rift between us once and for all.

And dance has given us a life we've always longed for. A life where five kids' dreams to belong have become a reality.

Through dance we found friendship.

We found a lasting bond so deep that no one and nothing has been able to break it. We found a home in each other's arms, and outside of our tight-knit fivesome we found a group of incredibly loyal, and fiercely protective men and women who'd back us up, no questions asked.

We found our true family.

Has it been an easy road to get here? No, not at all.

But it's a path I would travel all over again in this life, and the next, so long as I get to live it with the men I love. With Zayn, the boy who stepped onto that rundown playground when we were kids and saw a kindred spirit, unknowingly changing the course of our lives forever with his curiosity and kindness. With York, the boy who stood in the rain and held out the hand of friendship, waiting patiently for me to find the courage to entwine my fingers with his. With Xeno who fought so hard against his demons to keep loving me, *us*, despite all odds. With Dax who wrapped me up in his protection and kept me safe in his arms, sacrificing a piece of himself when he took a bullet for me years later.

God, that was the single worst experience of my life.

It haunts me still.

But he survived. *We* survived.

It's been five years since Dax was shot by my bastard brother. Five years since we opened Twisted Bullet, named after the slug that was pulled out of the mangled remains of his right forearm. Almost five years since we've *performed* together, like the old days.

It's been too long.

Now that's about to change, because irregardless of the pressures of everyday life, our souls will always be entwined through dance, the beats of our love will always remain a staccato rhythm across a scuffed and well worn studio floor.

We may have performed our finale on the stage of Stardom Academy in front of friends and family five years ago, but that was never going to be our last dance.

There was always going to be an encore…

DAX

"MOTHERFUCKER!" I shout, slamming my balled up fist against my desk, causing the double shot of bourbon to spill over the edge of my glass.

Kid's head snaps up as she looks at me from her desk situated on the other side of our shared office. Tonight, Kid and I are in charge of our club, Twisted Bullet, whilst Xeno meets with a supplier and Zayn takes care of York whilst he's recovering from the flu.

"Hey, what's up?" Kid asks, cocking her head to the side as

she closes her laptop.

I know she's concerned about me, and I love her for it, of course I fucking do. Still hurts my pride though. I'm off my game lately. The phantom pain from losing my right hand and forearm five fucking years ago still causes me issues even after all this time. It's doing my head in.

"Is it your arm?" she asks, knowing me only too well.

I heave out a sigh, rubbing at the stump. "It hurts."

She frowns, pushing back her chair as she circles her desk. "How bad?"

"Bad enough for me to lose my cool in front of you," I mutter.

"Why didn't you say something?" she asks as she strides over to me. I scoot backwards on my chair so that she can perch on the desk between my legs.

"Didn't want to bother you," I admit as she reaches for me, tipping my chin up. She shakes her head, her long brown hair rippling with the movement.

"We've been over this before, Dax. I love you. *We* love you. Don't keep your pain from us. I know you think you need to protect us, but you don't."

Scraping a hand over my face, I shrug. "Old habits die hard, Kid."

"I know, but no more hiding this from us. *Please?*"

"I don't even know why it still hurts," I say, worried that something else is going on. I know that phantom pain can be felt for a couple years after an amputation, but this long? "It's been fucking years, Kid. I'm over it."

"Then we'll get you an appointment with the doctor. He

can do some tests. Check you over, make sure there isn't anything going on that we need to be concerned about."

"Yeah, maybe," I agree reluctantly.

"Good," she replies, her thumb rubbing over my stubbled cheek as she regards me with a smile that still has the capacity to bring me to my knees in the best way possible. "I know what you need."

"What, you spread across my desk with my head between your legs?" I ask, the phantom pain fading a little at the thought of my tongue sliding through her pussy. Fuck, I'll never get enough of fucking her with my tongue... And my fingers... And let's not forget my dick. "Yeah... that's exactly what we both need." I conclude.

"Maybe later," she laughs, leaning over and pressing her lips against my mouth in a soft kiss.

I can't help it, I slide my arm around her back and pull her onto my lap, kissing her thoroughly, my tongue swooping into her mouth greedily.

"You don't get to tell me later, Kid," I state between kisses, enjoying the way she wiggles in my lap, feeling the heat of her pressed against my hard ridge.

"Oh no?" she questions, biting gently on my bottom lip and sending a rush of blood to my dick in response.

"Not when it's our night to have some alone time, even if that alone time is sitting in our office in the back of the club holding down the fort because York has the man-flu."

"Hey, it's not as if he can help it. He's genuinely unwell," she scolds.

"Which means he's going to have all your attention when

we get home. Am I right?"

"I'm just going to check in on him, but Zayn has already said that he'll make sure he's well looked after. This is our night, Dax. It's precious to me, to all of us. Barring any emergencies, it's the one thing we promised we'd always stick to. It's just me and you tonight, okay?"

"So let me show you just how much I love you, yeah?" I insist, not ready to give up just yet.

"I *know* how much you love me," she counters, brushing the tip of her nose against the bridge of mine, her peppermint breath fluttering over my skin.

"Then sit your peachy arse on my desk and let me taste you," I mutter against her plump lips, grasping the back of her head and kissing her harder. Before our kiss can evolve, she rests her hands on my shoulders and pulls back with a laugh.

"As tempting as that sounds... No."

"No?! Are you trying to break my heart? Or is it just my dick that you've got it in for?"

"Is it really that bad?" she snorts, shifting off my lap and dropping her gaze to my crotch. She smothers a smile at the very obvious boner in my pants.

"You know Beast told me that his dick nearly fell off from blue balls when Grim couldn't have sex with him for six weeks after Iris was born," I explain, adjusting my cock as she lets out a giggle. "The guy jerked off about five times a day and he still wasn't satisfied."

"I'm not surprised it almost fell off, jerking off that many times," Kid retorts with a burst of laughter. "Also, eww. I do *not* need that image in my head."

"I thought you liked Beast, all muscles and a body covered in tatts. He's every girl's wet dream, or so he likes to remind me despite knowing that there's no one else but Grim for him."

"I do like Beast, but not like that. Besides, I have all the muscles and tatts I need with you. *You're* my wet dream."

"And the others?" I tease, "Don't tell me you've gone off them. They'd be heartbroken. Me on the other hand–"

She shoves my shoulder. "That goes without saying."

"That you've gone off them?" I ask, enjoying our light-hearted banter.

"That they're my wet dream too, arsehole."

"Fine, fine. *We're* your wet dream. Speaking of which..." I drop my gaze back to my dick, which is straining impressively against my black slacks, "All this talk of wet dreams is making me harder. I'm afraid it's going to drop off if this issue isn't dealt with soon."

"You're dick is *not* going to drop off."

"It might."

"Stop being so dramatic."

"Tell that to my cock. He's either going to explode with frustration or hang limp with disappointment."

Kid rolls her eyes, then offers me her hand, which of course I take. Standing, I haul her close as she presses her body against mine and slides her free hand over my dick, giving it a gentle squeeze.

"Tell your cock that I have plans for us later that involve him coming in my mouth and again in my pussy, but for now I want to dance."

"You want to do what?" I ask, my head a little scrambled from her sinful words.

"I want to dance. With you," she enunciates, stepping back and traversing around the table, leaving both me and my cock bereft.

"Out there?" I ask, pointing to the door where our resident DJ is currently playing 90's hip-hop for our die-hard patrons. Sunday night is members night only, and it's heaving out there.

"Where else?" she asks, pulling open the door, daring me to deny her.

"It's been a while since we danced in front of people."

"Are you saying that you *don't* want to dance with me?"

"Absolutely-fucking-not," I reply, striding over to her and taking her hand before tugging her into the hallway beyond. "It's been too long."

"That's what I thought," she says, grinning widely.

"AND THERE'S me thinking you actually wanted to dance with me, when all you wanted was to battle," I say under my breath as DJ Foxy calls for space on the dance floor so we can go head-to-head.

Opposite me Kid shrugs, her black tank top tight over her pert breasts. She'd discarded her sheer black shirt behind the bar after knocking back a shot of vodka for dutch courage. Not that she needs it. Kid can still dance. We all can, it's just that we're a little... *rusty*.

Spending the last five years putting all our time and energy into the club and our other businesses has left little time for dance, and whilst we're all happy about the success of Twisted Bullet, there's no denying the fact that we're all suffering from the long arse days, with little respite to indulge in what all our hearts yearn for aside from each other.

"You needed a reminder," Kid says, striding onto the dance floor, her brow lifted in challenge as she spins around to face me.

"A reminder of what exactly?" I ask, as memories of that night when I faced Kid on the dance floor of Rocks come flooding back.

At that point, we hadn't seen each other for three years and the sight of her had taken my breath away. I was angry, fucking mad as hell at her, and hurt, so fucking hurt, but underneath all of that, I'd wanted her so badly I could barely breath. Battling her at Rocks had literally forced the oxygen back into my lungs, and despite how I'd acted towards her that night, it was the first time I'd felt at home in a long, *long* time. Though I wouldn't admit that to myself until months later.

She throws her shoulders back and narrows her eyes at me. "This is a reminder of the power you *still* have."

"I don't need a therapy lesson, Kid."

"This isn't a therapy lesson, this is a necessity. For me, as much as it is for you," she replies earnestly before nodding at the DJ.

Realising what's about to happen, a ripple of excitement rushes through the crowd as the opening beat to *In Da Club* by 50 Cent begins to play. In the first few months after opening, we danced regularly at the club, but as things got busier and our businesses grew we had less and less time to indulge. Tonight the members are getting a treat.

"This song," I begin, knowing the significance and loving her for it.

"I know," she whispers right before she flings her arms wide and steps into my space, challenging me, just like the good ol' days.

"Damn," I groan, seeing the fire in her eyes, the fucking *love*.

It makes me want her even more, if that's even possible. If it weren't for the couple hundred or so people surrounding the dance floor I'd fuck her right here and now. As it is, Kid makes her next move, a move that's burned into my memory like a tattoo on my very soul. I watch her in awe as she twists her arms up and around her head to the beat of the music, reenacting the very same steps from years ago when her anger and pain was as powerful as her love is now.

All I can do is watch. My love for her like a rolling storm.

It's powerful, this love. Electric.

It feeds my soul as much as dance does. It has always fueled me.

When I was a kid, dance kept me sane when my poor fucking excuse of a father thought the best type of parenting happened at the end of a brutal fist. It allowed me to deal with all the anger and hopelessness. Then Kid walked into our lives and she became the centre of our universe, the glue that held me and the boys together.

Fuck, and when we danced together, something special happened. Something *magical*.

We became the best of ourselves with her.

In a way, dancing with Kid *was* therapy.

I've missed this.

I've missed this feeling of dancing with my brothers, with the love of my life.

And I realise that I need it to happen more often. That we've allowed the monotony of real life to dictate our lives. It's time for that to change.

"What are you waiting for?" she asks, looking up at me from beneath her dark lashes.

My heart thumps to the beat of the song, and Kid lifts her chin defiantly, laying down a challenge.

One I refuse to back down from.

If she wants a battle, I'm going to give her one.

Then I'm going to take her home and fuck her until neither of us can speak.

Taking a page out of her book, I reach behind my head, grip the collar of my t-shirt and rip it off, leaving me bare-chested. Her eyes flare with heat as she bops to the beat, finding her rhythm.

"Get ready to lose, Kid," I say, stepping to my right, my gaze locking with hers as we circle each other, trying to psyche each other out as is customary, and expected, in a dance battle like this.

"What happens if I win?" she goads, popping and locking her body in a series of moves that has the crowd calling out her name and the DJ goading me.

"Looks like our queen has thrown down the gauntlet!" he roars, stoking the energy in the club, getting the crowd excited.

"What's the matter *Teardrop Dax*, scared you'll lose?" he adds, using my old nickname to bait me further. Arsehole. Just as well I like the fucker, or I'd knock him out for that.

"Are you scared?" Kid asks right before she performs a series of hip-hop steps to the music so smoothly that you'd assume she'd spent hours in the studio practising to make it look so seamless. Her gift is outstanding, and she's always been the best of us. The only reason I won the battle the last time we danced to this song was because she was taken by surprise.

This time, there's no way I'm going to win.

Not that it matters.

Because this isn't about winning. It's so much more than that.

Focussing on Kid, I let my body just react to the music, the beat dictating how I move my body. I don't worry about the fact I can't perform all the moves I used to do because of my partial amputation, I just take my cues from her and forget about my injury.

Kid keeps dancing, her movements raw, her energy like a bolt of lightning to my heart.

I'm helpless against it. Hopeless when it comes to this woman and the way she lights me up from the inside out. When she transitions from hip-hop to contemporary in one smooth kick of her leg, my feet move of their own accord.

I have no choice but to dance.

No, fuck that. I *want* to dance.

The crowd, sensing something special is happening, cheers louder, fuelling my need to just let the fuck go. It's time I join in on the fun.

Crossing my feet, I drop and spin, the force of the movement making the crowd blur as I turn then push back upwards, transitioning into a one-handed backflip.

Muscles that haven't been used for a while scream at me but I ignore them, determined to keep going, to immerse myself in the music, the beat, the energy, the freedom dancing gives me, the fucking joy.

I'm unstoppable, and as a result, the energy in the club builds, making the hairs on my arms stand on end. That buzz I used to get when I was a kid about to battle against another crew comes rushing back in, firing up my blood. Triggering this need to just move my body.

The crowd goes nuts. I don't hold back.

I dance into Kid's space, imitating her moves, urging her on, battling her. The grin on my face spreads as wide as hers as we dance with pure fucking joy.

I don't think about the pain in my arm.

I don't think about the fact I'm rusty as fuck and to the more discerning eye, have messed up a few moves. I keep dancing.

In return, Kid taunts me with one impressive move after another. She battles me with every last scrap of energy, urging me to dig deep, to forget about what I can't do, and forcing me to just dance.

I match her skill as best I can, and with every step I feel more like me.

The old me.

The me before I lost my arm to her cunt brother.

I've put on a brave face. I've worked through my demons as

best I can, and have lived happily with my woman and my brothers. I've been deliriously happy.

And yet, deep down, losing part of my arm has fucked with my head.

I know that.

I've tried my best to keep that part of me hidden.

But you can only push down your feelings for so long before they seek a way out.

Kid knows that, and she's giving me an outlet.

And despite joking about this being a form of therapy.

It fucking is.

It always has been.

For the both of us.

With one last attempt to win this battle, I run towards Kid, drop to my knees and slide across the floor, ending up at her feet. She looks down at me, her own skin covered in a sheen of sweat grinning as the crowd cheers and claps, their feet stamping as DJ Foxy announces her the winner.

"You were amazing," she says, dropping to her knees before me, clutching my face in her hands.

"I fucking love you," I respond, and with my chest heaving, sweat trickling over my skin, I slide my fingers into her hair and pull her towards me, kissing her with as much fire and passion as she's stoked within me tonight.

The crowd disappears as I fuck my beautiful girl's mouth with my tongue.

They no longer exist. It's only her. Just like it's always been. Just like it will always be.

We kiss and kiss and kiss, her hands everywhere, my cock

fucking straining against my zipper. It doesn't give a fuck we're giving another kind of show to the audience. It wants what it wants.

It's only when I feel a tap on my shoulder that I remember where we are. Reluctantly, I pull back and look up into the smiling eyes of my best mate.

"Xeno," I grin.

"You two need to deal with that," he says, looking pointedly at my boner.

Kid laughs, taking my hand as we climb to our feet. She steps in front of me, hiding my erection from the crowd who've started to pile back onto the dance floor as the DJ plays another 90's hit. Some of the patrons slap me on the back as they walk by, others wish Kid congratulations, and the rest just give us both a smile or a nod of acknowledgement.

"We've still got a few hours to go," I remind Xeno, as he sandwiches Kid between us both and presses a soft kiss against her lips in greeting. She lets out a satisfied moan, a look of devotion passing between them as he pulls away.

"Everything go okay with the supplier?" she asks him.

"All good. I'll fill you in tomorrow," Xeno replies, reaching up and squeezing my shoulder. "I'll see the night out. Go home. Make love to our girl, I'll see you both in the morning," he replies.

"You sure?" I ask, meeting his gaze and seeing the pride in them.

"You were fucking amazing, both of you. Now go home and celebrate."

We don't need to be told twice.

"HOW'S YORK DOING?" I ask as Dax slips into the bedroom forty-five minutes later.

"He'll live to see the morning," he replies with a smirk.

"Dax!" I scold, drying my freshly washed hair with a towel, another tied around my body. "Seriously, how's he doing?"

"Temperature's eased off, so has his cough. He'll be alright after another day in bed. Stop worrying. Zayn's on nurse duty."

"I should really go see how he is, and say hi to Zayn. I haven't seen either of them all day."

"You're not stepping out of this bedroom. You heard what Xeno said, and he's the boss."

"I thought *I* was the boss?" I retort, as I reach for the towel wrapped around my chest and pull it free. It drops to the floor, and cool air rushes over my too hot skin. Dax's mouth pops open and he ogles me for a good minute.

"Damn, Kid," Dax swears, stepping towards me, his gaze sliding over every inch of my naked skin. "You get more perfect every fucking day."

"Why thank you, you're not so bad either," I reply, licking my lips as I place my hand on his chest and ogle him right back. "You were saying something about me *not* being the boss...?"

"At the club, sure, you're the boss," he concedes with a cheeky smile, "But in the bedroom? I'm your *Daddy*, Kid."

"Daddy? Kind of kinky, don't you think?" I tease, even though him talking about being my Daddy in the bedroom, turns me the fuck on.

"Are you saying I can't do kinky?" he asks, hauling me closer.

"I'm down for kinky."

"Good, because you're my woman, and I'm your man... correction *Daddy*, and I want to take care of your needs."

"So what does that make Zayn, York and Xeno? Are they my Daddies too?"

Dax pulls a face. "York is too much of a kid at heart, Zayn ain't into *that* kind of kinky-fuckery, and Xeno..."

"Is definitely a Daddy," I finish for him, watching in amusement as Dax considers Xeno's 'Daddy' status. When he realises that he's got competition in that department he shakes his head.

"Okay, okay, he totally passes the Daddy vibe. But you snooze, you lose. I've claimed that title and he can fight me for it."

"I reckon you could share. It's not like you haven't before," I remind him.

"True enough, but tonight he ain't here. I am. So that makes me your Daddy for the next..." he looks at his wristwatch. "Four hours, give or take."

"Four hours?" I *do* need to get some sleep, I remind him.

"You will, after I've fucked you unconscious."

"Is that a promise...?" I chuckle as his fingers dig into my arse, and he presses his lips to mine.

He's so tall that I have to stand on my tiptoes to meet his hungry kiss. Anchoring myself to him, I wrap my arms around his neck, pressing my body against his as he parts my lips with his tongue and kisses the love right into me. There's so much love. I feel it right down to my toes, in the marrow of my bones. Dax loves me with his kisses and I love him all the way back.

"I will never get over how beautiful you are, Kid," he says after a minute or two of bruising, toe-curling, clit-throbbing kisses.

"You're not too bad yourself," I reply, reaching for the hem of his t-shirt, wanting it off. Needing to be skin-to-skin. He lets me remove it, sighing when my palms press against his pecs and I plant a kiss right on top of the angel tattoo in the centre of his chest. "Though I do have to admit, my muscles are screaming at me for some of those moves I pulled off tonight. Despite your sweet words, I'm a little out of shape."

"Ditto, Kid. Ditto," he replies, his hand sliding up my back and around my front where the heel of his palm presses against my collar bone and his fingers dig into my too tight shoulder muscles.

"Ah, that feels so good," I moan, loving the firmness of his touch, and how his hand feels so warm and certain against my skin. For a couple of minutes, he indulges me, massaging my shoulders, and I can't help but melt under his touch.

"As much as I want to hear those breathy little moans you make when I massage your body. I need to wash up. Go relax on the bed. I'm going to hop in the shower quickly," Dax says, sliding his hand down my arm, his fingers twining with mine, giving them a brief squeeze.

"Don't be too long," I say, watching him strip off his slacks, kicking his feet free from the material. Biting on my lip, I feel a rush of love squeeze my heart as he strides past me.

"Two minutes, max," he promises, stopping at the door of my ensuite bathroom, and turning to face me.

"No more," I add, my body zinging with desire and anticipation as he pulls his boxers down over his hips, his cock springing free.

"Like what you see?" he asks, his dick hardening at my leisurely perusal.

"Damn, *Daddy*," I respond, chuckling softly as he reaches for his dick, gripping the thick base.

"Two minutes," he reiterates, mostly to his cock that's pointing directly at me.

"I'll be timing you, because if you're not out in the promised time, I might have to deal with the ache in my pussy myself," I say, climbing onto the bed and settling against the headboard. I spread my legs just enough to give him a tantalising view of the place he loves to feast on the most.

"You wouldn't dare," he warns, pumping his dick a couple of times before reaching up to grip the door frame, showing me every inch of his beautiful body. "Take a good look, Kid. See how hard I am for you. How my dick leaks, wanting you so bad. Don't deny what belongs to me. *I* want to be responsible for all those breathy moans that turn me on so much."

"When you put it like that," I whisper, my tongue peeking out to wet my lips as I take my fill of him.

He knows I get as much pleasure out of looking at him as he does me. On many occasions, before making love, we've spent long minutes just staring at each other, appreciating what we see. It's kind of our thing. Something that belongs solely to us.

After his amputation, it became something we just did. I knew instinctively, despite how he used to try and reassure me otherwise, that he felt less than. That somehow by losing part of his arm, he became less of a man in my eyes.

The opposite couldn't be more true.

I've never seen what he's lost, I've only ever seen the masculine beauty of him. His broad shoulders, wide chest and strong thighs. His veiny forearm and hand, the strength of his biceps, his perfect dick that stands firm and virile from the trimmed thatch of hair at the base. I will never tire of staring at the perfect artwork that covers every inch of his skin, or react any differently to the way his presence makes me feel so *safe*. I love all of him, including his huge size twelve feet and the stump of his arm that reminds me every day just what kind of man he is.

A brave man.

A protective man.

A man who's willing to die for the woman he loves.

It's why this whole Daddy vibe works for Dax. He may only be a year or so older than me, but he has always been fiercely protective of the people he loves, a natural leader. He's compassionate, emotionally available, loving in a way that makes me always feel so safe. It suits him. Plus he's sexy as fuck, and domineering in a way that makes me want to surrender to him.

"Kid, don't make me come over there," he warns.

"What's going to happen if I do?" I tease, my fingers trailing slowly over my chest and the slight curve of my tummy, towards the thin strip of neatly trimmed hair covering my pussy. Teasing him is my second favourite past time next to perusing his body. I like being a brat, especially if it gets him going.

"I'll have to put you over my knee and spank your arse for disobeying me."

"Is that so?" My cheeks heat.

"You better believe it, Kid," he replies with a smirk, before twisting on his heel and giving me the perfect view of my favourite part of his body aside from his beautiful face, *his arse.*

"Okay, Daddy," I agree, chewing on my lip to hide my smile.

"And don't go falling asleep before I'm washed up. I want the pleasure of fulfilling my promise and making you come so hard you pass out," he throws over his shoulder, before moving out of sight.

I can't help it, I laugh. A feeling of happiness overtaking me.

How did I get so lucky? To be loved by one incredibly kind, selfless, thoughtful, protective, sexy-as-fuck man who can dance, is every woman's dream come true. But to be loved by four?

I don't care what anyone says, loving four men doesn't mean that I can only give them a quarter of my heart each, it means I have four times the capacity to love and be loved in return.

There is no limit to how I feel for my men, no ceiling.

It's endless, this love.

Eternal.

Forever and Always.

And today taught me a valuable lesson, that despite living a beautiful life with the men I love, despite building a business from the ground up alongside them, we have to make room for our other love, *dance*. It's as important to us as we are to each other. Today proved just how much, and with that an idea begins to form.

"Penny for your thoughts?" a familiar voice asks from the doorway.

It's Zayn.

The first thing I notice are the bags under his eyes, the second how he swipes a hand over his face as though trying to wipe away his obvious exhaustion.

"Hey, is something wrong?" I ask, shifting upwards, not in the least bit embarrassed by my nakedness. We've all spent so much time together naked as couples, as threesomes, as four-somes and fivesomes, that I'm comfortable in my own skin as much as they are.

"York's fine, don't panic. I just wanted to say goodnight. I've missed you today," he explains, giving me a heated look as he takes in my nakedness. I let out a sigh of relief but make a mental note to chat to him in the morning about his insomnia. We've all noticed how he's been surviving on only a few hours of sleep a night. He needs to rest, refuel. That seems to be a common theme and only adds to my resolve to make changes for us all, for the better.

"Where's Dax?" he asks.

"About to make love to our woman," he says, stepping out of the bathroom, completely naked, water sliding over his body as he rubs a towel over his chest.

"Shit, man. Sorry. I just wanted to say goodnight. I'll go."

"Don't be stupid. Say goodnight to Kid, she's been missing you today too," Dax says graciously.

"You have?" Zayn asks, striding towards me, melting my heart with his sweet, chipped-tooth smile. A couple years ago he made the suggestion of getting his teeth fixed, but decided not to when I said how much I'd miss his smile. It's a part of him that I love, an imperfection that's entirely perfect to me.

"Of course I have," I reply, my still damp hair sticking to my breasts as I shuffle towards the edge of the bed and sit up on my knees, wrapping my arms around him as he hugs me back. "You look a little tired. You okay?"

"I'm good," he replies quickly, changing the subject. "I heard about the battle you had with Dax at the club. I'm sorry I missed it. Did you whip his sorry arse?"

"Of course she did. This is Kid we're talking about," Dax says, dropping onto the edge of the bed as relaxed in his nakedness as I am. "How did you find out?"

"Xeno. He called me and said that you brought the house down tonight. Punters were going wild apparently."

Dax chuckles as I ease out of Zayn's hold. "Can't say I noticed, too busy getting my arse whooped by Pen."

"I bet. So how are you going to repay her?" Zayn asks, his dark eyes lighting with mischief and a heavy dose of lust.

"He's going to fuck me unconscious apparently. Aren't you, *Daddy*?" I ask, my cheeks blushing furiously as Zayn snorts with laughter.

"Now this I need to see," he says, running a hand over his stubbled cheek.

"Yeah, you're in for a treat," Dax says, reaching for me even though he's directing his attention to Zayn.

"You mean I can stay?" Zayn asks, looking between us as I take Dax's proffered hand, anticipation climbing up my spine.

It's not the first time Zayn has watched me make love to Dax, and it won't be the last. But each time it's still a huge turn on. There's something about one of my loves fucking me whilst the other gets off that sets my pulse racing and my pussy fluttering. They know that as much as I do.

"That's why you sought us out, didn't you?"

He laughs, holding his hands up. "Caught red-handed. You can tell me to fuck off. It's your night together. I won't be offended."

Dax raises a brow at him. "You want to watch me fuck our girl, I ain't gonna deny you. Take a seat."

Zayn grins. "Okay, where do you want me... *Daddy*?"

Laughter bursts out of my mouth, and Dax shoots him a look. "Tell you what, you can help me with something."

"Alright, what do you need?"

"An extra pair of hands," Dax replies, flicking his gaze from Zayn back to me. "You said you were feeling sore, let us give you a massage. Lie face down on the mattress. Put your head at the foot of the bed."

"It's *me* who should be giving *you* a massage," I point out, my gaze flicking to his stump. He hasn't complained of any pain since we left the club, but that doesn't mean he isn't hurting still.

"I'm good."

"Dax..." I begin, but he shakes his head.

"Be a good girl, and lie down on the bed," he orders gruffly.

"What if I don't want to be a *good girl*?" I ask, testing the waters, seeing how far he'll go with this roleplay.

"Like I mentioned earlier, I'll have no choice but to put you over my knee and spank your arse until it's as pink as your pussy for disobeying me. Then I'll make you take my cock in your mouth until you're choking on all those words denying me what's mine."

"Fuck, that shit's kinda hot," Zayn says, meeting my gaze with a surprised laugh.

"You're telling me," I reply, my pussy clenching with anticipation as I climb onto the bed and roll onto my stomach, making myself comfortable as I do exactly what Dax asks.

"That's it, Kid, let me reward you," Dax croons, his fingers lightly dusting up and down my spine. "You've been working so hard lately. I want to make you feel good."

How I love this man. He's so thoughtful. So attentive. So damn selfless. It's what I love about him the most. That and his incredible arse.

"We need some music," Zayn suggests as he mirrors Dax's movements, making me melt into the mattress as their fingers glide up and down my skin.

Damn, if I were a cat I'd be purring right now.

"I agree. Play *Move Closer* by Phyllis Nelson," Dax instructs, our built-in music system immediately switching on as the song trickles through the speakers.

"Good choice," Zayn comments, his fingers pressing into my calves whilst Dax pulls my hair off my back and starts gently massaging my neck and the base of my skull. The sultry voice of Phyllis Nelson slides over my skin as easily as their hands do, only adding to the sensuality of the moment. "That feel good?" Zayn asks.

"It feels amazing," I reply, relaxing further.

There's something so erotic about having two sets of hands on me at once and it isn't long before my breathing becomes shallow, and little breathy moans dance from my lips as they caress and knead my aching muscles.

"Good girl, let us take care of you," Dax urges, the tempo of his voice another caress as he fingers slide into my hair and he rubs my scalp, the sensation sending heat radiating through my body.

"Oh, fuck, that feels so good," I whisper, loving how his thick fingers dig into my scalp, sending tiny bolts of electricity zinging up and down my spine.

"Spread your legs a little, Pen," Zayn instructs, focusing on easing the tightness of my calf muscles as he works his way up towards my thighs, massaging my legs with firm yet gentle strokes. Every now and then his lips will brush against my flesh as he works on relaxing me, the soft tip of his tongue tasting my skin.

"That's it, relax for us," Dax whispers, his voice deep, melodic, as they continue to massage me.

"If heaven were a feeling, this would be it," I murmur, feeling my muscles liquidise with every touch. Every part of me is aware of their touch, heightened by their love.

"You took the words right out of my mouth," Zayn says, shifting position as he presses an open mouthed kiss at the base of my spine, his tongue laving my skin there. It's a spot he knows I love to be kissed, and on instinct I spread my legs further, telling him silently what I want.

A soft chuckle follows, and he says, "You'll have to ask, Daddy."

"Not yet," Dax replies, and I know without having to look at either of them that they're intent on teasing me tonight. Not that I mind, if this is the kind of teasing they're into, I'm all for it.

"You're the boss tonight," Zayn replies, kissing along the length of my spine as he works his fingers into the tight muscles of my upper back and shoulders. His touch is firm yet gentle at the same time, and I feel myself drifting into that strange place where you're so relaxed that sleep is tickling your consciousness, but you're so turned on that it would take very little to make you come, long and hard.

"You're so fucking precious to us, do you know that?" Dax whispers against my ear, drawing me out from the depths of my relaxed state. His voice thick and rough with emotion as he slides his fingers into the hair at the base of my skull, tightens his hold and tugs gently.

"Fuck," I moan, tingles scattering up and down my spine at the sudden sharp sting.

"Do you like that?" Dax asks, pulling on my hair again. My pussy clenches in response.

Why does that feel so good?

"Uh-huh," is all I'm able to utter.

Dax releases his hold as his thick fingers stroke through the strands briefly, then his lips meet my ear once more and he says, "I asked you a question. Now be a good girl and tell me how much you like us worshipping you like this."

"I *love* it," I say breathily as his fingers curl back into the strands and pull tightly. "Fuck, I love it when you pull my hair like that. Don't stop."

"What do you say?" he questions, fingers stilling. Even Zayn stops massaging my back, understanding Dax's cues too. They're making me work for it.

"Please," I beg.

"Please *what*, Kid?"

"Please, *Daddy*," I breathe, gasping as he tugs on my hair once more, and Zayn's fingers dig into my flesh.

"That's our good girl."

My body shivers involuntarily. The sensation of Dax's fingers loosening and tightening in my hair, combined with Zayn's hands massaging my tight muscles is almost too much to bear. I moan in pleasure as they work in tandem. Dax tugging gently at my hair while Zayn continues to caress and knead the knots from my muscles.

This goes on and on, until I'm nothing more than a bunch of nerve endings firing off all over my body. Who knew that having my hair tugged at the same time as receiving a massage could feel this good. Fuck, at this rate one light touch to my clit and I'll be seeing more than fucking stars, I'll be experiencing the birth of a new galaxy.

"Don't stop," I groan as Zayn briefly removes his touch and I feel the mattress dip as he adjusts position.

"Don't worry, baby. We got you," Zayn says, his hands sliding up the back of my thighs as he gently parts my legs and settles between them. I can feel the rough material of his jeans against the sensitive skin of my inner thighs, and my pussy quivers in anticipation.

"Zayn is going to continue to massage that peachy arse, and if he's a good boy, I might just let him have a taste of your pretty little pussy," Dax adds, his voice a mixture of heady lust and soft laughter.

"Hey, I'm *always* a good boy. It's Xeno and York who're the naughty ones," Zayn replies with a smile in his voice as he places a palm on each of my arse cheeks, squeezing gently.

"Let me be the judge of that," Dax chuckles, before pulling on the strands of my hair once again.

My lips part and I moan into the duvet, my eyes rolling in my head as waves of heat spark down my spine. I grind against the mattress, needing to rub my clit against something to ease the building pressure. I'm so fucking wet, and they haven't even touched my pussy yet.

"Tell me what you want me to do," Zayn says, his thumbs meeting along my arse crack as he spreads my cheeks. I can't see him, but I know he's staring at my pussy that's wet for him.

For them both.

"Fuck that's hot," Dax mutters, his fingers curling tighter in my hair, pulling, tugging, making me fucking crazy with need.

"I want to taste her. Let me taste her," Zayn says, his thumbs edging lower, swiping over my arsehole, rimming it.

"Jesus," I whisper, arching my spine, pushing my arse up off the bed, telling them both what I need. What I'm greedy for.

"Shall I let Zayn taste you?" Dax asks, his voice thick with desire.

"Please..." I cry as Zayn slips his thumb lower, circling my sensitive hole. He's teasing me, building tension, stoking the fire within. He could ask me to do anything right now and I'd do it for the release. "Please, I want to come. Make me come."

"On your hands and knees, Kid," Dax instructs, "Spread your legs, let Zayn see how your pussy gasps for him, for *us*."

"Fuck, yes, Daddy," I mutter, pushing up onto my knees as Zayn's thumb presses an inch inside of me, rimming my opening briefly before pulling back. "Don't stop, please don't stop."

"Say the words, Kid. Tell us what you want."

"I want you to lick my pussy, Zayn. I want you to make me come whilst Dax pulls my hair and watches."

"Whilst who watches?" Dax prompts as Zayn rubs the pad of his thumb lightly over my clit.

"Fuck!" I cry, pushing back against him, whimpering when he removes his thumb.

"Who, Kid?"

"Daddy, fuck! When you watch Zayn make me come, Daddy."

"Such a good girl, remembering how to address me. For that I'll let him taste you," Dax says, easing his fingers from my hair. "But I think I deserve something in return, don't you?"

"Yes," I pant, as I look up into the eyes of the man I love.

Fuck he's stunning. So fucking male. So very mine.

Dax cups my cheek, brushing the pad of his thumb across my bottom lip. "Open up for me, Kid," he says, voice rough and lusty.

It's intoxicating, the way he looks at me like I'm his whole world. There's nothing like that feeling of being loved so thoroughly, so intensely, and not just by one man, but by four. I'm loved by four beautiful, powerful men who belong to me as much as we belong to each other.

"Taste what you do to me," Dax continues. "I want you to feel my cock throbbing on your tongue knowing that you're the only woman on this planet who gets me as hard as this. I could fuck you every second of every day and never, ever tire of the way you make me feel. I feel like a god when I fuck you. Fuck, I feel invincible."

"Fuck, yes," I murmur, biting my lip as Zayn mutters something about Dax being a dirty, sweet talking Daddy, and liking it.

With saliva gathering in my mouth in anticipation, I lick the head of Dax's dick, savouring his familiar taste as he moans from the contact. Dax is big, his cock long and thick. I've sucked him off before, many times, the ache in my jaw is a familiar feeling after giving him head. I don't hate it. I love it.

"Take me deep. Choke on my dick whilst Zayn eats you out," he says roughly, before sliding his dick between my parted lips and letting out a guttural moan as I suck him deep.

Behind me, Zayn thumbs my outer pussy lips, gently pushing them apart, before sliding his fingers through my parted folds.

"Fuck, you're so wet for us," he says, his breath warm against my most sensitive skin as he gets up close and personal, but still doesn't taste me. Instead he inserts his finger inside of me, sliding it in and out in a teasing rhythm. "Your pussy is so fucking pretty," he continues. "How much do you want my lips on your pussy, Pen? Do you want my tongue to fuck your hole? Do you want me to suck on your clit, huh?"

I gasp around Dax's dick, and instinctively push back against Zayn's hand as he finger fucks me with smooth, even strokes, telling him without words what I'm desperate for.

"What are you waiting for, Zayn? Fuck our girl's pretty pussy with your tongue," Dax orders, his voice cracking as I swirl my tongue around his dick, tasting the salty pre-cum, feeling fucking powerful knowing what I do to him.

"Fuck, Kid. Just like that," he instructs, letting out a moan as he begins to rock against my tongue, his hand gently holding the back of my head as he moves inside my mouth, setting the rhythm.

Saliva drools from my lips as I suck him off, and I feel the soft tickle of Zayn's hair as he lowers his mouth to my pussy. Seconds later, the firm swipe of his tongue as he licks me from slit to crack has me almost self-combusting. I'm so fucking close to coming that I'm teetering on the edge of orgasm.

"Fuck, like that. Just like that," Dax groans, and at this point I don't know if he's talking to me or Zayn. Probably both.

If I could scream at the intense sensation I would, but all I can manage is a garbled moan as I take Dax deeper, my tongue stroking his dick as Zayn shifts positions behind me, not content with licking me up and down. Lying beneath me, he reaches up and grabs my arse cheeks.

"Fuck my face, Pen," he orders, wanting more than a taste, wanting to suffocate on my cum.

I hesitate, feeling a little unsteady as Dax deepthroats my mouth.

"You know better than that, Kid. Sit, don't hover," Dax grinds out, his voice thick with desire.

When I don't immediately do as I'm told, because I'm too busy trying to give Dax the best head of his life, he grips my hair roughly and slides his dick out of my mouth, forcing my head back to look up at him as his dick bobs in front of me.

"What are you–?" I pant, mouth parted, lust billowing as Zayn reaches up and swipes his tongue along my slit, taking my words momentarily, and my sight, as black spots of pleasure dance in front of my eyes. I press them shut, a moan releasing from somewhere deep inside.

"Sit!" Dax demands.

Still I hesitate, refusing to lower myself further, not because I don't want to feel Zayn all up in my pussy, but because I want to see what happens if I disobey Dax. I like how he's taking control, it turns me the fuck on.

It isn't long until I find out.

"Zayn, I do believe that Kid needs to be reminded who's her Daddy, don't you?"

"Couldn't agree more. What do you have in mind?" he replies, smirking up at me as Dax releases my hair and I look down at him. I recognise that look. Zayn might be more vanilla than the others–if you call vanilla partaking in orgies regularly with your three best mates–but he's more than happy to try out new things.

Fuck. I'm in trouble. Good trouble. The kind of trouble that has me passing out from a mindblowing orgasm, just like Dax had planned.

"What happens to our naughty girl when she doesn't do as she's told?" Dax muses, fisting his dick, jacking himself off at a leisurely pace. His cock glistens with my saliva, and my cheeks heat at the way the veins in his hand pop beneath his tattooed skin, how his thick thumb slides along his slit, mixing jewels of pre-cum with my saliva.

"We teach her a lesson," Zayn replies, and my skin zings with anticipation.

It's not the first time they've ganged up on me in this way, and honestly, I like it. I know I'm safe with them. I know they'd never hurt me, not like my brother used to do. This is only about my pleasure, and truth be known, I like testing them. It's fun... *and* rewarding.

For all of us.

"That's correct," Dax replies, dropping his dick and grasping my chin instead, tipping my head upwards.

Our gazes clash and I can see the heat radiating from his eyes as he looks down at me. "Now slap that fine arse until she does as she's told," he orders, his fingers gripping my jaw.

"Yes, *Daddy*," Zayn smirks, and on the next beat, grips my hip with one hand and slaps me with the other.

Hard.

I lurch forward, but forget the sudden sharp sting the second Zayn pulls me down onto his face and starts eating me out with such savage intensity my pussy starts pulsating around his tongue, within seconds I'm close to free-falling off the precipice I was teetering on. Wildly turned on, I buck against his face, sliding the most private part of me against his welcome mouth and tongue.

"That's it, take it like a good girl," Dax orders as Zayn eats me out, his mouth and lips, sucking and tasting, licking and fucking.

"Fuck me," I moan, my head falling back as my hips rock and my tits bounce, riding his face without restraint just like they wanted me to.

"Keep going, Kid. I'm going to fist my dick until I come, and when I do I'm going to empty my cum in your mouth and you're gonna swallow it down for me like a good, obedient girl."

Dax's voice rolls through me, but I can't answer him because the feel of Zayn's teeth gently scraping over my clit at the same time he slaps my arse hard enough to leave a mark, pushes me over the edge.

I come hard, my pussy muscles clenching as I cry out, wave after wave of pleasure flooding my senses making me almost blind with it as I judder and twitch against Zayn's face. With my head thrown back and my mouth open on a scream, I clutch onto Zayn's hair, anchoring myself to him as wet heat drips from me into his open mouth.

Zayn grunts beneath me, tasting my cum as he grips my hips tighter, his fingers digging into my skin, urging me to ride out my orgasm all over his face.

When I open my eyes, Dax is still standing before me, stroking his cock. "Now you taste me," he says with heated eyes and dirty intentions.

"Fuck yes," I moan, easing upwards as Zayn slides out from beneath me and shifts on the bed behind me. Sliding his fingers along my shoulder blade, he moves my hair out of the way and kisses me at that sensitive spot where my neck and shoulder meet.

"That was so fucking hot," he mutters against my skin, arm circling my waist as he grasps my breast, squeezing gently.

"We're not done yet," Dax says, rubbing the pad of his thumb over the thick, engorged head of his cock. The slit glistens, his balls tightening against his body. "I'm gonna come in our girl's mouth."

"I want you both to come," I reply breathily, wanting to feel full of them. Needing them both. "But only if you allow it?"

Dax's nostrils flare, and he nods sharply before cutting a look to Zayn behind me. "I'm gonna take her mouth. You take her pussy. And when you're done, I'm going to fuck her too. Then I'm gonna hold our girl until she falls into a deep, satisfied sleep."

"Yes, *please*. Do it," I beg, gasping as Dax grabs my hair and pulls me towards the edge of the bed. On all fours, I line up my mouth with his dick, licking the tip as I part my legs giving Zayn enough room to position himself between them.

"It's my lucky fucking night," Zayn says with a chuckle, the unmistakable sound of his zipper being undone. "I only came for a goodnight kiss."

"Then you'd better make sure you fuck our girl good," Dax

growls, before sliding his cock into my mouth, right at the same time as Zayn slips inside of me, carefully not to thrust too hard given my position.

My pussy instantly clenches around Zayn's cock, while Dax's thick shaft fills and stretches my mouth, and I moan against his length, grinding myself against Zayn as I do. For a moment they both settle there, allowing me to adjust, to revel in the feeling of them taking me in such a dirty, feral way. Then Zayn starts to gently rock his hips, and the action helps me to suck Dax off with the perfect rhythm.

"Ahhh! Yes!" Dax cries out, his hand cupping my cheek, as Zayn rocks me back and forth on his cock. "Like that, just like that."

"You like that, Daddy?" Zayn asks without a shred of humour in his voice.

I can feel his fingers curling into my hips as he sets the pace of our combined pleasure, his cock swelling inside of me with every slip and slide, the sloppy, wet sounds of our fucking only adding to the intensity of this moment.

"Yeah, fuck I do," Dax grunts, his cock jerking in my mouth, the salty taste of precum hitting my tongue, turning me on. "Keep that pace, Zayn. Fuck our girl whilst she sucks my cock."

"You got it," Zayn replies as his movements become more intense, blending into one continuous wave of pleasure that builds higher and higher within me.

"You've got it, *who?*" Dax asks, his voice thick with lust.

"You've got it, Daddy," Zayn repeats gruffly, his fingers digging into my hips.

"Good boy," Dax adds, and fuck if my clit does a happy

little twitch at the deliciousness of this moment. Hearing Zayn acknowledge Dax in this way is a huge turn on for me, and them both considering how their cocks swell.

"Make me come," Dax chokes out, his fingers tightening in my hair. "Suck me harder."

Hollowing out my cheeks, I suck hard on Dax's cock whilst I squeeze my internal walls tightly around Zayn's dick, triggering his orgasm first.

"Pen!" Zayn roars, jerking inside of me as his orgasm takes him over the edge, and me with it.

My eyes roll back in my head as a galaxy of stars twist and tumble, vibrant and startling behind my closed eyelids as I moan around Dax's cock. A few seconds later Dax follows suit, filling my throat with his hot release as he grunts in satisfaction. I swallow greedily, savouring the taste of him as he judders and jerks, his fingers curling in the strands of my hair, until eventually he pulls free leaving a trail of cum and spit connecting his dick to my lips.

"Fuck, Kid," he murmurs, cupping my cheek, his thumb pressing against my swollen lips as he swipes the evidence of our arousal from my lips and tastes it. "The things you do to me."

"*Us*," Zayn adds, pulling out of me gently. "The things you do to us."

"Yeah, our girl," Dax adds, dropping onto the bed with a look of contentment on his face as he looks between us both. He smirks, raising a brow at Zayn.

"What?" Zayn asks.

"You can call me Daddy anytime you like, mate. Just saying."

Zayn barks out a laugh, punching Dax lightly on the shoulder. I giggle at the love between them both, my heart swelling with it.

"It was in the moment. I got carried away," he says, though I see the interest in his eyes, the curiosity of what this could mean.

Dax shrugs, winking at me before turning his attention back to Zayn. "Well, if you ever want to join in like that again, we ain't gonna turn you down, are we, Kid?"

"Absolutely not. I love getting thoroughly fucked by my men," I reply a little breathily as I sit

back on my haunches. It takes me a moment to calm my racing heart, so I reach for them both, my hand resting on each of their thighs until eventually I can gather myself enough to speak.

"All better?" I ask, biting down on my swollen lips, my aching pussy dripping Zayn's cum.

"Much better," Zayn agrees, watching his release slide down my inner thigh, his own dick glistening with my cum as it rests against his chiselled abs.

"Fuck, Kid, that was nothing short of mind-blowing," Dax says, watching me as I press my thighs together and try and scoot off the bed.

"Something blew, but it wasn't your mind," Zayn quips with a smirk.

More laughter bubbles up my chest, but it only seems to encourage more of Zayn's cum to slide out of me. "Give me a second," I murmur, but I don't have time to get off the bed before Dax is reaching for me. His firm grip circling my wrist.

"Where do you think you're going?"

"I need to wash up."

Dax pushes up onto his stump, reaching between my legs and gathering Zayn's come in his hands, sliding it back up inside of me. "Didn't I say I wanted to fuck you?"

"But I need..." I gasp, my voice trailing off as his slick fingers start to pump in and out of my sensitive hole, spreading Zayn's cum over my pussy.

"You need to lie down so I can fuck you unconscious, remember? Besides, what's a little sex fluid between friends?" he adds with a devilish glint in his eyes.

"Amen to that," Zayn agrees, chuckling as Dax tugs me onto the mattress and hauls me back against his chest, spooning me. I let out a delighted squeal as he cups my throat gently and nibbles on my earlobe. "But this time, I'm out," Zayn continues, "I'm gonna go check on York, make sure he knows how much fun we've had without him tonight."

"That's mean," I say, frowning a little.

"Call it karmic justice. He wouldn't stop going on about how perfect that long weekend you had together, *alone*, was, and how many times he got to make love to you," Zayn adds pointedly.

"You three got to go to Vegas, it was hardly a chore," I argue.

"It was a business trip, Pen, and without you there with us, it was most definitely a chore."

"That was a month ago, Zayn. You should be over that by

now," I gently point out to Zayn while Dax feathers kisses across my shoulder blade and neck, trying his very best to distract me.

To be fair, it's working.

"Well *I'm* not over it, and I'm feeling petty," Zayn replies with a chuckle before pressing a chaste kiss against my lips and winking at Dax. "Enjoy my love-juices, mate."

"Get the fuck out of here. You've overstayed your welcome," Dax banters back.

"Love you," Zayn quips, and even though he's looking at me, I know he's talking to Dax too.

We've long since gotten over our inability to express our love for one another verbally. Saying those three words to each other is the easiest, most natural thing in the world now.

"Love you back," we both reply.

Zayn's grin is the last thing I see before Dax hooks my leg back over his hip, and slides inside of me in one firm stroke, my eyelids fluttering closed on a moan.

"That's it, take Daddy's cock like a good girl," he growls, fucking me from behind, and by fuck, I mean make love.

THREE

I Hope You Dance

XENO

"AFTERNOON, HOW ARE YOU FEELING?" I ask as York steps into the kitchen looking better than he has in over a week. To be honest, as much as we've all ribbed him for having 'man-flu', it's a relief to see the colour back in his cheeks.

"Put it this way. A couple days ago I felt like I'd done ten rounds in the gym with Beast. Now I feel half human, though this lingering headache is doing my head in, literally," he complains, rubbing at his temple and messing up his already wayward hair as he takes a seat at the kitchen island.

"You were pretty ill there for a while."

"Ah, were you worried about me?" York jokes, his smile dropping when he sees the expression on my face, and realises that for me being able to control my emotions, which includes concern for the people I love, is something I'm still working on. "Sorry, man. I know how hard it is for you."

"I'm just glad to see you up and about again," I say, giving his shoulder a brief squeeze.

Even after all this time, through years of friendship and love, it's still hard for me to keep a lid on my emotions without it coming out in a way that isn't appropriate or what's deemed *normal*. Truth be known, I've been battling with my concern for York and trying not to blow up in rage and frustration from my wayward emotions. The only way I've been able to keep a lid on it is by throwing myself into work.

"I appreciate your concern, Xeno," he says, acknowledging my feelings but not pushing the matter further, knowing only too well that if I want to talk, I'll do it in my own time.

"You want some coffee?" I ask, changing the subject for now.

"I'd love a coffee. Give me all the caffeine. I don't want to see another lemon, honey and ginger drink for the rest of my goddamn life."

"Yeah, not the same as a good cup of coffee," I agree, pouring him a mug of the newly brewed liquid, stirring in a heaped teaspoon of sugar and topping it with full fat milk, just the way he likes it. "There you go."

He takes a sip, then lets out a long sigh. "Fuck, now that's what the doctor ordered, and not that disgusting shit you guys forced me to take two days ago. What the fuck was that stuff, anyway?"

"Something Cynthia made. Grim swears by it."

"Cynthia as in the *Deana-dhe's* missus?"

"The very one," I confirm. "She sent it all the way over from Ireland when she heard how ill you've been."

"How did she find out?"

"Pen told Grim. Grim told Cynthia. Well, Cynthia *and* Christy. You know how they love to talk."

"Well it tasted like shit," he complains.

"That might be so, but to be fair, your temperature started to ease off and the coughing stopped within hours of you taking that tincture. I was sceptical when I received the package and the instructions from Cynthia, but it worked. Grim thinks she's a genius. According to her, she can cure any ailment with her herbal medicine."

"Yeah, and what does Beast think?"

"He's as impressed by Cynthia's ability as The Masks are, and you know what those fuckers are like, they don't mess around with fakes or frauds. Cynthia has known Jakub, Konrad and Leon most of her life, and you know she spent time at Ardelby castle taking care of the Numbers before Christy walked into their lives and made them free them all."

"No wonder the Deana-dhe locked Cynthia down. Someone who's gifted like that is a valuable asset."

"She is, but they married her because they've been in love with her since they were kids, even though for a period of time they were shits to her," I correct.

York pulls a face. "Of course they did. Us men can be stupid, stubborn dicks."

"Yeah," I agree.

We might have all loved Tiny since the moment she stepped into the basement of 15 Jackson street, but we treated her badly for a period of time too. It's something she forgave us for years ago, but despite that it's something I've never quite forgiven myself for, especially since I was the hardest on her.

"That's why Beast teamed up with the Deana-dhe and The Masks a few years back? To fetch Cynthia back from those cunts, the Skulls, right?" York asks, taking another sip of his coffee. "It all makes sense now."

"You know Grim and Beast, they're always willing to help good people."

"Good people? I thought you only tolerated the Deana-dhe?"

"Their reputation has always made me wary of them, but I respect them for gathering a small army to hunt down and annihilate the men who stole their woman. It's nothing we wouldn't do."

"Agreed. Do you think Cynthia's the one that made the drug we took that time at Tales?" York asks, remembering that night we danced with Pen under the influence of a drug the Deana-dhe manipulated us into taking.

"Without a doubt," I reply.

"To be fair, that shit was incredible," York muses, his attention wandering. "Dancing with you both was like a fucking dream, but super intense at the same time... And the sex. Fuck man, it *was* intense."

"Yeah."

York looks over at me and grins. "Don't tell me you've forgotten what that felt like?"

"Believe me, I haven't," I admit. "Point is, someone who has the ability to alter the mind's perception and heighten the body's ability to feel pleasure with natural ingredients, without any side effects, is someone gifted for sure. I've no doubt her medicine is what pulled you through this shitty virus."

"You're right. I feel better than I should. Great actually."

"Not as great as I felt after having the best sex of my life last night," Zayn says, as he steps into our open plan living space from the door on the other side of the room and throws his arms above his head in a stretch. If I wasn't already packing rock hard abs, a man could get a little jealous of his physique.

"Oh yeah?" I question, remembering I sent home Dax and Pen to enjoy *their* date night.

It's a quarter past one in the afternoon, and he looks like he's just woken up given he's wearing his sleep joggers and nothing else. To be fair, I've only just rolled out of bed myself after staying at the club way beyond closing time so I could catch up on some work.

"Have you been wanking off again?" York asks, smirking. "You know what happened to Beast when he wanked one too many times during that dry period with Grim."

"You do know that if Grim finds out that Beast discussed their sex life, or lack thereof, after Iris was born she'll shoot us all, right?" I point out. "I do not have a death wish."

"Oh come on, it's not as if she doesn't do the same with Pen and the others on their weekly girls date. I bet Grim knows all the spicy little details about our sex life," Zayn points out.

"Point taken," I agree, chuckling.

"Anyway, as talented as I am at handling my own dick, York, no, I wasn't wanking off," Zayn smirks, a huge grin spreading across his face as he strides over to us both and slaps York on the shoulder before giving him a hug.

York shoves him off, narrowing his eyes at him. "Care to elaborate."

"Dax and Pen invited me to play along with them last night when they got back from the club."

"What the fuck? That's not fair," York pouts, popping his lower lip. "Not only has this damn flu kicked my arse, it's also prevented me from joining in on all the fun."

"I wasn't about to turn Pen down, nor was I willing to upset *Daddy*," Zayn says, his grin spreading wider as he drops that little tidbit.

"*Daddy?*" York and I blurt out in unison.

"The fuck?" York eyes me, the brief annoyance at missing out replaced with amusement.

"Yep, *Daddy Dax* was looking after our girl *very* well last night. Pen seems to enjoy it, and he fits the role perfectly, so why the fuck not?"

"Erm, excuse me," I say, pressing a finger against my chest. "If anyone's the Daddy of this group, it's me."

"See, I told you," Tiny giggles as she enters with Dax, her hand entwined with his.

My fucking heart jackhammers in my chest at the sight of her in a pair of grey sleepshorts and matching vest top. She has her hair pulled up into a messy bun and her face free of makeup. It's all I can do not to stride over to her and pull her into my arms, so I can kiss her breathless, or maybe even bend her over the back of the sofa and fuck her senseless.

Even after all these years, I still have a really strong emotional and physical reaction to being in Tiny's presence. The love I feel for her is so huge, so overwhelming, that it takes a lot of self-control, and understanding from the others, to handle it. But like everything else, the five of us have worked through all of our difficulties and are closer for it. Even so, despite their love and support, I still have bouts of almost uncontrollable emotions, and I feel an episode coming on now.

"Mate, I don't deny you've got Daddy potential, but *I've* claimed that title. If you wanna dispute my status, then we'll have to figure out a way to determine who's the Daddy..."

"I'm game," I reply, needing the distraction. I'm not one to back down from a challenge, even though we both know that this is just lighthearted banter, nothing more. "I'm sure Grim will let us fight it out in the cage."

"Oh stop it," Tiny says, slapping the back of her hand against Dax's chest before making a beeline to York who's doing his best impression of an abused and abandoned dog, giving her puppy eyes. "How are you feeling?" she asks, sliding between his parted legs and pressing the back of her hand against his forehead.

"Better now you're here," he replies, loving the attention as he wraps his arms around her back.

I roll my eyes and Dax shoves him on the head as he walks by. "Stop laying it on so thick, dumbass."

"Hey, leave him alone, he's just recovered from the flu. He deserves some attention," Tiny scolds, pressing a kiss against York's mouth that soon turns indecent.

Dax chuckles. "Yep, he's *much* better now."

"Flu my arse," I add jokingly, that lightheartedness a momentary reprieve from the sudden swell of love.

It's all I can do not to press the heel of my palm against my chest to rub at the ache there.

Instead, for the next few minutes I watch Tiny as she fusses over York, chatting to him quietly as Dax and Zayn start pulling food from the fridge to make a late breakfast, or is that an early lunch? The way she dotes on him makes my heart swell to almost painful levels, and I have to turn away, placing my mug in the dishwasher as a distraction. I'm not sure why I'm struggling today trying to keep a lid on my feelings, but I am.

It's not that I don't want to express my emotions, or am trying to hide them like I used to do before, it's just that they feel really intense today, so intense that I'm not sure how they're going to come pouring out of me. Perhaps it's because I've been worrying about York, maybe it's just because every day my love continues to grow for Tiny and my best mates that it's hard to keep those feelings contained. Either way, it's a battle for me to keep myself together, and when my hands start to shake I realise I need to take myself out of the room and get myself under control.

"Shit, I just remembered I needed to send an email to the suppliers. Firm up what we discussed last night. If I don't do that now, I'll miss the deadline for delivery for the event in two weeks," I say quickly.

"I thought everything was covered for that?" Dax asks as he takes the diced pepper from Zayn, and throws it into the pan, adding whisked eggs to make an omelette.

"It is, I'm just ordering more as a precaution. I'd rather have too much than not enough. This is a big deal for us and the club. We've never hosted a dance competition of this calibre, and with international dance crews battling it out, I want to be fully prepared," I reply, folding my arms across my chest and hoping no one notices how fucking twitchy I am.

"Fair enough. Let us know if you need anything, or want to run through any plans," Dax adds, before turning his attention back to preparing our lunch.

"Will do," I reply, then stride across the room, avoiding eye contact with Tiny as York pulls her back into his arms, giving me the opportunity to escape.

"THERE YOU ARE," Tiny says less than half an hour later as she enters our studio. "Dax saved you some lunch, but you better be quick because York has his appetite back and he's been eying your portion for the last five minutes."

"I'll be there soon," I reply, masking my growing anxiety by pretending I'm sorting shit out in the cupboard. Right now, I'm holding onto a length of silk that was stashed there some time ago after Clancy and the dancers from Tales borrowed our studio to do a dress rehearsal. I vaguely remember them wearing nothing more than swathes of silk. I hold it up to her. "I'm just sorting through this shit."

"And you're doing that because…" Her voice trails off as she approaches me.

"It needed doing," I reply, my voice tight. "Just give me a minute and I'll come eat."

But instead of leaving she says, "Xeno, talk to me."

I should've known better than to try to pretend that nothing's wrong. She knows me better than anyone, and she always seems to have this sixth sense when I'm about to spiral.

Fuck, I love her for it. I really fucking do.

The *love* she has for me is part of the problem, *and* the solution.

"I'm good. I just need a minute to get myself together," I say, realising it's useless to try and pretend nothing's happening.

"And I gave you several," she replies softly. "I know when you're feeling overwhelmed, Xeno. I recognise the signs. You don't need to do this alone, but I gave you space to see if you could. You aren't able to do that right now. So let me help you."

"Tiny…" I warn, not because I think I'm going to hurt her, but because I'm losing my grip on my ability to hold back. I need an outlet, and fucking without restraint right now feels like it might be the only thing that *will* help.

Reaching for me, she slides her hands around my waist, hugging me tight as she rests her cheek against the centre of my back. When I get like this, she always allows me the space to try and manage my emotions myself. For the most part, I can do that, but today she knows as well as I do that physical touch and human connection is what I need the most. It isn't always a sexual connection that I need either. Sometimes a hug and her undivided attention is enough.

Not today.

Today I need more.

But I'm also conscious that she spent the night making love to Dax and Zayn, and I'm not about to coerce her into having sex with me for selfish reasons, so instead I say, "If you stay, I'll want to fuck you. It'll be rough, Tiny. I won't hold back, and I don't want to assume you want that right now. So please, let me do this my way."

Her arms ease from around my waist and she steps around me, her big brown eyes looking up at me knowingly. "You need me. I'm *not* leaving."

"Tiny, I can't be gentle. Besides, you don't owe me your body. I have no right to use you like that, and I certainly don't want a pity fuck," I grind out, my fingers wrapping around the length of silk in my hand, pulling it taut.

Her gaze drops from my face to my hands, her fingers pressing gently against mine. "When have I ever given you a pity fuck, Xeno? I wouldn't be here if I didn't want to help you work through these feelings."

"It doesn't matter. Fucking you in these circumstances would feel like one anyway. I'm not in my right mind," I add, causing her to wince. "You know I don't mean half the stupid shit I say. Ignore me."

She nods, forgiving me instantly. "Then we need to find another way."

"Fuck. I haven't felt this out of control in a long time," I admit, hating that's true.

It's been creeping up on me lately, this feeling of being out of control, *anxious*. Over the years, with Tiny's help, I've learnt how to manage my reactions to my emotions, how to ride the wave. Lately that wave has turned into a storm, and I feel like a small boat being churned on a violent ocean of emotion, helpless against its power.

"You're not the only one," she replies, reaching up to cup my face. I stiffen at her touch, not because I don't want it, because I do. So fucking much. "Dax hasn't been feeling great lately either," she continues. "It's partly the reason we battled last night, to take his mind off it, and to show him he's still capable."

"What's happening with him?" I ask, hearing the panic in my voice and hating it. This isn't me. Well, it is, but it isn't the side of me that I feel uncomfortable showing despite how safe I feel with Tiny. She's never once judged me, and has only ever embraced every part of me, even the flaws.

"Phantom pain. He's going to call the doctor today, get an appointment."

"Should I be worrying?" Even as I say the words, that ball of anxiety in the pit of my stomach gathers momentum. I know it's a sign of my love and concern for Dax, as well as my inability to rationalise my emotions, but that doesn't make it any easier to live with.

Tiny reads my expression, understanding immediately what's happening within me. "Xeno, let it out. Don't bottle this up. We can work through anything. You know this."

"I hate feeling like this," I say, gritting my jaw, my teeth grinding against each other as I wrap the silk tighter around my fists, cutting off the circulation in my hands, wanting to hurt myself. It's an old habit, one I've fought to rid myself of, and for the most part I've succeeded.

Not today.

"I know," Tiny acknowledges, gently unfurling the silk from my fingers. I let her, trusting her in this moment because I can't trust myself. "Let me take that. I've got an idea."

"This is bullshit," I blurt out.

"You're overwhelmed. You don't have to be ashamed of that, Xeno. York has been sick. We've all been working so hard at the club, on the other businesses. We've not had a break in five years, and the little time we do have together is so precious that all we want to do is fuck."

"You don't want to fuck?" I ask as she steps behind me.

She laughs softly, her reflection in the mirror making my heart squeeze tightly. "Of course I do. I don't think that will ever change. *Not ever*," she reassures me. "But there's been something vital missing. Something we *all* need."

"What's that?"

"What have we been missing?" she fires back softly.

I meet her gaze, and it finally dawns on me what she's getting at. "*Dance*," I say.

"Exactly. When was the last time we danced together as a group, the five of us?"

"I can't remember..." My voice trails off as I understand the significance of that. "*Fuck*, Tiny."

"Is it any wonder you're finding it hard to deal with your emotions? That York has been so ill with this flu and hasn't bounced back as quickly as he should've? That Dax is struggling with phantom pain. Zayn hasn't been sleeping all that well either lately, don't tell me you haven't noticed how tired he's been? Our proverbial well is empty. We've been so busy living this hectic, *wonderful*, draining life that we've forgotten what's fundamental to the five of us. Our *need* to dance with *each other*. It's always been our outlet, and not dancing together is taking its toll on all of us."

"How have I not noticed what's been missing?" I ask, mainly to myself.

"What we've *all* missed," Tiny replies, gently squeezing my arm as she runs the length of silk through her fingers. "I don't regret this life, or the past five years since we opened Twisted Bullet. There's nothing about it that I wouldn't do over again. I'm so proud of us all, of what we've built, the family we've become, the home we've made together. It's just I wish we had carved out more time for our first love, the love we all had before we loved each other."

"Then that's what we'll do. We'll make time," I reassure her.

She nods, rising up onto her tiptoes to plant a kiss on my cheek. "Starting right now," she says.

"Now?" I mutter, my eyebrows meeting in a frown.

"Now," she repeats, before sliding the silk tie over my eyes and knotting it at the back of my head. Before I'm able to ask her what she's doing she says, "Play *Work Song* by Hozier."

FOUR

Work Song

XENO

"THIS SONG," I say, feeling the beat pounding in rhythm to my heart, reminding me of that night when I'd stepped into the studio at Stardom Academy whilst Tiny was dancing blindfolded.

Fuck, she'd been a vision.

Startling.

Pure.

Intense in her movements.

Certain in her ability.

My heart had hiccupped in my chest, swollen with longing, that for a moment I'd thought I might die from the sheer size of it. Christ, just hearing this song takes me back there. Conjures up those confusing, contradictory feelings that I'd felt back then.

"Do you remember how you felt dancing with me that night?" she asks, her fingertips dropping from the length of silk and sliding down my spine. She leaves me blind, my vision taken from me momentarily. It only seems to make my emotions swell even more.

My breath hitches and I nod, swallowing hard as I fight the urge to rip off the blindfold and pin her to the studio floor.

"Talk to me, Xeno, tell me what you felt," she encourages, sensing I'm about to bolt, bringing me back to the moment.

"I was mesmerised by you, Tiny. I was drawn to you by some invisible pull that I couldn't explain. Still can't," I begin. "All I knew at that moment, despite how much I thought I hated you, was that it felt *right* holding you in my arms. I couldn't not dance with you."

"I know, I felt that too," she whispers, her arms wrapping around my waist as she presses her front to my back, her hips swaying to the beat as she reminds me in this moment how blissful it is to dance with her, how *fucking right*.

Instinctively, my body moves in synchronicity, taking cues from her subtle steps, her gentle coercion, the sensual way her body knows mine so well. "I *knew* that stepping into the studio with you would burn me, *hurt* me," I continue, "But there was nothing I could do to stop myself. I couldn't even if I wanted to."

"Is it hurting now, dancing with me?" she asks, moving

around me, her leg sliding between my thighs as she positions herself between them, her warm breath feathering across my neck, sending chills scattering across my skin. Chills that erupt into flames as her crotch presses against mine.

"No. It doesn't hurt, Tiny. Not anymore."

"Good," she murmurs, taking my hands in hers, gently circling her hips, encouraging me to follow her lead this time.

The lack of vision is disorienting at first, but eventually I begin to find my way, her gentle touches and cues guiding me. As we dance, I allow myself to surrender to the moment, moving to the music, our bodies so in tune that there's no need for words as our feet glide across the studio floor. Yet despite the easy way we move with each other, with every step my emotions become bigger, larger, *more* overwhelming. The familiarity of dancing with Tiny has always soothed my soul, but right now being this close to her whilst I'm in this frame of mind only fires the need in my blood.

I want to fuck, not dance.

My steps falter, and my fingers grip her tighter as my cock hardens, lengthening painfully as it pushes against the zipper of my jeans.

"Tiny, I–" My voice catches as I press into her, holding her closer as my need to fuck takes over.

"Keep dancing," she urges, sensing the change in me, but fighting against it, trying to bring me back around.

"I need you," I grind out, the swirl of emotion growing, building, drowning me.

If I don't find a way to distract myself it's only going to get worse. So I allow that other part of myself to step forward, this wild, animalistic side of me that's wrapped up in these over-whelming, overpowering emotions. It's snarling to be free. Free to fuck wildly, violently, so that it can obliterate these feelings that will tear me apart if I let them.

But Tiny refuses me. She refuses to entertain that violent part of me like she has so willingly on other occasions. This time she keeps me moving, keeps me dancing, her intoxicating scent tantalising me. I know what she's trying to do, I understand better than anyone, but dancing with her right now, like this, is like fuel to a fire.

Every press of my hips against hers, every brush of her thigh against my own, every teasing sweep of her nipples against my chest is agony. It's pure agony.

My cock swells. My fingers bruise.

Fuck.

"I. Need. You," I repeat, anger tainting my words, heating them up, making them painful.

I'm not angry at her, I'm angry at myself, at this fucking infuriating way that I can't deal with my emotions like everyone else.

"No, you *need* to keep dancing," she replies, her fingers slipping from mine as she steps back.

I lurch forward, reaching for her, my knees buckling, my dick aching, my heart fucking thundering. "What are you doing, Tiny?" I ask, my emotions spiking in my chest from her absence, tiny blades carving into my heart.

"I'm letting you dance, *alone.*"

"No," I reply, my voice raised, tremulous, angry. "Come back."

"You need to do this without me. Trust me on this," she insists, her voice further away.

I reach up to remove my blindfold, my fingers hovering over the material, stilling only when she shouts at me, the pain in her voice lancing my chest.

"No! Keep dancing!" she commands, the kindness in her voice replaced with sharp edges.

I'm tempted to ignore her, but something stops me. Something nags deep inside, but instead of listening to it, I make a demand of my own in one last ditch attempt to get her back in my arms. It worked once before, why not now?

"Dance with me!"

"Not this time, Xeno," she replies gently, Hozier's haunting voice settling over my skin, taunting me with memories as my heart slams against my rib cage in a desperate attempt to reach the woman it beats for. "This time you dance with your emotions alone."

And just like that, the past collides with the present. Her absence is filled with the ghost of her memory, reminding me of all the pent up emotion that had begun to leak from me the moment I'd danced with her blindfolded in the studio all those years ago.

That was the start of it. My unravelling.

Tiny is reminding me of that moment, not to taunt me, but to show me that we've been here before, dealing with big emotions, and we survived. Love will always hurt me as much as it soothes me, and Tiny will always be the one to remind me of my *own* strength, just like she's doing now.

Dancing together might give us joy, it might complete us,

but dancing solo? *That's* where we found our souls, our true strength.

We have to start there first.

"Move your body, Xeno. Don't think. Let the music guide you," she encourages."Forget about the past. Forget about your feelings for the moment. Forget about me. Just dance. Remember who *you* are. Draw strength from that."

I'm tempted to remove the blindfold, to chase her across the room and relieve myself of my emotions temporarily whilst balls deep inside of her. I could fuck them into submission, gorging myself on the woman I love, with a heart so fucking damaged that it tries its best to kill me on the regular.

I don't.

And I don't forget about her either.

I force myself to relive that moment I stepped into the studio. How it had felt back then to watch the girl I both loved and hated move with such passion and fire it had completely disarmed me. I had watched her with such awe and reverence that my heart had swelled with emotions it hadn't allowed itself to feel for a long, long time. It's with that memory in mind that I start to move, though it isn't bachata that guides my steps, but lyrical.

"That's it, Xeno, dance," Tiny encourages as I bring my curled fists into my stomach, bending at the waist, imitating how it feels to live with my big emotions, how they often wind me, taking my breath with their hugeness.

I could stop there, breathless by my emotions, gasping for breath in a sea of feelings, but I don't. Instead, I force myself upright, reaching up with my left arm, swimming against the tide, fighting for breath as I leap into the air.

Once I shake off some of the heaviness of my feelings, my steps grow more confident and deliberate, and as I press my palms together, it's almost as if I'm cradling a ball of emotion that's swirling with fear and anxiety in my hands. It fizzles there, a part of me, yet outside of me.

With one powerful push, I send the sensation tumbling away, propelling myself backward in the process, but I'm not throwing away my love, I'm releasing the stress and anxiety that makes it seem too huge to handle. Too overwhelming.

Because I *can* handle it.

Loving Tiny, loving York and Zayn, loving Dax is *easy*. It's the fear of that love hurting me somehow, causing me pain, that I can't handle. It's fear of losing the people I love, fear of being out of control that overwhelms me.

That's what I'm trying to let go of now as I dance, the fear. Nothing else.

With every step, I brush that fear off. I push it down. I force it away. My movements are contained, controlled, and decisive as I dance. Bending my knee, I lift my foot off the ground, bring my arms back then stamp down, in an attempt to squash the fear. I push harder, striving for control and that sense of relief, release.

This isn't me ignoring my feelings. This is me acknowledging them, thanking them for what they are, and letting the ones that no longer serve me go. Fear holds me back. I understand that better than anyone, and as that realisation slides through my body, like an undulating wave, my arms roll in one singular, fluid movement.

Of course nothing is ever easy, and this fear that's so entangled with feelings of love tries its best to hang on. It builds once more inside of me in a last ditch attempt to bring me to my knees, to make me turn in on myself. But I refuse to let it.

Resting my palm against my chest, I gather that rotten emotion and force it upwards and out of my mouth. It tries to smother my face, but I grasp it in my hand, pushing it away.

I battle against it, grasping that invisible ball with one hand as I move around the studio, still blindfolded, still trusting every step as I dance.

That wild, unhinged part of me snarls and growls in confusion as I dance.

It wants Tiny. It wants to release itself in her. It wants to hear her cries and her moans, blotting out the noise of my emotions.

It's angry. *Scared.*

But with every step that anger becomes determination. With every sway of my hips, and kick of my legs, that anxiety unfurls into understanding.

This is who I am. This is a part of me that will never change.

I can't hide from it. I can't pretend it isn't there. I can't force my emotions into neat little boxes, chaining them up beneath hours of work, or appeasing them temporarily with violent fucking.

There is no fix. No bandaid. No cure.

Tiny might be able to provide a safe place to listen, she might be a willing participant in aggressive consensual sex. My best friends might indulge my need for violence in other ways by fighting me in the ring. They might guide me with their friendship and hold me accountable with their love. But at the end of the day the only person with the power to deal with all these painful emotions is me.

That's what I do now.

Gripping my wrist, I force all that fear away from me, but it holds on. Fuck, it holds on.

Still I refuse to let it overpower me.

I refuse.

I fight against it until eventually I win.

Stomping my foot, I place my fingers to my lips and release this mounting fear that has been building up over the last few months with a heartfelt kiss.

Letting it all go.

I. Let. It. Go.

And with every exhale I become still. My body relaxes, and my arms loosen at my sides as an inner peace washes over me.

Soothing me.

Calming me.

Leaving me free to listen to the thumping rhythm of my heart as it beats in time to the music.

The relief is palpable as I reach up and remove my blindfold, blinking back the sting of the studio lights as I search for Tiny, instantly finding her.

She stands across the other side of the studio with a huge smile spreading across her face. A smile that's so fucking beautiful and filled with pride that I am helpless against the pull of it, against the pull of her.

My soul cries out for her.

My body yearns for every inch of hers.

I no longer have that ripping, tearing need to annihilate my emotions by temporarily fucking them out of my system. What I have is this warm swell of love, so fucking pure and uninhibited that I all I want to do is express that the best way I know how.

"Tiny," I mutter. "Dance with me?"

"Always," she replies, stepping towards me as I move towards her.

We are opposites in so many ways, Tiny and me, but in the way we love? We're not so different. She might be able to handle that love better than I can, but she sure loves as big. I feel it now, her love, it's like a fierce embrace, solid, grounding, stable, protective, *pure*.

Sliding my fingers down her arms, I notice the way her skin rises with goosebumps, reacting to my touch so viscerally. It's always been this way between us, this connection that we share is so much more than physical, emotional even.

It's soul deep.

I know she feels it with the others too.

A long time ago I struggled with that, believing that true love, soul deep love, can only be felt between two people. That it isn't possible to feel that way for more than one person.

But it *is* possible.

I see it in Tiny's eyes as she looks at Dax with the same deep, intense, heart-pumping love that she's looking at me with now. I see it when she laughs with York until she's crying, clutching her stomach as he clutches her, their love shared through pure joy and laughter. I see it when she spends hours talking with Zayn, setting the world to rights, so comfortable in his presence, so at ease in his company, so at home in his love.

She has enough love for us all, and in turn we love her and each other.

There's no jealousy. There's no bitterness or greed.

There's just us.

Taking her hands in mine, and with our gazes locked together, we move closer and closer until our bodies are barely an inch apart. Yet it still feels like miles begging to be bridged.

My breath hitches in time with hers, a knowing look passing between us, but instead of immediately diving into a kiss, I take her hand and spin her beneath our lifted arms.

I meant what I said. I danced alone, now I want to dance with her.

"I'm so proud of you," she whispers as I pull her closer, our lips just barely brushing against one another.

With our hips swaying, and her soft breath fluttering over my skin, she looks up at me from beneath long dark lashes, her right leg sliding out in an arc behind her as she dips low. Another smile blooms across her face, and this time the swell in my heart feels healing.

She heals me every day with her love.

"I love you, Tiny," I say. The words are so easy, so free.

This time when I say it, there's no pain, there's no fear, there's just this *knowing*. I won't kid myself into believing that I won't ever get to this point again, because I know I will. This is who I am after all, but knowing I've relapsed and got through it again gives me power and a sense of hope that one day loving Tiny, loving my best friends, won't be as frightening or as painful.

"As I love you," she whispers back, lifting back up, hooking her leg over my hip and leaning into my hold until our bodies slide against each other.

At some point the music stops but we don't; instead, we melt into each other's embrace and continue to glide around the studio without missing a beat, dancing in time to some inner rhythm only we can hear.

The rhythm of our love.

Then, as if drawn by a magnetism beyond us, our lips meet again for a kiss so deep it feels like ages have passed since the last time we held each other in this way. The same electricity that had bound us together as kids, now binds us even more tightly. Desire takes over both of us until all rational thought disappears, leaving no place for fear or doubt.

"Thank you," I whisper.

"For what?" she replies, reaching up and brushing the hair out of my eyes.

"For knowing me. *Truly* knowing me," I reply, my hands slowly travelling up her sides and as I look deep into her eyes, I see all of those beautiful memories reflected back at me from that first night we met until now. Memories that have been burning brightly inside of me ever since then.

"Thank *you* for letting me in. Thank you for loving us, for loving me back," she replies before pressing her lips against mine.

I open up to her searching tongue, stroking back, with my

fingers gently grasping her jaw, holding her in place, loving her with every last breath in me.

She gasps, I moan.

We both feel it.

That connection.

The raw edges of my heart barely hold on under the onslaught of such heightened emotions. I feel bruised from them, aching, but in a way that reminds me that I'm capable of feeling and surviving, that I'm capable of loving and not collapsing under the weight of it.

We stumble back across the studio floor, barely noticing where we're going as our clothes are discarded piece by piece. Her vest top and shorts, my t-shirt and joggers are pulled off as we kiss and fumble, laughing between gasps and moans.

My hands palm her breasts as we hit the far wall, my lips burning a path across her jaw, down her neck, my tongue tasting the hollow that sits above her collarbone.

"Yes," she whispers, her fingers sliding down my chest, sending sparks flying over my skin as she cups my dick, squeezing once before pumping me up and down, up and down. My eyes lose focus as she jerks me off. A pool of electricity gathers at the base of my spine, making me almost mindless with the need to come.

"Christ, you need to stop that" I utter, even as I rut into her hand. She giggles and I reach between us, knocking her hand out of the way and cupping her pussy instead, silencing her with two fingers as I slip them inside of her easily. She's so wet, so open to my touch, so willing. "I *will* come if you keep touching me that way, and I don't want to. Not yet."

She gasps, head pressed back against the wall momentarily as I finger fuck her, crooking my fingers, reaching for that spot inside of her that makes her wild.

"I want you to. I want you to come," she replies breathily, licking her lips, holding in a groan as she accepts the hard press of my mouth against hers.

"Not until you do," I reply, dropping down her body, my mouth finding the hardened nub of her nipple, sucking it deep, latching onto it greedily as I pump my fingers inside of her.

Her hands fly to the back of my head as she presses my head tighter against her, urging me to suck harder, to graze my teeth against her in the way she likes.

I don't deny her. How can I?

I'd give her the world if I could because she has everything else. She took my heart and made it hers years ago, and she's owned my body and soul since then.

"Xeno, fuck. Xeno, I need you," she cries, her hips rocking against me as I slide lower, kneeling between her parted legs

"You've got me, Tiny. Fuck, you've got me," I reply, lifting her leg over my shoulder, burying my face in the slickness of her pussy.

She cries out. I suck her clit into my mouth.

She jerks against my face. I rub that spot deep inside of her.

She screams. My dick leaks, weeping for her pussy.

"Enough! I need you inside me!" she shouts, forcing my head and hand away, dropping to her knees as she grips my dick and climbs my body.

I adjust myself beneath her, bringing my legs out as she angles my dick towards her hole.

"Fuck!" I cry as she takes me to the hilt, her knees cracking against the hardwood floor as she rides me.

"Like this," she moans. "I will love you like this, always, Xeno. For as long as you'll let me."

"Goddamn it, Tiny," I groan, my heart swelling with love as my cock thickens with lust. She tilts her head back, her lips parting as she takes me in, grinding, riding me hard, like she has everything to prove, even though there is nothing she could do to ever make me stop loving her. "You know I'm no match against you. There's nothing that will ever stop me from loving you. Not my stupid, broken heart. Not anything, you hear me? You have me."

She cries out at that, her pubic bone hitting mine as she falls forward, taking me with her. My back hits the floor, her fingers curl into my shoulders as she fucks me into the ground.

Funny how she prevented me from fucking her violently, and here she is doing exactly that.

I'm not complaining, she has needs, ones I'm willing to fulfil.

Gladly, wholeheartedly. Forever.

Holding onto her hips with one hand and clutching onto her arse with the other, I help her, driving up into her relentlessly, rocking my hips up to meet each brutal thrust. We fuck like that until I can't breathe. Until sweat drips down my face and my heart is beating out of my chest.

"I'm going to come," I hiss, feeling it gathering, building, growing, ready to blow my mind.

"Come. Please come, please!" she pleads, her fingernails digging into me, leaving angry red crescents in the flesh of my shoulder as she rides me, fucking me, taking me so deep I feel it in my throat.

I hold onto her hips, clutching her against me as I come with a cry.

Shuddering, shaking, spurting my cum deep inside of her.

Her body quakes and she moans my name, falling over me as she swallows my cries, kissing me deep, fisting me tight, drawing out my pleasure with her own.

"I love you. I love you. I love you," she whispers against my lips, her pussy contracting hard around me, squeezing me as she comes. Coming for me, for us, *together* as we always do.

"OKAY, GIVE IT TO US," York says, resting his bare feet on the coffee table as we all gather around for a family meeting later that evening. "What's this all about? Did I forget to put the toilet seat down again? I mean to be fair I've been sick as dog, you can hardly blame me–"

"Let Pen speak," Zayn scolds, cutting him off with a light tap to the back of his head.

"Ow you fuckwit, no need to be a bully," York retorts, shoving him back.

"Children, children, can we have your attention please?" Dax interjects, glancing my way when he sees that I'm not laughing at their playfulness this time. Usually I find their banter and boyishness endearing, but there are things I want to discuss with them all and I need their undivided attention.

"Yes, *Daddy*," Zayn and York reply in unison, earning them both a death glare.

"I'm never going to live this down, am I?" Dax grumbles, swinging his arm over my shoulder and pulling me into his side.

Xeno chuckles. "You know you could always hand the title over to me."

"I told you, fight me for it," Dax retorts.

"Okay, okay, that's enough," I say, resting my hand on Dax's thigh and giving it a gentle squeeze, not because I think he's going to lose his cool, but because I want to get this conversation moving.

"Sorry, Kid. Tell us what's on your mind."

Taking a sip of my water, I place it on the coffee table and say, "I've been thinking a lot about us lately, and I wanted to discuss something with you all."

York shifts forward in his seat, the smile that always brightens his face dimming a little. "Hey, I'm not sure I'm liking the sound of this..." His voice trails off as he looks at the others for any signs that he should be worried.

"Wait, no. It's nothing like that," I reassure him, knowing where his thoughts are going even when he hasn't voiced them out loud. "I love you all so so much, forever–"

"And always," the four of them reply.

"And always," I repeat, remembering the day we came up with this saying.

It was about six weeks into the refurbishment of the club and I'd had an argument with Xeno and York over what tiles we should use in the ladies toilets. It had gotten pretty heated, pretty quickly, the stress of the build and the ongoing surgery to Dax's arm taking its toll on us all, and coming out in surprising ways. The three of us had ended the argument *making up* in the VIP room on the first floor. Whilst naked and satiated Xeno had told me I was their forever, and I'd responded that they were my always despite our argument. It had stuck. Ever since, whenever one of us says, *forever*, the rest of us reply, *and always*.

"What then?" Zayn prompts, cocking his head to the side as he regards me.

"Dax has been getting phantom pain again," I begin, and I feel him stiffen beside me. "But that isn't the reason why I want to talk. Well, not the only reason anyway."

"You didn't say anything," York accuses Dax, concern painting his handsome face.

"It's not a big deal," Dax replies with a shrug, his hand absentmindedly cupping his stump. "I called Hudson this morning. He pulled some strings and I've got an appointment with the consultant in a couple days. They'll do some checks. I'm not worried. It is what it is."

York huffs out a breath. "I'm not worried either, mate, but I am pissed off you've been keeping this to yourself."

"Well now you know. I've got it under control. Don't stress."

"See that's the thing. You *are* stressed," I point out, giving his thigh another gentle squeeze.

"I'm not," he protests.

"We *all* are," I continue, cutting him off as I look up at him, then across to Xeno who's gaze flickers with understanding. "Xeno's been having a hard time lately too."

We all look over at Xeno who puffs out his cheeks, blowing out a long breath before giving a sharp nod of his head in acknowledgement. "I have," he admits.

"You know we got you, bro," Zayn says in an attempt to reassure Xeno. "If shit gets too heavy, we're here."

"I know that," Xeno replies, swiping a hand through his hair. "Tiny and I worked through some of it earlier today. I'm good."

"Ah, so that's why you took forever to come and get lunch, you were *eating* elsewhere," York says with a grin, his smile falling when Dax leans over and flicks his ear.

"I know you've been off your game lately because you've had the flu, but can you reel in the jokes for one minute and let Kid speak? This is important."

"Sorry, Titch," York says, giving me a sheepish smile. "You know me, banter is my way of dealing with heavy shit."

"I know, and I love you for it," I say, reaching over and giving him a kiss on the cheek before continuing.

"Love you back," York whispers, shifting his head so he can capture another kiss on my lips before letting me curl back into Dax's side.

"As I was saying, I think we're *all* a bit stressed, and before either of you try to deny it," I say, pointing first at Zayn. "Don't think I haven't noticed how tired you are because of your insomnia."

"I swear it's just a blip," he says, but I know when he's lying and he's lying now.

Zayn always holds eye contact, until he's lying, that is, and then he looks everywhere else bar me. But I let that go as I turn my attention to York.

"And you got as sick as you did because you're rundown trying to juggle training new staff and overseeing the rebuild of Chastity Nightclub with Zayn."

York doesn't bother to deny it because he knows it's true.

"What about you, Pen?" Zayn asks, focusing his attention on me now. "You said we're all stressed. So are you?"

I don't avoid the question. I face it head on. "Not stressed per say, just a little overwhelmed. Maybe feeling a little more tired than usual, I guess."

"Fuck," Dax mutters, hauling me closer to his side and dropping a kiss to my head.

"My sentiment exactly," York adds, pinching the bridge of his nose. "We've not been paying attention. That's on us. What can we do to help?"

"This is what I wanted to talk to you all about," I say, glancing over at Xeno who gives me an encouraging smile. After our brief discussion earlier he already knows what I'm thinking. "I miss us."

Zayn frowns. "*Us?* You have us. Forever and always, remember?"

"What I mean to say is that I miss the 'us' when we were kids. The 'us' that brought us together, and I think... No, I *know* that not dancing together as a crew is having this awful affect on us all. In different ways maybe, but the outcome is still the same. I miss it. I miss dancing with you all," I admit.

The room falls silent whilst they digest what I've just said. Xeno is the first to speak.

"Earlier Tiny pointed out something fundamental to me. She said that before we had each other, we had dance. That was our coping mechanism, our escape, a way to express all the shit we'd buried inside," he says, looking between us all. "It kept us all on an even keel, then when we found each other, and we formed our crew, dancing became our joy, our way to communicate with each other without even needing to speak. It gave us true happiness, and I'm not saying we're not happy, we *are*. Fuck, you're my family. This life is *everything* I wanted, more than I'd hoped for..." Xeno's voice trails off and he clears his throat before continuing. "The thing is we've pushed aside that one crucial piece of our relationship because we've been so busy striving to build our lives together that we've forgotten what truly matters. It's not the money, or the success of our businesses, it's *us*. Dance is a vital part of *us* just as much as our friendship, and our love for each other is, and I for one want it back."

"I miss it too," Dax admits, glancing over at Xeno who gives him a warm smile, a look passing between them. My heart swells with love for these men, for how they understand without words needing to be spoken what the other is thinking. With his fingers trailing up and down my arm, Dax continues. "I didn't realise how much I missed dancing until Kid and I battled last night," he says, reaching around and pressing his palm against the middle of my chest. "And if I'm truly honest, I've avoided dancing because of my injury. I can't do all the things I used to be able to do before. I can't lift you Kid, the way I used too, and that's fucking hard to deal with."

"Oh Dax," I cry, a lump in my throat forming. "Dancing with you is so much more than just a couple of lifts. You know that, right?"

"The sensible part of me knows that, but try telling the rest of me that. It makes me feel…" his voice trails off as he chews on his lip.

"Just say it, mate. We ain't gonna judge," York says, not a hint of a smile or a joke anywhere near his lips. For all his banter, he knows when it's important to just listen, to be supportive, and I love him for it. I love them all for sitting here and listening, talking, *loving* each other like real men should.

Dax turns his body towards mine, his arm slipping out from behind me as he reaches for my face, cupping my cheek. "Like I can't take care of you."

"But you can. You have. You *do*, Dax."

"What if someone came for you again? What then, Kid?"

"You'll protect me, just like you did that day, and we'll do the same for you because this isn't a one way street," I reply vehemently, curling my fingers around his hand and pressing a warm kiss against his palm. "I've seen how hard you've fought through your recovery, how you've adjusted to this new version of yourself despite how traumatic it's been. There's no doubt in my mind that not only will you dance as well as you always have, you'll kill any man who tries to hurt me, or any of us. That is who you are. You're our protector, you're *my* avenging dark angel–"

"Remember, you're the Daddy," York adds, a smile bleeding across his face and into his voice.

Dax chuckles and Zayn grins.

"Okay, okay, he's the fucking Daddy," Xeno concedes, seeing the funny side.

We all laugh then, and the sound is freeing.

"Okay then, so what now?" York asks. "I'm all for making this work, but realistically, we've got three clubs to run and barely any time to do much else but eat, sleep and fuck."

"We delegate work to other people then carve out much needed time for the five of us," I say. It's such an obvious solution that I don't understand why we never thought of it earlier. "It's not as if we don't already have people stepping in and managing the clubs when we've got other business to deal with. Why not give them more responsibility?"

"Because Xeno is a control freak," Zayn points out.

"I'm willing to let go of some of the control to make this work," he replies with a rueful look on his face.

"You are?" York glances at me and raises his brows, before returning his attention to Xeno. "Okay, who are you and where's the real Xeno?"

Xeno shrugs. "It's not a big deal. I've already got a few people in mind."

"Who?" Dax asks, shifting position as I settle back into his side.

"Gray for one," he replies.

"Gray works for Grim and Beast," York points out.

"Actually, they've been trying to get him to take on more responsibility at Tales, but he won't," Dax says. "Beast told me the other week. I think he was a bit put out that Gray said no."

"Why?" Zayn asks. "He's worked for them for years."

"Why do you think?" Xeno says, looking at me briefly. I know what he's thinking, because I'm thinking it too.

"Lena?"

Xeno nods. "He's a goner for her."

"But *why* hasn't he made a move? I'm pretty sure Gray has been in love with her for a while now," York asks, shifting on the sofa as he leans forward. He loves a good gossip, and when Beast and him get together they're like a couple of old maids, nagging over a cup of tea.

"She's in love with him too," I add. "Whenever he pops over to the club whilst she's working, she gets this look on her face."

Zayn pulls a face. "What look?"

"Possessive," I explain. "God forbid any girl tries chatting him up. The last time that happened, Lena *accidentally* spilled a whole tray of drinks over the poor woman who dared approach him."

Zayn laughs. "Okay, so they like each other. What's the issue? They're both adults."

"My guess is that Gray can't get over the fact that he was asked to protect Lena when she was a kid whilst we were dealing with your brother," Xeno continues. "He's a good man. He doesn't want to look like some kind of pervert going after her now given their history."

"It's not as if he made a move, *any* move when she was a child. He still hasn't and she's an adult, She's twenty now," Zayn points out.

"Much to Lena's annoyance," I add, blowing out a breath. "She hasn't said outright to me that she loves him–Lena has always played her cards close to her chest–but I *know* it hurts her."

"I can see why he might feel the way he does," Dax says, "But we all know Gray, the man is a straight-up good guy. He's been looking out for Lena even after the whole thing with your brother was sorted. He dealt with that arsehole Jack who broke her heart when she was seventeen."

"Lena still doesn't know about that," I say, chewing my lip. "She thinks he was beaten up by some guy who mugged him, not Gray, who gave him a good arse-kicking for even daring to raise a hand to her."

"Maybe he should have a conversation with Beast. Didn't he have a similar situation with Grim?" York suggests.

"Gray's not much of a talker," Dax adds, "But I guess it's worth a shot?"

I shake my head. "No. Let's leave them to sort this out their own way. I don't want to interfere. Things will work out if they're supposed to work out."

"So you don't think I should offer him the management position at the club?" Xeno asks, giving me a look that suggests he knows what the answer will be.

"I didn't say that," I reply, hiding a smile. "We'll offer him the job. If he takes it, then we'll see how working together every night of the week works out for the pair of them."

York chuckles. "Not interfering?"

I can't hide the smile this time. "Let's just say we're giving fate a helping hand and leave it at that."

"Fair enough," he agrees with a wink.

"Okay, so I'll speak with Grim and Beast first, then if they're okay with it, we'll offer the job to Gray. That means we'll have a lot more time on our hands," Xeno says.

"What about the other clubs?" Zayn asks, running a hand through his hair. "Pierre is still learning the ropes at Jewels, and Chastity nightclub is nowhere near ready for opening in a couple of months. The builders have eight of the ten rooms done, but they've still got to finish the whole upper level."

His voice rises with the stress, and I wriggle out of Dax's arms, dropping down on the sofa next to him. Wrapping my arms around his waist, I say, "You definitely need a break. Samantha has the construction team in hand, right?"

"She's assured me it will get done. That there's enough time..."

His voice trails off as I press a kiss against his cheek, snuggling into his side as I breathe in his familiar scent. "Then you've got to trust her. We hired her for a reason. She's the best project manager in London."

"You're right," Zayn agrees, letting out a slow breath as he hugs me closer. "Maybe Xeno isn't the only control freak in this family."

York nudges Zayn with his elbow. "Mate, if I didn't already know you two weren't related I'd be convinced you were brothers."

"Then I'm the brother with the bigger dick," Xeno says, expression deadpan.

All four of us whip our heads around and stare at Xeno.

When his lips begin to twitch and he can no longer hold in the laugh, we all join in.

For the next five minutes, my four men argue over who has the biggest cock until finally I intervene by saying, "It's not the size that matters, it's what you do with it that counts."

"Hear that?" Zayn questions. "Our woman has spoken, and her word is law."

"That's only because you've got the smallest dick," York smirks, bringing his arms up to protect his face when Zayn picks up a cushion and swats him with it.

"And I *know* what to do with it," Zayn counters, before pulling me back into his arms and kissing the breath from my lungs.

When we come up for air, I say, "He's not wrong."

"I'm still the biggest," Dax mutters under his breath, shrugging when I shake my head at him in amusement. "It's not a lie if it's true," he adds.

"Okay, okay, enough dick talk. You know I love every one of your dicks as much as I love each of you," I say with a grin. "But we've gone off topic a little here. The point I was trying to make before talk of cocks took over is that I want to dance with you all, and I think we should put something together for the dance competition we're hosting."

"That's in two weeks, Tiny," Xeno points out with a frown.

"I'm aware of that. I think we can pull it off."

"We're not kids anymore," Dax says, glancing at his stump, his jaw gritting. "Last night showed me I'm not as flexible as I used to be."

"Pretty sure you're flexible enough, going by last night's

antics. Zayn hasn't shut up about how much fun you had," York adds, popping his bottom lip like a petulant child before grinning. "I'm in!"

I lean over Zayn and kiss York on the cheek, loving his exuberance, appreciating his faith in us. "Thank you."

"Always, Titch. I'm in on this one hundred percent. Fuck, anyone else getting that excited butterfly feeling in your stomach?"

"That's the food Zayn and Dax made earlier," Xeno quips, a half smile lifting his lips. Regardless, I hear the caution in his voice.

"You've changed your mind?" I ask Xeno.

"Not about dancing with you all. Of course not." He looks up at me from beneath his heavy brows. "Performing for an audience is a whole other ballgame. It's been a while."

"Exactly," I insist, meeting his gaze. "Which is precisely why this opportunity is so perfect for us. I want to do this. I *need* to."

"Then we do this," he says with a brief nod of his head. "Whatever you want, Tiny. I'm in."

"Zayn?" I ask, pulling out of his hold so I can read his expression.

"I've already got a million ideas," he says, giving me my favourite chipped-tooth grin.

"Perfect, then there's no time like the present," I say, jumping up, warmth blooming inside my chest as I look at each of my men in turn.

"If you keep looking at us like that I'm not sure we'll make it to the studio," York says, pushing to his feet, and biting his bottom lip as he looks at me suggestively.

"Keep that thought in mind," I murmur as he steps closer, dragging me towards him.

"Does that mean you want to–?"

"Dance first, and if you've still got enough energy loverboy, then we'll see about later," I reply, stepping back and striding towards the other side of the room.

"What the hell? Did you just turn me down?" York says with a faux hurt expression on his face.

"Good things come to those who wait," I sass back, throwing him a promising smile.

"Well, when you put it like that," he responds. "But I call dibs on being the big spoon. It's been a while since I've been able to wrap myself around you. I've missed it, Titch."

"Come on, let's do this," Zayn says, dropping his arm around York's shoulder as Xeno and Dax climb to their feet. "We promise you can be the big spoon, right guys?"

A look passes between Dax and Xeno. Xeno grins, "So long as it's alright with *Daddy*..."

SIX

Stupid Cupid

YORK

"SO WHAT'S THIS ALL ABOUT?" Beast asks amiably, jiggling Iris on his lap as we sit in Grim's office at Tales the next morning.

She giggles, her dark waves bouncing over her shoulders. She sure is the cutest, five year old kid. Not sure how Beast helped create her, then again, Grim's the one with all the looks, so there's that.

"We've got a favour to ask…" I say, my voice trailing off as I try to figure out the best way to tell Beast we want to steal his most loyal employee.

"Why so serious. We're all friends here," Beast points out, looking bemused.

"It's about Gray," Xeno begins, glancing over at Pen, then me.

"What about him?" Beast asks absentmindedly as he tickles Iris under the chin when she tugs on his beard.

"We want to offer him a job," Pen blurts out, causing Beast to snap his head up.

He narrows his eyes at us. "You poaching one of my men?"

"No, we'd never ask him to come and work for us without your approval first. That's why we're here," I add, leaning forward to grab Iris's teddy that she dropped on the floor and passing it back to her.

She gives me a wide grin that melts my heart. Fuck, I don't know how Beast can be so chilled out when it comes to Iris. I know if we ever had kids, I'd be the most protective. I know everyone thinks I'm the joker of the group and the most light-hearted, but God help anyone who ever falls in love with our children, let alone dares hurt them. Then again, Beast has literally cut out the hearts of the men who hurt Grim, so I've no doubt he'd be a tough nut to crack when it comes to future suitors for Iris.

"Good to know," Beast replies, waiting for me to continue.

"We wanted to ask whether you'd be okay with that," I explain. "If you're not cool with that, no hard feelings. We'll find someone else."

"Okay with what?" Grim asks as she steps into the office, a

clipboard in her hand that she immediately drops onto her desk so she can press a kiss against Iris's head, then Beast lips. She's been working closely with Clancy and the dancers here at Tales on the performance they're putting together for the big fight that's coming up this Saturday night. Neither Beast nor Grim will tell us who's fighting, but it must be a couple of heavy hitters–literally–for them to be so secretive about it. Of course, we're attending so we'll find out soon enough.

"They want to poach Gray from us," Beast explains as Grim perches on the edge of her desk, her leather clad legs crossed at the ankles as she looks between the three of us. Grim always dresses badass, her aesthetic totally gives off *don't fuck with me vibes*, and I'm here for it. In a totally platonic, friends kind of way, because no one comes close to how I feel about Titch. Except maybe my best mates, which is a given.

"Really? Okay, that's not what I was expecting when you said you wanted a meeting," she says, frowning a little.

"Yeah, and I'm not sure how I feel about it to be honest," Beast adds as Iris cuddles against his broad chest and sticks her thumb in her mouth. "Gray's worked for me since he was a kid. He's family. Besides, he didn't even take *my* offer of a promotion. What makes you think he'll take yours?"

I catch Pen's eye and she nods, giving me permission to elaborate. "Lena."

"Lena?" Beast questions, adjusting Iris in his arms as her eyelids start to droop.

"Ah, I get it," Grim remarks with a knowing look.

Beast looks over at her. "Get what?"

"You can't be serious?" Grim chuckles, rolling her eyes.

"And there's me thinking you were pretty insightful when it comes to Gray."

For a moment Beast looks blankly at Grim, but then it suddenly dawns on him. "Oh shit! So this is some kind of elaborate match making opportunity because Gray can't pull his finger out of his arse and finally admit what he feels for Lena. I get it now."

"*Arse,*" Iris mutters in her half-sleep state and we all laugh.

"Well, it's partly why we want to offer him the position of managing Twisted Bullet for us, but not the main reason," Pen explains with a rueful smile.

"What's the other reason? You lot opening up yet *another* club? If we didn't fucking love you so much, we'd start getting pissed off at all the competition," Beast says.

"Fuck, no," I reply, swiping a hand through my hair. "That's the *last* thing on our minds."

"What then?"

"Dance," Xeno says.

"Dance?" Beast snorts. "If it hadn't slipped your notice, Gray has two left feet. Did you not see how fucking awkward he was at our wedding? The guy might be a badass, but he ain't no dancer."

Pen giggles. "Not Gray. *Us.* We want to dance."

"And you need to hire Gray to do that?" Grim asks, cocking her head.

"Yeah," I confirm. "We haven't danced since we opened up Twisted Bullet. It's taking a toll."

"But why haven't you danced?" Beast asks, shooting us a

questioning look. "Ain't that your thing? I mean, don't you all just go home and prance about in your studio or whatever?"

"Okay, first of all we don't prance, big guy," I admonish with a shake of my head.

"Well, I don't fucking know. It felt like prancing about to me when you forced me to learn that dance for our wedding."

"That's not what you said at the time," I retort with a smirk. "Pretty sure you said something along the lines of, 'fuck man, this dancing lark is better than sex.' Right?"

"What? Better than sex with *me*?" Grim questions, feigning hurt as she presses a hand against her chest and widens her eyes.

"Don't listen to that conniving bastard, I did *not* say that dancing is better than having sex with you. Nothing is better than having sex with you," he says, glaring at me.

I hold in a laugh. "What, not even having sex with yourself?"

"Shut the fuck up, man. You're gonna get a guy in trouble!" Beast grinds out.

Grim shakes her head, leans over and whispers something in Beast's ear, something that's clearly dirty given the look on Beast's face. He's getting lucky tonight, that's for sure. Beast clears his throat, smothering a smile.

"You know it, baby," he murmurs, before turning his attention back to me. "Okay, so you guys want to dance, and you need the time to do that, hence wanting to hire Gray?"

"Exactly," Xeno agrees. "We've been focusing on the clubs, and we haven't had time for each other in the way that's important to us as a family. We're hosting a dance competition at the club in a couple weeks. We want to put together a performance."

"You're entering the competition?" Grim asks.

"No, that's against the rules as hosts. But we do want to perform. We need to," Pen adds.

Xeno nods in agreement. "So we figured Gray would be the best person to ask. He spends a hell of a lot of time at Twisted Bullet anyway–"

"Because of Lena," Beast fills in.

"Precisely. We all know he's trustworthy, smart, and can handle any issue that might crop up. We couldn't think of a better person to take over the reins," I add.

"How long? Is this a temporary thing, or a more permanent job offer?" Grim asks as she considers our proposal.

"We were thinking of a three month trial, if he agrees of course," Xeno replies. "After that it depends on whether you guys are happy to let him go and, of course, if he wants to stay. I know he's integral to your team, and I appreciate what we're asking here. Like York said, you can say no and we wouldn't be offended."

Grim flicks her gaze to Pen. "You need this, right?" she asks knowingly.

Pen nods. "We do. We wouldn't ask if it wasn't important."

"Then I'm okay with it," Grim replies. "You did us a huge favour looking after Iris when we needed you to. Fuck, you were willing to be her parents should anything have happened to me and Beast. This is the least we can do."

"Hey, you know we did that without needing anything in return, right? You're family," Pen says, reaching forward and gently stroking Iris's hair off her face as she sleeps peacefully. "Iris is my goddaughter, I love her as if she's my own."

"*We* love her as though she's our own," I add, glancing at Xeno who's looking at Iris with a fierce kind of protectiveness that we all feel towards her. Those few weeks we looked after her whilst Grim and Beast went to rescue Christy from the Masks–which, as it happens, turned out to be a wasted journey given she fell in love with the fuckers–showed us all how much we wanted to be dads.

"We know that," Beast adds, clearing his throat.

"Is that a tear?" I joke, noticing how his eyes appear to glisten

"Fuck, yeah, it is," Beast retorts, swiping at his face. "Being a dad makes you fucking soft."

"I disagree. Becoming a dad has made you the best version of yourself," Xeno says, meeting Beast's gaze. "Iris couldn't have a better dad. She'll grow up knowing how much she's loved. Some of us didn't get so lucky."

"Thanks, mate," Beast mutters, hauling a sleeping Iris closer against his chest. "Fucking scariest thing I've ever done, and I'm constantly fucking questioning everything I do when it comes to this sassy girl of ours, but I wouldn't change a thing. She owns us both, and I think she already knows it."

"Damn straight she knows it. She's her mother's daughter after all," Grim adds.

Beast chuckles. "You ain't wrong there, love. Point is, maybe you guys should try it one day. I think you'd make great dads, and we already know Pen would be a brilliant mother. Pretty sure it was due to her that Iris survived those couple weeks in your care."

Pen's cheeks flush and Xeno chuckles. "If I had my way Tiny would already have a belly full of our kid."

"Well, sign me the fuck up," I pipe up. "More than happy to help make a baby. Frankly, I was more than happy last night, but these fuckers were all tired after spending the afternoon putting together a routine that they all fell asleep as soon as their heads hit the pillow."

Titch winces. "Sorry about that, I was knackered."

"There's always tonight," I reply, wiggling my eyebrows, before pressing a kiss against her lips.

"Now who needs a room," Beast quips, smirking as we pull apart. "How would that work anyway?"

"How would what work?" Xeno chuckles knowing full well what Beast means.

"Don't tell me you need a lesson in how babies are made?" I joke.

"You know what I mean, arsehole. Like, if you did want to have a baby, who gets the honour of planting the seed, so to speak?"

"Jesus, Beast, personal much? You don't have to answer that," Grim says, giving his shoulder a shove.

"That's simple," Pen says softly before meeting Beast's inquisitive gaze. "If we ever chose to have children, it would happen as it was meant to, and we wouldn't do a paternity test because as far as I'm concerned they'd all be her father."

"*Her?*" Grim asks, cocking her head to the side.

"Or him," Pen adds with a smile. "Either way, it wouldn't

matter to us who the biological father is, because I know they'd all take responsibility for any child we have together, and they would love them as fiercely as we love each other."

"Damn straight," I say, squeezing Titch's thigh.

"I second that," Xeno adds.

Beast whistles. "Your set up is fucking fascinating to me, but I ain't one to judge. You do you. I think you'd make fucking great parents, and just so you know, Iris could do with a playmate."

"She already has a couple of playmates, so ignore Beast. No pressure here," Grim adds.

"George and Sebastian are little toerags and not a good influence on Iris," Beast retorts, referring to Asia's younger brothers that she and her guys have parental responsibility for. "Plus they're too old for her."

"Oh, don't be so mean," Grim admonishes. "Those two boys are lively, sure, but they have good hearts just like their older sister. Besides, Ford is responsible for their care too and he's my brother and there's no way he'll let them get away with any poor behaviour around Iris."

"Hmm," Beast mutters. "Well I've got my eye on them. One wrong move and I'll–"

"You'll do absolutely nothing. They're kids. Iris loves them," Grim points out.

"Exactly, and kids grow up into adults, Not sure you'll be as relaxed with them hanging out with Iris when they're all grown up."

"They're family," Grim adds with a shake of her head.

"Not by blood," Beast stutters.

Grim shakes her head, rolling her eyes. "Okay, so making babies aside, we're happy for you to offer the job to Gray, and if he wants to keep it, then we're cool with that too. Aren't we Beast?"

"Yeah, we're good," he agrees, getting to his feet. Iris murmurs in her sleep and he lifts her in his arms and presses a kiss against her cheek. "Got to get sleeping beauty home for a good night's rest before the hoards arrive."

"Hoards?" Xeno asks.

"Asia, Ford and the gang are visiting so they can enjoy the fight at Tales this weekend. So is Christy and The Masks," Grim explains.

Pen smiles. "So you've got a full house then?"

"Yep, this one won't get a wink of sleep whilst those toerags–"

"Beast!" Grim warns.

"Whilst George and Sebastian are staying over. If you thought Iris was sassy with us, you ain't seen nothing. She's *Miss Sassypants the Second* when they're about."

"I hope you're not suggesting I'm *Miss Sassypants the First*," Grim accuses.

Beast smirks. "If the shoe fits, darling."

"Well, it sounds like Iris can handle them all on her own," I comment with a grin.

"Yeah, that's what I'm worried about," Beast scowls in response.

"Mate, I think you should relax," Xeno says, laughing as Beast pulls a face.

"Say that to me again when you become a dad," he quips

before striding out of the room and into the club, a sleepy Iris resting peacefully in his arms.

We follow Beast into Tales, and despite the hustle and bustle going on around us, Iris doesn't stir as their team gets the club ready for this weekend's fight. The club is situated in a huge warehouse, providing ample room to house over two hundred seated guests, three bars, a huge cage to fight in and whatever props they need for the dancers to use in their performance.

It's an impressive set-up and we've learnt a great deal from Beast and Grim over the years.

"I'm just going to say hi to Clancy. I haven't seen her for a while," Pen says, motioning towards her friend who's over on the far side of the warehouse going through her routine with Grim's dance troupe for this weekend's performance.

It's unique for an underground fight club like Tales to have dancers perform before and after fights, but it has proven successful. Grim's fight club is renowned for hosting the best fights, accompanied by the best shows in the whole of the UK. It's why the club is heaving most weekends.

"I'll come with you, Pen. I need to firm up some final details with Clancy for the show anyway," Grim adds, joining her.

"We'll wait in the car," I call after Titch.

"Won't be long," she replies, throwing me a smile over her shoulder before disappearing.

"Gray's over there," Beast says, jerking his chin towards Gray who's speaking to a couple of the guys on the security team on the other side of the warehouse. "You may as well take the opportunity to grab him. No time like the present and all that."

"You don't mind us having the conversation now?" Xeno asks.

"Nah. I gotta get Iris home whilst Grim finishes up here anyway. See you at the fight this weekend?"

Gripping Beast on the shoulder, I give it a friendly squeeze. "Wouldn't miss it for the world."

"Good. Catch you later."

"Looking forward to it," Xeno says, before twisting on his heel and striding towards Gray.

"You think he's gonna say yes?" I ask, falling into step beside him.

"If you were offered a job to work as the manager of the woman you were secretly in love with, would you turn the job down?"

I laugh. "No. No, I would not. I'd jump at the chance. All those moments working late nights together. All that tension. Fuck me, I'd *love* it."

"Precisely," Xeno retorts, side-eying me with an amused smirk. "Let's see if we can play Cupid."

"Mate, I've got my bow and arrow ready. Gray ain't gonna know what hit him."

"Yeah, where Lena's concerned, I really don't think he knows just what he's getting into."

"Shh, enough talk of Lena," I say, squashing a grin as we get within hearing distance of Gray. "Let's do this shit properly. Titch will kill us if we give the game away."

"Afternoon," Gray says as we approach him, and the two

members of security give us a nod before wandering off. "You need me for something?"

"You could say that," Xeno says.

"Okay," he replies cautiously, folding his arms across his chest. "Shoot."

Xeno side-eyes me, and I suppress a smile at the thought of shooting an arrow into Gray's heart just like Cupid would.

SEVEN

Sisters Are Doing it For Themselves

PEN

"THANKS FOR THIS," I say to Grim, taking a sip of my drink as I lean back in my seat and soak in the atmosphere of her kitchen.

It seems like a million years ago when this house was once the headquarters of the Skins, the gang the Breakers belonged to as kids. Grim and Beast brought the property and made it into their home, completely transforming it a few months before Jeb, the leader of the Skins was taken out.

Instead of the cracked and chipped plaster, leaky sink and

mold on the floor and ceiling that I remember so well, the walls are now painted a comforting shade of mocha, giving the space a baked-earth feel. The large wooden table, that we're sitting at now, stands central to the room, with oak cupboards running the circumference. Vibrant, patterned tilework adorns the back-splash above the oven and countertops adding to its homely ambiance. Over the years Grim has re-decorated the kitchen several times, this is my favourite by far.

"I figured you needed some girl time when we had that chat in the office the other day," Grim replies knowingly, tucking a wayward strand of hair behind her ear.

Even when she's make-up free, her hair piled up on top of her head in a messy bun and wearing a tracksuit that's seen better days, she still manages to look badass. Most days I wish I had my shit together like she does. She makes everything seem so effortless.

"You figured right," I agree with a nod, my gaze drifting to the glass of wine in my hands as I take a sip.

"That's a lot of testosterone you're having to deal with on a daily basis. There has to be a balance, and hanging out with the girls is just the tonic you need, am I right?" she asks.

"Hey, there are plenty of perks being surrounded by men," Christy says, nudging me with her elbow, her differently coloured eyes sparkling with amusement. "I can think of three very large perks, actually. *Four* in Pen's case."

"We're not talking about how many times you're getting fucked," Grim retorts, throwing a look at her sister. "That's one conversation too far."

"Oh right, sorry. I keep forgetting you still think I'm a virgin who hasn't had any experience with one cock, let alone have taken three... *At once."*

Grim snorts. "Either your men have tiny dicks, or you have a detachable jaw."

"I wasn't talking about my mouth," Christy grins, cocking a brow as she knocks back the rest of her wine.

I choke on my drink, smothering a laugh at their banter. When I first met Christy a few years back she seemed reserved, thoughtful, but we've gotten to know each other over the years and she has a dirty sense of humour that amuses me.

Grim wrinkles her nose. "You want to watch out for that, after giving birth to a tiny human, I know what it's like to have a vagina that's not as tight as it used to be."

"Eww, gross! You might not want to hear about my sex life, but I definitely don't want to hear about your bucket-fanny."

"Christy!" I exclaim in shock, then bark out a laugh as Grim shoots her a horrified look.

"I can't believe that you just insinuated my vagina is the size of a bucket!" Grim scolds, aghast.

Christy shrugs nonchalantly. "Hey, I'm only repeating what you just said, things tend to loosen up a bit down there after having a baby. It's not a big deal. You can always do kegels or something. Just ask Cynthia, she'll tell you the same. Faith was a huge baby, but I bet your arse *she's* been doing her exercises."

"Thanks for the advice," Grim deadpans, rolling her eyes. "But I *know* how to look after my vagina thank you very much! Anyway," she says, redirecting the conversation back to me. "I hear Gray took the job offer."

"He did. To be honest it didn't take much persuasion," I reply, still feeling a little guilty that we stole him from them.

"We all know how he feels about Lena. Makes perfect sense," Grim retorts, not in the least bothered that he's agreed to work at our club instead of taking the job Beast offered him.

"Ah, I wondered when that would happen," Christy comments, a knowing look on her face.

"You've seen something?" Grim asks, leaning forward in her seat to grab her glass of wine and taking a sip. She eyes her sister over the rim of her glass, waiting for her to elaborate.

"You know I can't say," she replies, all the laughter from earlier replaced with a seriousness that gives me goosebumps.

Christy is known for seeing things that haven't happened yet, Initially I was sceptical, but there's no doubt in my mind she's as special as Grim has always said. It's why I ask her what I do next. "Have I done the right thing?"

Christy wraps her hand around mine and squeezes gently. "Your instincts when it comes to the people you love are spot on. Don't worry about Lena. Things will work out the way they're supposed to."

I release a sigh of relief. "Thank goodness. I just want her to be happy, and honestly, she's been miserable these past few years pining after Gray while he kept his distance."

"I know the feeling," Grim chuckles. "Beast tortured me until I shot him, and then he let me wallow for two years after that. *Bastard.*"

"Not sure I blame him," Christy says, grinning when Grim picks up an olive from the bowl on the table and chucks it at her.

Dodging the olive, Christy's smile drops to a more sombre

expression. "These men were sent to torment us," she says, and I've no doubt she's remembering the tumultuous start to her relationship with The Masks, which eventually blossomed into a beautiful love story.

"They sure were. But we're strong, badass women capable of taming the wild beasts in our lives," Grim says, holding up her glass of wine and inviting us to clink our drinks together.

"Cheers to that," I agree, raising my glass.

"And to multiple cocks," Christy adds playfully.

We all laugh heartily.

"Hey, what did we miss?" Asia says as she steps into the kitchen, Clancy following behind her.

"Hey Clancy," I say, giving my friend a welcoming smile.

"Hey, Pen. Ladies," she replies, taking the glass of wine that Grim offers her, and dropping down in the seat opposite me.

"So what were you all laughing about? I thought Beast had rocked up in his birthday suit again," Asia says, shivering at the memory as she takes her own glass of wine and sits down next to Christy.

"You've seen Beast naked?" I snort, glancing at Grim who pulls a face.

"By accident," Asia replies quickly. "Last night he was heading out of the toilet, and I was trying to enter. I got an eyeful of his dick jewellery. Believe me, it's not something I'll forget in a hurry. That thing looked fucking lethal."

"He's got a pierced dick?" Clancy asks, her face lighting up in amusement. "The saucy old bugger."

"Hey, enough of the old," Grim counters, smothering a smile as we all look at her in a mixture of disbelief and awe.

No wonder she's happy with just the one dick when it comes with added features. "He's in his prime, thank you very much."

"Now I understand why the thought of more dicks is a no go for you, sis. You've been getting fucked by the Rolls Royce of dicks all this time!" Christy exclaims, clearly tickled by the thought.

"Oh my god, Christy, do *not* tell him he has the Rolls Royce of dicks, his head will get so large he won't fit through the door," Grim pleads.

"By the sounds of it, your door is big enough to accommodate the largest of heads," Christy quips, waggling her eyebrows.

"Jesus, fucking christ," Grim mutters, and we all fall about laughing once again.

"Seriously though," Asia says after we calm down a bit, "Some days I'm just exhausted with all the dicks."

"Surely not. You love your guys," Christy says.

"Of course I love them, but you know how it is. If you're men are anything like mine, they're horny fuckers most of the time, and whilst I enjoy having a lot of sex, sometimes I could just use a good night's sleep," Asia explains, pulling a face that has us all giggling.

"I'm telling you ladies you need to include another woman in your harem. She can take up some of the slack," Clancy points out.

"Are you offering?" Grim asks, nudging Clancy with her elbow.

Clancy offers her a wink back. "Hey, I've got my hands full

with River and Lola. Besides, Pen turned me down the last time I offered to help her out, didn't you, Pen?"

"Damn straight I did, you horny bitch. I'm a little territorial when it comes to my men, and as much as I love you, Clancy, I'm not sharing them," I say adamantly.

"Your loss." Clancy shrugs, shooting me a wink so I know she's only joking with me, and that she'd never overstep where my men are concerned. Besides, she's so stupidly in love with Lola and River, that she wouldn't dream of upsetting the balance of their incredible relationship.

"Don't listen to Clancy," I say, waving away the ridiculous idea, because if Asia is anything like me and Christy I know she wouldn't want to share her men with another woman despite everything she's said. "There are other ways to deal with your situation."

"Oh yeah? What's the solution?" Asia asks, "Because my v-jay-jay needs a well-earned holiday."

"A schedule," I reply, deadly serious. "One that includes you getting a night off every week."

"A schedule?" Asia smirks. "*You* have a schedule?"

"*We* have a schedule," I correct. "Each of my guys has a dedicated night a week alone with me, and then we spend two nights together as a group, and then I have a night to myself. Like tonight for example. It's worked so far."

"Well, shit, that seems so... *simple*. Why didn't I think of it before?"

"It works for us. There's no harm in giving it a try," I offer.

Asia shifts forward in her seat, her purple streaked hair a sleek curtain that falls forward over her shoulder as she moves.

"As soon as I've got a moment alone with the guys, I'm going to have a chat with them about it. Thanks, Pen."

"You're welcome." I grin and reach for an olive, popping it in my mouth before immediately spitting it out into my hand. Eww, tastes foul. Must be off. I pop it into the napkin on the table, thankful no one's noticed the fact I nearly threw up.

"Okay, so now we've got that sorted," Grim says, turning her attention back to me. "How's the choreography going with you and the guys? I'm not gonna lie. I'm excited to see you perform together again."

"Wait, you are? *When?*" Clancy asks, snapping her eyes to mine. "That's great news!"

I smile softly, loving their enthusiasm. "The weekend after next we're hosting a dance competition at Twisted Bullet. We're not entering, but we are performing that night."

"George and Sebastian will be dancing too, in Rose and Ivan's troupe," Asia blurts out, a look of pure pride crossing her features.

"They are? You didn't mention it," I reply.

"We wanted it to be a surprise, but I guess I let the cat out of the bag," Asia laughs with a shrug.

"When I heard Rose had entered her troupe in the competition I had wondered whether you guys would be attending to support them. I know how close you all are with Rose and her men. I can't wait to see George and Sebastian dancing too."

"Me either," Asia replies, her face lighting up as she talks. "Rose has been teaching George and Sebastian ballet for the last few years. They love it. I think Luka–shit, I mean, *Ivan*, has had a massive influence on them. They want to be ballet dancers just like he was."

"Wait a minute, are we talking about *the* Luka Petrin? Luka Petrin as in the greatest male ballet dancer of all time?" Clancy says, her eyes widening at Asia as she sits forward in her seat.

"The one and only," Asia confirms, looking sheepish, "But I really shouldn't have let that slip. He's known as Ivan Sachov these days."

"No shit!" Clancy replies, clapping her hands together in glee, her red curls bouncing around her face as she jiggles in her seat. "This is *amazing*! River is gonna shit a brick when he finds out."

Asia pulls a face. "Whoa," she says, looking a little panicked.

"Shit, what?" Clancy asks, picking up on Asia's worried vibe.

"According to Rose, after his late wife died, Ivan kind of lost himself a bit. So whilst it's cool for River to know, please don't let it go any further. He doesn't want the press to hound him or Rose for that matter. This is important to them and to my little brothers."

"Shit, of course not! I've never said a word about the dodgy patrons of Tales, you can totally trust me," Clancy says.

"Clancy is very trustworthy," Grim confirms, "If not a little excitable."

"I swear, your secret's safe with me," Clancy deadpans, lifting her fingers to her pursed lips and miming a key turning in a lock.

Asia's shoulder's relax. "I appreciate it, Clancy."

"But I can meet him, can't I? I swear I'll be on my best behaviour," she adds.

"I'm sure that'll be fine," Asia agrees.

"I can't bloody wait," Clancy blurts out, unable to contain herself. "Meeting Luka, watching you and the guys perform, and your cute little brothers dance. It's going to be an epic night..." Her voice trails off as she looks at Grim and pulls a face. "Erm, can I have the night off boss?"

Grim chuckles. "I'm closing Tales that night. There's no way I'm missing it."

Clancy throws her arms around Grim's shoulders, hugging her tightly and planting a kiss on her cheek. "You really are *the* best boss."

Grim's cheeks redden. "Pack it in, I have a reputation to uphold," she scolds, but I see the gleam of appreciation in her eyes. Grim might've been brought up around dangerous men, but she's a woman's woman through and through, and we all adore her for it.

"I'd love it if you could *all* attend, Cynthia and her guys too if she can?" I ask, looking between Christy and Grim who know her best, and can extend the invite. "Get the whole gang together?"

Over the years we've spent time together at events and special occasions, and whilst I'm not as close with Cynthia and her men, they're like family to Christy and Grim, so by extension that makes them important to me too.

"I'm sure she'd love it," Christy says. "I'll call her tomorrow."

"Do you think Hudson, Louisa and the guys would want to come too?" I ask Grim.

"They're away until after the fight, but I reckon they'd enjoy a night out when they get back. I'll ask them."

"What about Malakai and Connie?" Asia asks. "It'd be good to see them too."

"Yeah," I agree. "If they could make it that'd be great."

"Sure thing. I'll give Malakai a call too," Grim agrees.

"Great," I reply, unable to hide the smile spreading across my face. "I'm really looking forward to this. It just feels... right, you know?"

"Girl! I am so happy for you. I know you've been wanting to perform with the guys again for ages now. What finally changed?" Clancy asks.

"A few things actually. I noticed that we'd all lost a bit of our spark. It kind of crept up on us."

Grim cocks her head to the side. "You never said anything. I've been with Beast forever, I know plenty of ways to keep the spark going in a relationship."

"There's nothing wrong with our relationship per se, or our sex life for that matter. This is something else entirely. Something deeper, I guess."

"Dance is the keystone to your relationship," Christy says, her voice soft with understanding. "I get it. I still dance for my men too."

"It is," I agree, a smile touching my lips even if it is a little melancholy. "I've missed performing with them. I miss the way it makes me feel. I know they feel the same way too. We've just been so busy working and building this life together—a life I wouldn't change for the world," I hasten to add, "That somewhere along the way we forgot what gives us the most joy."

Clancy nods knowingly. "I totally get it. I'm not sure who I'd be without dance. I'm so grateful to be able to do a job I love everyday, thanks to you, Grim," she says, nudging Grim with her shoulder, but refraining from hugging her this time.

"Listen, hiring you was a no-brainer. Your choreography is insane and the club has benefitted from it greatly. So long as you still want to work for me, you'll have a job for life."

"I appreciate it, Grim," Clancy says.

"So are you going back to your hip-hop roots?" Asia asks, steering the conversation back to me.

"We're still working through the choreography at the moment, but of course it wouldn't be a Breakers performance without some break dance in it," I grin. "We've got a few surprises up our sleeves too."

"Well, I for one can't wait," Clancy says. "I know it will be the perfect encore."

I meet her gaze, nodding my head in agreement. "You bet you arse it will."

EIGHT

Cry To Me

Zayn

"SHALL WE TAKE A BREAK? I'm beat," I say, my fucking heart thumping in my chest as I grasp my knees and drop my head between my shoulders. Jesus fuck, when did I become so damn unfit?

"What's the matter, no stamina?" York teases as he grips my shoulder, chuckling.

"I swear to fuck, York, if you comment that I haven't got any stamina one more time…" I warn, only half joking. Most days I love York's humour but today I'm fucking cranky.

"This is what happens when you spend more time behind a desk than on the dance floor, mate."

I shake my head, standing upright. "Listen, it's been a while since I danced for three hours straight without a break. I'm not a kid anymore," I remind him.

"Yeah, I agree, especially with that island forming on your head." York swallows a smile and backs away from me, his hands aloft. "Only pointing out what's plain as day, *Grandad*," he adds, rubbing salt into the wound.

"What fucking island, you cheeky bastard?" I retort hating that I lift up my damp hair and check for a receding hairline in the mirror behind him.

"See," York smirks, pointing at my forehead which, by the way, does not have a fucking island.

"Fuck you, you wind-up merchant," I snap, "My hair is as thick as it's always been, but you'll get a punch to the nose if you keep saying shit like that."

"Boys, boys, boys. Enough of that," Pen admonishes, stepping back into the dance studio with a tray of drinks that she left to get a few minutes ago.

We've been working hard at our portion of the routine, and it's looking good so far, though we still have a way to go. I'm not concerned that we haven't got it down just yet, we've got time. To be fair, dancing with each other is like riding a bike for other people. It doesn't matter how long it's been since you've ridden, once you hop back on, muscle memory kicks in and you're all good to go. Except instead of a casual bike ride on a Sunday afternoon around the local park, this is more like the Tour de France. I'm fucking beat.

"Why are you arguing anyway?" she asks, taking a sip of her favourite peach ice-tea as she looks between us.

"York said I have a receding hairline!" I protest.

Pen looks at my forehead, her gaze trailing lower until we lock eyes. "You're hot as fuck, Zayn Bernard, don't let anyone ever tell you otherwise," she says, placing her drink back on the table and striding over to me. As she passes York, she shoots him a glare. "Quit winding him up."

"Well *he's* been winding me up for days about how much fun he had with you and Dax," York pouts, crossing his arms as he watches Pen pass him by.

When she cups my face and plants a heated kiss against my lips, I take her cue, pulling her closer and kissing the breath out of her lungs.

"Well, fuck. Should I leave?" York mutters, and this time we both hear the hurt in his voice.

Pen steps away from me, and turns to face York. "Come here, *Yorky-baby*," she says, her voice low, soft, sultry-as-fuck. Pretty sure his cock is reacting the same way as mine.

"I was only kidding," he says, giving me a wry grin as he steps closer. "You know me, always the fucking joker."

"We know," Pen says, reaching up to cup the back of his head and pulling it down to hers. "Kiss me, you idiot."

His arms circle her waist, the bare skin of her back, and tight lycra leggings a fucking temptation that's hard to ignore. Dancing with Pen has been cathartic, sure, but also the biggest turn-on. I don't even know how any of us managed to keep our hands off of her for so fucking long when we were kids.

Despite York being a cheeky fucker, I refrain from touching

her, allowing them this moment. We've been together for so long, friends for even longer, that it's easy to read the signals, to know when to join in and when to back off. I love that about our relationship. I wouldn't change it for a thing.

"You know, I've started to get a complex," York mumbles against her lips, his hands trailing down her back, stopping short of grabbing her arse. "Didn't think you liked me much anymore."

"Of course, I like you," she replies, and I smile when she reaches behind her back, puts her hands over his and slides them lower, then adds, "I more than like you, I love you, York. I love you so much."

"Even when I wind everyone up?" he jokes, his hands gripping her arse tighter as he pulls her closer.

"Even when you wind up the others."

"Don't tell him that, he'll never stop," I groan, rolling my eyes.

York smiles, winking at me. "It's part of the charm."

"No one makes us laugh like you do. *We* love you. Don't we, Zayn?" Pen adds, dropping a kiss to his lips that he accepts with a groan.

"I suppose he's alright," I joke.

Truth be known, he's been like a bear with a sore head for the past week or so, and we both know it's because he's missed being intimate with Pen. As much as we love each other, and we love to share, alone time with Pen is as important to each of us as spending time together is.

I can relate. It's not easy sharing the woman you love with

three other people, but it is manageable because we love each other as much as we love her.

When York deepens the kiss, I take that as my cue to leave. I've already encroached on Dax's time with Pen this week, not sure if I can get away with it a second time.

"I'll go take a shower. Then I'll start dinner. Xeno and Dax should be back from the hospital soon," I say, winking at York when he comes up for air, his face flushed.

"Appreciate it, Zayn," York says, dipping his head. "Sorry about earlier. I was only joking. You're still a handsome bastard."

"Love you, mate. Now give our girl an orgasm, then come join me in the kitchen. I'm making Paella."

"Paella? Delicious," Pen says, twisting in York's arms to face me whilst he wraps his arms around her waist and kisses her on her bare shoulder.

"Hopefully," I laugh. "It's been a while since I made it. Thought it'd be nice."

Pen's smile softens. "It's Dax's favourite dish."

"I know."

"That's thoughtful of you," York acknowledges.

I shrug. "Figured he'd appreciate a home cooked meal tonight."

"Are you worried about what his consultant might've said?" Pen asks, her hands sliding over York's arms as she regards me curiously.

"Nah. He's gonna be good, this is Dax we're talking about," I say, not sure who I'm trying to reassure more, them or me.

Pen's mouth pops open as though to protest but I shake my head. "He's got this, okay?"

"Okay," she nods.

I lift my eyes to York, swiping a hand through my hair. "Take Pen's mind off it. I'll see you both in a bit."

"THAT SMELLS AMAZING!" York exclaims, his cheeks flushed and eyes bright as he enters the kitchen with Pen forty-five minutes later. Pen, on the other hand, wrinkles her nose.

"Thanks, I think?" I reply, my gaze roving over Pen who gives me a small smile. "You okay?"

She's wearing her pyjama shorts and tank top with thick knee high socks, looking sexy as fuck fresh out of the shower.

"Yeah, of course I am!" she says, almost too brightly as she strides over to the sink and pours herself a glass of water. "Just a little thirsty."

"Mate, I've sure worked up an appetite," York says, throwing his arm over Pen's shoulder and drawing her into his side once she's got her drink. He's wearing grey joggers and nothing else and whilst women are my preference, scratch that, *Pen* is my preference, I appreciate he's a good looking man. Besides, we've spent so much time together sharing our girl and making love as a group that there have been several occasions where we've enjoyed the closeness of each other whilst loving our girl, and I ain't ashamed of any of it. Love is love, right?

"I bet you have," I comment, throwing him a wink as Pen settles into his side. "Are you feeling... better?"

"There's no better cure for *grumpy-arse-itis* than alone time with our girl," he throws back with a smile.

"Can't disagree with you there," I say, wondering if they fucked before or during their shower. Knowing York, it was likely both considering his enthusiasm for sliding around in slippery soap suds. There's been a couple of occasions over the past few years he's gotten overzealous with his use of body wash and almost gave himself a concussion when he slipped and fell. Both times he saved Pen from the same fate, his instincts to protect her overriding the instinct to protect himself.

I guess we're all the same in that regard.

"When will dinner be ready?" York asks, his stomach grumbling in protest.

"I'm going to let the paella simmer on low for a while," I answer, rinsing the chopping board and placing it on the drainer with the other washed dishes. "When Dax and Xeno return home, it should be ready to eat."

"Did you speak to them? I got a missed call on my phone," York says, pulling his phone from his pocket and resting it on the kitchen island as he grabs the bottle of Pinot I put out, and pours us all a glass.

"Yeah. Should be home in about forty minutes," I say, reaching for the integrated touch screen on the fridge and turning the volume down on the radio so we can talk.

Pen shakes her head when York offers her the glass of wine. "Not for me. Water's fine. Did Dax say anything to you about how the appointment went?"

I shake my head, wiping my hands on the towel. "He said

he's good, and that he'll fill us in when he gets home. That's about it."

"Okay," Pen nods, but I can't help but notice the worry in her eyes.

"This is Dax we're talking about. If there's anything going on, then we'll figure it out together, just like we always do," I say, striding over to her and pulling her into my arms. She smells of cocoa butter body lotion, and lemon zest. I can't help it, my cock stirs.

"I know that. I do," she replies, wrapping her arms around my waist. "Doesn't stop me from worrying though."

"The big guy's gonna be fine," York says, trying his best to reassure her. "I swear to fuck, he's got nine-lives."

"You're right," Pen agrees, leaning back and looking up at me. "Thanks for cooking dinner tonight. Thanks for choreographing such an incredible routine. Thanks for being you."

"Yeah, ditto to that," York adds. "Thanks for the alone time too, mate. I needed it."

"I figured," I reply, meeting his gaze with understanding. "You've been a miserable shit for days now. "

"Well, I'm sure as fuck not miserable anymore," he retorts, accepting my banter with the good humour it was intended.

"Thank fuck," I retort. "You weren't the easiest to live with when you were sick."

"I'm not a good patient, sorry about that," he replies, giving me a rueful smile.

"No sweat."

"Is there anything that you need me to do? I can set the table for dinner if you'd like?" he offers.

"Knock yourself out." I grin, dropping a kiss to Pen's head. "Hmm, you smell good."

"Thought I'd better wash up after getting hot and sweaty in the studio."

"Hot and sweaty with me, you mean," York quips as he sets the table for the five of us.

"Are you satisfied?" I ask, smirking when York throws me a disgusted look.

"Excuse me, when have I ever left our girl *unsatisfied?*"

Pen giggles. "I'm very satisfied, thank you. Why do you ask?"

"Just making sure..." My voice trails off as Pen looks up at me, her fingers feathering over my two-day old stubble. "What?" I question.

"Nothing, I just love us, that's all," she replies, and despite her concern for Dax, there's a lightness in her eyes I've not seen in a while.

"I love us too," I reply, lowering my face to hers and brushing my lips against her cheek. "I'm sorry it's taken us so fucking long to rectify what's been missing."

"Don't apologise to me. You've nothing to apologise for. I've been happy. I *am* happy. I love our life, and what we've built together. You're my heart, my family. Besides we have the rest of our lives together to love each other, to laugh, to–"

"Fuck?" York interrupts.

"I was going to say to dance, but that too," she replies with a laugh.

I draw her back into my arms, wanting to hold her close, needing the reassurance of her hug. Never thought I'd be a needy fucker, but when it comes to Pen, I definitely need her. Pretty sure the others feel the same way too. Not sure how we ever walked away from Pen, and then stayed away for three years, but I'm sure as fuck glad we swallowed our pride and made our way back to her.

"Oh, I love this song," Pen says, drawing me back into the moment as *Cry to Me* starts to play on the radio. "It's from Dirty Dancing."

"Isn't that Camden's favourite movie?" York asks, as Pen starts swaying her body to the music.

"And Asia's I think," Pen adds, looking up at me with a soft smile as I lower my hands to her waist and she runs her palms up my arms, grasping the back of my neck. We stare at each other, bending our knees as we dance, mimicking the scene we both know so well.

"Pretty sure *we've* all watched it a few times too," I tease, a playful grin spreading across my face as we stare at each other. She doesn't need to say a word because as her fingers play with the short hair at the nape of my neck, I already know what she wants.

"Dance with me?"

"What here?" I reply, just like Johnny did in the movie.

Pen bites on her lip. "*Here.*"

"Oh, fuck yes," York says, catching on quick as we re-enact the scene we all know so well.

Tucking my leg between Pen's thighs and with my hands gripping her rib cage either side of her breasts, I slowly lower her backwards. Our hips press together with the movement. There's no mistaking my hard-on as her hands slide over my shoulders and down my arms, and she drops her head back, exposing her beautiful neck.

Fuck I want her.

As she slowly rises, York rounds the kitchen island and leans against the countertop, watching us both intensely. Our eyes meet and I see the same love and passion reflected back in them as I draw Pen tightly against my chest, my fingers sliding into her damp hair as we dance.

"I want you," I murmur, my lips warm against her ear.

I know I'm being greedy, but I can't fucking help myself. When she's like this, relaxed and warm in my arms, not a stitch of make-up on and wearing her sleep shorts, I can't help but want her.

"Then have me," she replies breathily, as I fold over her, loving how she feels in my arms as we rock to the music.

Smiling into her hair, my lips glide down her neck as she exposes it to me. Kissing a trail of heat across her skin, I feel my heart pounding against my rib cage, but instead of taking the opportunity to start something right this second, I whisper, "Keep dancing."

She smiles softly as I lean into her, urging her backwards. Taking the cue, she drops her head back once more as I lean over her, then pulls back upright as we mirror the movement. We rock like that backwards and forwards until York steps up behind Pen, his hands finding her hips as our eyes lock.

"You've forgotten a step," he says, crouching slightly, as he runs his hand down the back of her left thigh and hooks his hand behind her knee.

"Pretty sure we were getting to that part," Pen says,

laughing softly as York guides her leg over my hip, releasing it to me. I grind against her, feeling the heat of her pussy through the thin material of her sleep shorts.

"Fuck," Pen moans, pressing her lips against the base of my neck, as York squeezes her arse.

"The island," I say, glancing at the surface, and the bottle of wine and glass in my way.

York takes the hint and moves them to a safe place. I lift Pen up, depositing her on the surface with a soft kiss against her parted lips.

"What are you doing?" she grins, her cheeks flushing with colour as her hands slide down my arms that are now caging her in.

"I'm hungry," I reply, licking my lips as I push between her legs, my palms gliding up her thighs, the smoothness of her skin making me itch to taste her.

"Me too," York adds, standing beside me, our intentions clear.

"Then I guess you better eat," Pen replies huskily, looking between us, "But not before you satisfy one of my needs first."

"Oh?" York questions, knowing full well what she's getting at.

Our Pen has a kink of her own, and we're always happy to oblige. Like I said, I love our family, I love my best friends, and over the years that love has developed for all of us in surprising ways. Ways I'm more than comfortable indulging in. Our only rule is that we don't share each other unless Pen is there. Ultimately she's our number one priority, and the beating heart of all of us, and that's the way it's going to stay. But when she's here with us, asking for what she desires, all bets are off.

"We got you," I reply, leaning forward briefly so I can press a kiss against Pen's lips before turning to my best friend. "Kiss and make up?" I joke, referring to our earlier spat.

York laughs softly in response, his gaze flicking between my eyes and lips as he reaches for the back of my head with one hand and draws me closer to him. Pen's thigh is the only thing preventing our bodies from meeting entirely.

"I swear I was joking," he mutters, his fingers curling into my hair as he caresses my mouth with his soft lips. Cleanly shaven, York's skin is smooth against mine, I can't say the same in return, but if Pen can take a little stubble rash from our kisses, pretty sure my best mate can too.

Pen lets out a soft moan as she watches us tease each other. The fact she's so turned on only makes me harder, and I rock my hips against her thigh to get some much needed friction.

"I love you both so much," she murmurs, reaching forwards as she pops the button of my fly and unzips me.

"Fuck," I mutter, and when her hand reaches inside and wraps around my cock, our soft kisses turn into demanding ones, and I groan into my best friend's mouth, welcoming his tongue with my own as Pen pumps my dick.

It's not long before I'm close to coming, and Pen knows it. Right at the moment stars begin to form behind my closed eyelids, and sensations swirl at the base of my spine, she withdraws her hand. I gasp, and York pulls back, his own eyes heavy-lidded, his lips swollen from our kisses.

"What?" he questions, lust-blind from our encounter.

Pen smiles, her cheeks a deep rose as she moves a hand between the two of us and cups York's chin, encouraging him to look at her.

"York," she breathes, "I need you to get on your knees for me."

"For you, anything," he replies without hesitation, his eyes darkening with desire.

Kneeling, his gaze never leaves hers as Pen shifts forward on the counter so that she can reach for my cock and guide it into York's mouth. I groan loudly as his lips wrap around me tightly, my body tingling from the pleasure flooding through it.

"That's it, baby, take him in your mouth," Pen coos, as York sucks on the tip of my dick, fucking teasing me with his talented tongue, making sure the head is laved with attention before moving onto the shaft itself.

"Fuck, York," I groan, grasping the back of his head as he takes me fully into his mouth. "Fuck, that feels so fucking good."

"Make him come, York. Make him come all over your tongue," Pen gasps, her fingers diving beneath her cotton shorts as she begins to finger-fuck herself on the counter.

"You do not come, you hear me?" I grind out, looking at her, my cock swelling at the feel of York's mouth wrapped around my dick and the sight of Pen getting off. Her head is thrown back, the straps of her top sliding down her shoulders as she rides her hand.

"Pen!" I demand, my gaze coasting upwards, the edge of her cotton top caught on her pebbled nipples.

Her eyes snap open, her mouth parts. "I won't come until your mouth is on my pussy and you can taste how wet I am for you both," she pants, slowing the pace of her hand as she meets my gaze then drops it to watch York sucking me off.

"Fuck," we both groan. Pen with her eyes fixed on York's mouth wrapped around my dick, and me fixated on her fingers pumping into her pussy.

"Tell me how much you love this," I demand, fucking breathless.

"I'm so turned on. God, look at the way he sucks you off, Zayn. I love the way you grasp his head so tight, how you force your cock down his throat because you can't get enough. Does it feel good to feel his mouth wrapped around your cock?"

"It feels fucking amazing," I cry out, wrapping my other hand around the back of York's head and rocking into his warm, wet mouth.

He gags, and I almost come there and then.

"Oh. Fuck. Yes!" Pen cries her hand moving faster as she grinds her hips against her fingers, totally forgetting her promise to us.

"York, Pen's ignoring me," I heave out, feeling my balls tighten as that familiar, overwhelming sensation, gathers at the base of my spine. "I need you to finish this so we can taste our girl's excitement, then fuck her until she begs for us to stop."

York grips the base of my dick, hollowing out his cheeks as he looks up at me. I don't need to see how he wanks himself off to know that he's enjoying this encounter as much as we are because I already see it in his eyes.

He's fucking loving this.

"Make me come, York," I demand, dropping my chin to my chest as I watch how he smiles around my cock. Fuck, he's good at this. "Make me come so we can be inside our girl together. I want to feel your cock slide against mine as we fuck Pen. I want to feel your dick pulse as she squeezes us both tight."

"Fuck, yes. I want that too," Pen cries, her breathy moans and frantic movements telling me she's close to coming herself.

"Do it. Fucking make me come, York!" I growl, gripping his hair tight in my hands, my stomach muscles tensing with the first stirring of my orgasm.

With his eyes locked on mine, York releases his dick and grasps my balls, gently rolling them in the palm of his hand then slides down my dick, choking on my cock.

The second the sensitive head of my dick meets the back of his throat, I throw my head back and come with a guttural roar, my whole body quivering as I pump my release into his mouth. Wave after wave of pleasure grips me tightly as I come and I jerk against York's face, unable to control myself. The wet, slippery sounds of him sucking me off and the feel of his tongue lapping at my sensitive flesh is almost overwhelming. Fuck, he's *really* good at this.

"Oh my god!" Pen cries, and I force myself to look at her.

"Don't you fucking dare, come!" I order. "That orgasm's ours."

Pen's eyes snap to mine, and her chest heaves. For a moment I think she's going to ignore me, but she slowly removes her hand from beneath her shorts. I can't help but notice how her fingers glisten with her arousal.

"Good girl," I whisper. "I promise it'll be worth it."

Releasing my cock, York smirks and rises to his feet, a smile playing on his lips as he presses a hard kiss against my mouth before saying, "You don't need to tell me I'm a ten out of ten, because I can already taste your approval on my tongue."

I swipe a hand through my hair, tucking myself away with the other, "We all know that the only person who deserves a ten out of ten is our Pen, but I'll give you an eight point five for the effort," I joke back.

We all laugh, but that laughter dies down when we round on Pen who slides off the counter with a coy smirk.

"I think the sofa will be more comfortable," she says, her cotton shorts riding low on her hips as she saunters past the kitchen table and towards the couch, slipping off her tank top as she moves. When she reaches it, she looks over her shoulder at us both, and says, "What are you waiting for?"

My pulse quickens, and my cock swells with every heartbeat as York and I stalk forward, slipping off our clothes until we're both naked.

Settling on the sofa, I watch York as he kisses Pen, gently kneading her breasts whilst the pad of his thumbs circles her peaked nipples. She moans into his mouth, and I can't help but reach for her, pressing hot kisses to the base of her spine as I tug at her sleep shorts, pulling them over her hips and sliding them down her legs.

Naked before me, I palm her arse cheeks. Needing to taste her, I drop a kiss to the firm muscle of her arse, biting her gently. She gasps and York backs up against the coffee table, taking a seat, his dick bobbing between his legs. The tip leaks pre-cum as he guides her face to his so that she bends at the waist, exposing herself to me fully whilst he kisses her thoroughly.

I move quickly, my tongue grazing her delicate flesh in slow circles. Reaching up, I gently part her labia and flatten my tongue against her, licking her from clit to crack. She moans, pushing back against my face, begging for more as her hole contracts, desperate to be filled.

"Please," she moans, looking over her shoulder at me and widening her stance.

"You want our dicks, baby? You want us to fuck you?" I ask between licks, gripping her hips, teasing her with my tongue.

"Yes. Please, yes. I want you both to fuck me. I want it so bad, I can't wait a second longer," she cries, but her pleas are swallowed by another kiss from York who tugs on her breasts as she rocks against my face, gripping York's thighs to keep her steady.

Fuck she tastes good. So fucking good.

Pen's breath becomes increasingly ragged as she rocks against my face, her whole body quivering until she's suddenly tight with tension, teetering on the edge of an orgasm. Her cries are punctuated with pleas, and I know she's ready to take us both.

Pulling back, I say, "Sit on my cock Pen, let me feel you fist my dick before York slides inside of you and we fuck you together."

"Yes. Fuck, please. I just want to come," she moans as I lie back on the sofa and catch York's wicked gaze.

"Oh Titch, you're gonna come so hard with our dicks pressed together as we fuck you and each other."

"Yes," she whimpers, straddling me. Her hair falls over her shoulders, sticking to her damp skin as she hovers above me.

I reach for my cock, holding it at the base, watching as she lowers herself onto my dick, wrapping me in her tight warmth.

"Fuuuuccckkkk," I groan, my fingers gripping her hips, preventing her from rocking against me. I'm so fucking turned on, it's not going to take much for me to come.

Sucking in a sharp breath, I slide my hands to her waist and around her back, urging her to press her chest against mine. We've been here before on so many occasions, and as she lowers herself to me, I spread my legs, dropping one foot to the floor and making room for York.

"Go easy," I warn York, as her internal walls grip my cock. "She's tight."

He nods, his gaze meeting mine briefly before Pen presses her lips against mine in a wet kiss. Our tongues dance, and we both moan as I feel York's fingers sliding inside of Pen, edging her open, readying her for another cock. His knuckles press against the base of my dick, his fingers pressing against my shaft as he moves them in and out of Pen, adding more delicious friction against my already sensitive cock.

"Fuck, York, that feels good," I groan.

He chuckles. "I'm a man of many talents."

Pen drags her mouth away from mine, pressing her lips against my shoulder, her tongue snaking out to taste my perspiration. "Please," she whimpers, moving against us both. "Need you."

"Do it!" I demand, unable to wait a moment longer. Fucking lust-crazed, love-drunk.

"I got you," York replies, leaning his body over hers, angling his dick against her entrance. "Ready?"

"Yes," Pen hisses, and I can feel the firm press of him against my dick as he removes his fingers and slips inside.

Pen gasps against my skin, her teeth biting down on my flesh, her core tightening around us both, grasping tight, making my eyes fucking roll in my head at the glorious feeling.

"Fuck!" York and I exclaim in unison as the firm ridges of his dick slide against mine and his balls slap against my own as he seats himself inside of her fully.

We still for a moment, allowing Pen to adjust, to take us without pain, and when her teeth release my skin and she moans in pleasure, I know she's ready for more.

"That's it, baby. You take us so good," I croon, keeping still as York slowly fucks her from behind. Sliding out to the tip, he gently pushes back inside of her, the feel of his dick rubbing against my cock has me crying out alongside Pen.

It's like he's fucking me too.

Feeling like this, so fucking close like this, it's *everything* I never knew I needed. The first time we shared Pen like this, it had blown every other experience out of the water. There's nothing like being inside of her with someone I love as much as I love her.

"Fuck, I love you both so fucking much," I say, reaching for York's arse as he leans over Pen and looks down at me, his white-blonde hair falling into his eyes.

"I love you too, brother," he replies, smiling down at me, his cock sliding against mine. "And I love you, Titch," he adds, lowering his mouth to Pen's shoulder, biting down gently.

She shudders against us both, her body reacting to that deep orgasm I can feel building between us.

"I'm so close. I'm so close," she pants, her mouth parting on a moan as her pelvis presses against mine, her clit rubbing against my abs.

Reaching up, I cup her cheeks. "Look at me. Look at me when you come," I demand as our eyes lock.

She gasps. York thrusts deeper.

I bring her mouth to mine, kissing her hard, gripping her hair tight, swallowing her moans. Fucking feeding off on them, feeding off her pleasure, York's pleasure, our pleasure.

York thrusts again, and she screams into my mouth, her body trembling as I rock my hips to meet his, pushing us both even deeper inside of her.

We fuck her like that, sliding against each other, the ridges of our dicks adding more sensation as she grips us tight. York bears down on her, I push up, Pen rocks between us.

We're a tangle of limbs, of sweat–slicked skin, breathy moans, and deep groans.

We're frantic and impassioned. Crazy for each other.

"Please... Oh god, please. I want to come," Pen cries, as I release her hair and York grabs her thick strands, arching her neck for me. I push up onto my elbows, licking and biting her skin, laving at the frantic pulse in her neck as York takes control and fucks us both.

"I'm going to come," Pen cries out in pleasure, her orgasm breaking as York slams his mouth against mine, thrusting harder as his tongue fucks my mouth and Pen's internal walls ripple around us both.

"Fuuuuuccccckkk!" York cries, coming first.

He bites down on my lip and I feel the warmth of his cum cover my dick as Pen gasps, shuddering and shaking against me, her pussy squeezing and releasing our dicks as she draws out my own orgasm.

It's fucking brutal.

Breathtaking.

Eye-rolling, fucking mind-blowing.

It rips through me, blinding me momentarily as I release inside of Pen, my dick pulsating as she wrings me of every last drop of come. The sound of my voice is guttural, fucking primal as I come, back arched off the sofa, York's arm wrapped around my back as he supports us both, my forehead pressed against Pen's shoulder as my heart tries to find a slower rhythm.

"Jesus, fuck!" I exclaim, flopping back onto the sofa, taking Pen with me.

She laughs, York chuckles and we stay pressed together with sweat-soaked skin until our heartbeats have calmed, and our breathing is less ragged.

"That was incredible!" I exclaim, laughing softly as York gently slips out of Pen and wraps his arm around her waist, dragging her upright with him. Her cheeks are flush and her limbs loose as he gently helps her to stand.

"I might need another shower," Pen laughs, biting her lip as our joint arousal glistens on her upper thighs.

"I'm down with that," York quips, pressing a kiss against her cheek as she rolls her eyes.

"Down boy, I've had quite enough dick for one day."

"Fair enough, she's taken quite a pummeling today," York jokes, pulling Pen closer for a hug while I slip away to get some towels to clean ourselves up with. When I return a few minutes later, they're snuggled together on the sofa, contentment radiating off them both.

DAX

TIPPING MY HEAD BACK, I look up at the grey billowing clouds above me, blinking at the early evening sky as the sun begins to drop beyond the horizon and fat raindrops start to fall.

"This is bullshit," I exclaim as the heavens open and the rain drenches me in seconds. I'm standing on the roof of our apartment building avoiding the people I love because I can't face them right now. I'd sooner get struck by fucking lightning than explain to Pen, Zayn and York just what the fuck is up with me.

Xeno had stayed silent for most of the appointment, but he'd sat by my side throughout it all as the doctor explained what's going on. The irony is, there's nothing wrong with me. Not physically anyway. The doctor ran all the tests, he triple checked the results and he came up with the same conclusion. Physically, I'm fit.

It's my head that's the problem.

I'm fucked up.

All this pain is as a result of post traumatic stress disorder. I haven't gotten over what happened to me. I haven't accepted the loss of my arm, or the fact that I almost died. I haven't faced the emotions of such a loss. It's only an arm, right? I've got another one.

That's the kind of stupid shit I've been telling myself over the years.

It doesn't matter that I can't tie up my own fucking shoelaces on my own. It doesn't matter that I choose to eat pasta over my favourite meal of steak and chips because I don't have to take twice as long cutting the damn meat one-handed. It doesn't matter that my right bicep is slimmer than my left through lack of use. It doesn't matter that my balance is off when I dance, or that I can't throw Pen up in the air and catch her like I used to do.

It doesn't matter.

And yet it does.

It fucking matters to me.

And I've pushed all these feelings down deep. I've suppressed them. I've refused to listen to that taunting voice in the back of my head telling me I'm not fucking worthy.

I figured this was the deal, that it wasn't physical, but being told that by a medical professional is a punch to the gut.

I'm supposed to be fucking strong.

I'm supposed to be the one everyone turns to. I'm supposed to be the one who can protect Pen. I'm supposed to be the one she can lean on, that my brothers can lean on.

I'm the motherfucking *Daddy*.

"Jesus, fuck," I laugh, and the sound is broken. Empty.

It kills me.

"Dax?"

My heart stops as a crack of thunder sounds overhead and I lower my head, my eyes landing on Kid who's wearing nothing but her sleep shorts and a baggy hoodie, three sizes too big for her.

"What are you doing up here?" I ask, meeting her gaze as the fire door closes behind her.

"What am *I* doing here? What are *you* doing here?"

"I'm thinking," I say curtly, turning my back to her, feeling like a fucking arsehole. I don't speak to her like that. I never cut her off. I never shut her out. Fuck, what am I doing?

"During a storm?" she questions, her voice gentle, tentative. Afraid. I chew on the inside of my cheek, tasting blood. "Dax?"

Fuck.

"I need a minute. Just give me a minute." My voice cracks and I hate it. I fucking hate it. With my back still turned on her, I try to pull myself together.

"No," she replies instantly. "You don't need a minute. You *need* your family. You need the people who love you. Dax, Xeno told us what the doctor said."

"I asked him not to," I reply, refusing to face her, my gaze focussing on the view of my hometown stretched out beneath us.

"He's worried about you," she counters softly. "He loves you so much, Dax. We all do."

"I know that. I *know*," I press, feeling her presence as she approaches, the heat of her body as she tentatively reaches for me, her fingers lightly grazing my arm.

"Don't do that!" I shout, twisting to face her, stepping back and wrapping my hand around my stump.

"Don't do this," she replies, eyes wide, her hair stuck to her head as the rain pelts us both. Her teeth chatter as she stares at me. Hurt. Confused.

"I'm not doing a damn thing. I just need a fucking minute, Pen. Just a minute."

"It's Kid," she whispers, correcting me.

I see the hurt in her eyes and it guts me. Fuck, how it guts me.

Pressing my eyes shut, I pinch the bridge of my nose. "I just... This is a lot."

"I know. I know it is, but we'll get through this together. We'll get you a therapist if you don't want to talk to me, to the guys."

"I don't want a fucking therapist!" I shout, unable to help myself.

Another thundercrack sounds overhead making Pen jump, or maybe it's me that's terrifying her right now. Maybe it's me. Fuck, what if it's me?

"Kid, I'm sorry," I say, meaning it. "That was out of order."

"It's okay. You're upset. You're trying to figure this out, but I'm telling you, Dax, you don't have to do this alone."

"I can't be weak, Kid."

"You're not! Dax, you're the strongest man I know. Don't you see what I see, what we see?"

I shake my head, swiping a hand over my face. "It's not real. I'm not fucking strong. It's all a fucking front."

She shakes her head. "That's not true."

"But it is. That day I woke up in the hospital and saw what I'd lost, I vowed to myself that I would never, *ever*, let you see how much it affected me. I vowed that I would remain your dark angel. But it's not real. I'm not that man anymore."

"You're right, you're not," she replies, reaching up and wrapping her fingers around my stump, holding me tight. "You're more. You're everything. You're the man I love, we love. You're Dax."

"Pen..." My voice trails off as she slides her hands up my arms and cups my face. "No. Listen to me. You're Dax. You're the man who saved my life."

"You saved your own life, Kid," he retorts. "Your brother never stood a chance. You were so fucking brave that day."

She shakes her head vehemently. "I'm not talking about that night when I killed my brother. I'm talking about the night I first met *you*."

"What do you mean?"

"You saved my life that night when I had nowhere to go and I ended up in the basement of 15 Jackson Street."

"I didn't do anything," I counter.

She smiles softly, her thumb gently caressing my stubbled cheek. "But you did. You *all* saved me that night."

"You're just saying that to make me feel better."

"No, I'm not. I was scared. No, I was terrified that night. Not only had my brother beaten me black and blue, my own mother did nothing to protect me, and somehow I'd ended up in the basement of the Skins' clubhouse with four boys I barely knew. Four boys who accepted me without question. Four boys who took me in, sheltered me, and loved me like I was worth loving."

"Kid..." My voice trails off as she presses the pad of her thumb against my lips, silencing me.

"That night when I looked into your eyes, and I saw a soul the same as mine, a soul that was hurt by the people who should've loved him the most, I knew I had something worth living for," she continues.

I swallow hard, the memory of that girl so far removed from the person standing in front of me, bringing tears to my eyes. It was like looking in a mirror back then, and seeing all the things I'd tried to hide from myself. I'd instantly wanted to protect her, that's never changed.

"So you see, I'm not talking about that night you took a bullet for me. I'm talking about that boy who let me lean my head on his shoulder because I was too emotionally exhausted to keep my eyes open a second longer. I'm talking about the boy who whispered the words; 'See a penny pick it up, all day long you'll have good luck.' I'm talking about him. You made me feel special, that a kid with nothing to offer but herself was a lucky charm worth keeping hold of. You're still that person, Dax. You're still him."

Bringing my hand up to cup her cheek, I lower my forehead to hers. "I don't know if I am..."

"If you can't believe me, believe what's in here," she replies, pressing her hand against my heart. It thumps beneath her palm, firm, strong, true. "It's the same kind, sweet heart that loved a girl who didn't believe she was worth loving. It's the same brave heart that took a bullet for her, sacrificing a piece of himself. It's the same heart that has loved and protected his best friends his whole life. That hasn't changed. It never will. Do you understand?"

I grit my teeth. "I want to believe that's true. It's just..."

"It's just what?" she whispers, rain falling over her face, merging with the tears that I know burn her eyes, just like my tears are burning mine.

"It's just *hard*," I say helplessly, unable to verbalise what I truly feel.

"I know," she whispers, pressing her mouth against mine as she wraps her arms around my neck and pulls me close.

I taste the salt on her lips, the strength of her belief, the faith she has in me, and I allow myself to believe her words, to let them sink in, to truly *hear* them.

I saved her.

And in return her friendship had saved me. All the hours we spent together laughing, dancing, getting up to mischief, and the love that blossomed between us as a couple, and as a group. We'd saved each other once. Our love can do that again.

Blowing out a sharp breath, I pull back, swiping wet tendrils of hair off her face. "Kid."

"Yes?"

"Will you watch me dance?"

"Here?" she asks, tipping her head to the side.

"Please?"

She presses another soft kiss against my lips, then nods. "I'll watch you dance forever."

"And always?" I question.

"And always," she replies as I draw my phone out of my pocket and find the song I'm looking for. Turning it up to full volume, I hand it to her.

"Halo?" she whispers, the tears in her voice matching the ones that fall from the sky in a deluge.

"This dance was a breaking point for me," I explain.

"It was?"

"I'd brought you back to the flat after Xeno acted like a dick towards you at Chastity's," he continues, reminding us both of that fateful evening. "It made me so fucking mad how he treated you that night, and it reminded me how *I'd* always been your protector. That was when I told myself that I was done pushing you away. I was done being ruled by my past, by the brutality of my father's fist. It was the moment I admitted I never stopped loving you. That I was strong enough to love you. That I'd do anything to keep you by my side."

"And now what does this mean to you?"

"All of that and so much more," I reply, before holding my arms out horizontally to my side and pirouetting in the rain.

The rush of cold air and the needling rain as it hits my face is nothing in comparison to the swirl of emotion in my chest, or the tornado of feeling as I dance. Each step comes back to me as I move, as though embedded in my very psyche. I dance with this need to just let go, to prove that I'm still capable, that I'm worthy of Pen's love.

I feel her watching me, just like I did the night I decided I no longer wanted to hold hate in my heart for the only woman I'd ever loved. She'd watched me with a fierce gaze back then, her eyes following my every movement, greedily drinking me in, just like she's doing now.

That kind of focus I feel from her now is the kind that makes you feel like you're the only person in the room. It's what keeps me dancing despite stumbling on the slippery ground as I lose my balance. I ignore the slink of defeat that tells me I can't dance like I used to. I ignore the pain that rushes up my arm, telling me that this is pointless.

I simply dance.

With a bruised heart, beating so damn hard I feel it's going to break free from my chest, I dance.

Flying across the concrete roof, I spin on my feet, my arms flaring wide as I feel that familiar magic unravelling. The kind of magic that takes over your body when your soul is doing what it was always supposed to do.

Over the past five years I stepped back from dancing, pretending that like the others I was too busy working to have time. The truth is, I avoided it. I avoided it because I was scared that I'd be less of a dancer. It didn't matter that I performed at Stardom Academy just a few months after I was shot. I'd convinced myself that was a fluke. A last hurrah. That with time my ability would deteriorate, that I would forget how to move, forget how to dance with my best friends, with Kid.

Then I'd convinced myself I didn't *need* to dance. That it didn't fuel my soul and give me joy.

I'd turned my back on it.

But I'm done lying to myself.

It's going to be hard.

It's already hard.

But I'm going to do this. For Kid. For my brothers. For me.

Just like before, every beat of the song, and all the words Beyoncé sings are expressed through my movements. I leap into the air, performing a grand jeté, my powerful legs splitting wide, and as I do I throw my head back and roar into the night's sky.

My anger at what I've had to endure comes ripping out of me. It feeds my steps as I move with a lightness and grace that I haven't felt in years. I'm expressing myself the best way I know how, the only way I can, and I *feel* all these emotions swelling inside of me.

Grief, pain, hate.

Love, kindness, acceptance.

I dance with an open heart, accepting all these emotions as I flip backwards, one handed, tumbling like a gymnast. I dance with brutal honesty, as I share my story once again with Kid.

Twisting and turning, I move my body with as much fluidity as I can muster, revealing the depths of my love for Kid, sharing the bottomless pieces of my soul.

Right here on the roof as a thunderstorm sounds overhead, and rain pelts me with ice-cold needles, I show Kid all the debilitating feelings I've held inside. I spin and kick, letting out a strangled cry as I fall to my knees, mimicking the steps from all those years ago. Except now they represent the internal battle I have with myself daily. When I curl over, clasping the back of my head, I'm not protecting myself from a brutal, cruel father, I'm protecting myself from the self-doubt, the self-hatred, the words I've told myself over and over and over again.

You're not worthy.

You're not strong.

You can't dance like you used to.

You're not her dark angel.

I cover my head, shaking with cold, with emotion, with adrenaline as I reach up, my hand opening and closing to the beat of the music, timed with the pounding of my heart.

Then I slam my fist onto the floor.

Thump.

Thump.

Thump.

Thump.

With every beat of my heart, with every crash of my fist against the concrete roof, I feel a surge of power, of strength, of self-belief.

Lifting my head, I pin Kid with my stare. Our gazes clash and I feel this wave of love that's fucking powerful.

"Dax," Kid breathes, her eyes glistening with more tears, tears that streak down her face as she chokes on a sob when I begin crawling towards her, hauling myself along on one hand and a painful stump.

"Get up, Dax," she cries. "Don't crawl to me. Don't you dare fucking crawl."

Gritting my teeth, I nod my head.

That's enough.

I'm strong. I'm powerful. I'm Dax.

Pushing up on my hand and knees, I slowly climb to my feet, unfurling.

Transforming.

I'm not a broken man. I'm not someone to pity.

I will face my fears head on.

I *will* overcome.

"That's it," Kid gasps, stepping towards me, a wobbly smile forming on her lips. "Finish this."

So with a heaving chest, I jerk my chin, grit my jaw and fling my arms wide and stamp my feet, squashing the doubts, the self-loathing, all my fucking insecurities.

"Dax," she laments, and I feel the connection between us pull taut.

"Kid," I croak out, flexing my fingers, my gaze focused and fierce on hers, and just like before, she doesn't hesitate, she *runs*, leaping into my arms.

And I do what I always do. Will *always* do.

I catch her.

TEN

Your Guilty Pleasure

DAX

"IS EVERYTHING OKAY?" Xeno asks as we step back into the flat, our clothes stuck to our skin, completely drenched from the rain. He leans back against the kitchen island, placing the dishcloth on the draining board. Dinner has been cleared, and the dishes washed and stacked on the side.

"It will be," Kid replies, squeezing my hand tightly. Her faith in me, her love, it's humbling.

"Good. Are you hungry? I made sure York didn't eat your

dinner too," he says with a wry smile, motioning toward the two covered plates on the counter.

"Not right now. I think we could both use a shower," I say, wrapping my arm around Kid's shoulder and giving her arm a rub. She's shivering now, her teeth clacking from the cold.

"Where are York and Zayn, anyway?" Kid asks as she wraps her arm around me, trying to keep warm.

"Sophie called. Something cropped up with the build at Chastity Nightclub. Zayn and York have gone to sort it out," Xeno explains.

"Should we be worried?" Kid asks.

"No, it's just a refit issue in one of the VIP rooms. They won't be long."

"Okay, that's a relief," Kid murmurs, sensing the atmosphere change in the room.

We both know Xeno struggles to deal with emotional stuff, not because he doesn't care but because he cares too much. Supporting me today took a lot of courage, but I'm feeling a little too vulnerable right now to give him the reassurance he needs.

"They're worried about you, Dax..." He hesitates, smoothing a hand through his hair before saying, "I'm worried."

"I know, and I'm sorry to concern you all." My throat bobs as I drop my gaze. Fuck I'm emotional today.

"Don't be sorry," Xeno interjects, pushing off the counter. "How we deal with this is on us. Not you. We worry because we love you. You know I get tangled up in all those feelings because I'm fucked up."

"You're *not* fucked up. You just handle things differently,"

Kid says, her voice full of so much love as he approaches us both. Honestly, some days I don't know how she does it, handling all of our emotional needs, not to mention our physical and mental needs. She never complains, is always so fucking compassionate and patient. We're fucking lucky to have her.

Pulling her closer into my side, I drop a kiss to her damp hair. "Kid helped me to see a little clearer, and I think I'm going to be okay. You just got to bear with me, while I work through this,"

Xeno nods, reaching for the back of my head as he brings his forehead to mine. "We'll be there every step of the way. I love you, Dax," he says, and I feel it, his love.

It's intense, fierce, yet comforting all in the same breath. He's always looked out for us, and when I think back to all the shit we've gone through over the years as friends, as *brothers*, I know it must've been so fucking hard on him to deal with in the early days when we didn't know how much he suffered or the best way we could help him cope with his overwhelming emotions.

"We love you too," I reply, breaths mingling, meaning it wholeheartedly.

Our love has evolved over the years. It began as friendship then developed into a brotherly love, and now it's something infinitely deeper. I don't want to put a label on it, because love in any form doesn't need an explanation. What we share is unique to the five of us and so long as we're all happy then that's all that matters to me.

"You know, you should really take that shower, I don't want either of you getting sick like York," he says after a beat.

"Yeah, I think that's a good idea. Want to join us?" I ask, knowing he needs physical reassurance in this moment as much as I do. Besides, Kid needs his love as much as we need each other.

"If that's okay with Tiny," he replies, searching her gaze.

She smiles up at us both, taking our hands in hers. "Of course it is. Come on," she says, guiding us both across our living space and into the hallway beyond.

A few minutes later I step under the warmth of the spray, groaning as it hits my chest. With my hand pressed against the tile, I duck my head beneath the water, enjoying the gentle massage it gives my neck and shoulders.

"Can I wash you?" Kid asks, stepping into the shower unit behind me. When Kid moved in five years ago we had one of our four bathrooms converted into a huge shower room, removing the bath and extending the shower so it could fit the five of us comfortably. With five separate shower heads, and a bench running the length of the wall, we've had a lot of fun in this space.

"Please," I reply, remaining where I am, needing to feel the reassurance of her touch.

As soon as her palms rest against my shoulders, her fingers massaging the tense muscles there, I let out a low groan. "Fuck, that feels good, baby," I say as her hands move down my spine, massaging gently as she goes. When her fingers dig into my lower spine, her hands smoothing over my arse, squeezing the muscle, my cock stiffens,

"What do you need?" she asks, her voice soft, full of promise.

I turn beneath the spray, gripping my cock and sliding my fist from the tip to the base as I look down at her. Water cascades over her breasts from the shower head to her left, and behind her, leaning against the far wall is Xeno. He watches us both, gaze heated, his cock long and hard.

"Control," I say simply. "Right now I need control."

She nods, understanding the words left unspoken. Rising up onto her tiptoes, she presses a soft, lingering kiss against my lips, her hands resting against my pecs as my heart thunders beneath her touch. Her belly slides over my dick, and it takes everything in me not to lift her off her feet and fuck her against the tiled wall.

But right now I need more than a quick fuck.

"Whatever you need," she replies, before pulling back and turning to face Xeno.

"Can you give Dax control, Xeno?" she asks, knowing that more often than not he likes to take the lead. In a group setting, it's a habit we've fallen comfortably into. Xeno takes the lead in the bedroom, and we all follow. It's not until recently I've wanted that to change, at least some of the time anyway.

He nods once, his gaze flicking from Kid to me and back again. "Yes."

"Thank you," she whispers, and then does something extraordinary, she drops to her knees. With her arse pressed against her heels, head lowered, hands folded in her lap, she waits.

"Fuck," I mutter, my balls tightening at the gift she's given me, that Xeno has. For a moment, I contemplate what I should do next as I admire the beauty of Kid's submission. It's a powerful and humbling sight to behold.

"Tell us what you want," Xeno says, his eyes meeting mine.

There's an openness in his gaze, a willingness to explore this new dynamic. He doesn't call me Daddy, and I'm okay with that, but I do see the loosening of his muscles and the way he gives himself up to the moment, and that's what matters the most.

"You're okay with this?" I ask, needing his confirmation.

"I think..." His voice trails off as he considers what he's about to say next. Biting on his lip, he leans his head back against the tiles, and I wait, giving him a moment. Eventually he lifts his eyes back up to meet mine. "I think I want to try and relinquish control. I want to know what that feels like. Though it might be hard at first," he admits.

"I can understand that," I reply, feeling so fucking honoured that he's willing to try this for me. "I know this can't be easy, but I swear to you, Xeno, I'll take care of you."

"Okay," he replies, then slowly he drops to his knees too. Head bowed, hands folded in his lap, he waits, a mirror image to Kid.

My heart squeezes painfully in my chest as I stare at them both. Fuck, I love them so much. Just like I love York and Zayn. I'm so fucking grateful that I have them all in my life, that we're able to share our pain, our love, our fear and joy. That I can be me, the real me in their presence.

Taking a deep breath, I push off from the wall and stand beside them both. Water pounds against our skin, the only sound apart from their gentle breaths as they kneel before me.

"Look at me," I demand softly, my eyes grazing over Kid's breasts, following the curve of her hips and stomach as she blinks up at me. "I want you both to submit to me wholly and completely," I say, looking between them both. "But I understand that you may need a safe word, not because I intend to hurt either of you, far from it, but because I need you both to know that you're safe with me. I will honour your desire to withdraw your participation at any point. Do you understand?"

"Yes, Daddy," Kid says.

"I understand," Xeno replies.

"Good. The safe word is *lyrical*, okay?"

"Okay," they repeat.

"Now," I continue, "I'm going to tell you what I want, and you're going to obey. If you refuse, and choose not to use the safe word there will be punishment. Do you understand?"

"Yes," they reply in unison.

Licking my lips as my gaze travels from the strip of hair between Kid's legs, to Xeno's erection. He's as turned on as I am. "You will only touch yourself, me, or each other when I say, and not before."

Kid nods, but Xeno opens his mouth to protest. "Is there a problem, Xeno?" I ask.

"I want to touch, Tiny. I want to touch her now."

"No."

"But—"

"I said no, Xeno."

He grits his jaw, but does as he's told.

"Good boy," I murmur, testing the words, liking how they sound. "I know this is hard for you, but to thank you for obeying,

I'm going to reward you. Place your hands on your thighs, Xeno. Whatever you do, leave them there. Remember no touching until I say, okay?"

"Okay," he replies, following my orders as he rests his palms against his thighs.

Focussing my attention back on Kid, her gaze flicks to my cock fisted in my hand. "You want a taste?" I ask her.

"Yes," she replies.

"Open your mouth, my love. Poke out your tongue," I demand, then gently slide the tip of my cock into her mouth. "Suck me."

She sucks. I groan. Xeno swears.

"Fuck, Tiny. Fuck," he grinds out, his fingers curling into fists on his thighs.

"Keep your hands where they are, Xeno. No touching. Watch Kid take me all the way to the base. See how she enjoys sucking my cock. Imagine how it feels. How wet and warm her mouth is, how she hollows out her cheeks and slides her tongue around my dick. You know what bliss it is to fuck her beautiful mouth, so you'll know how much I want to come right now."

Kid follows my orders, sliding her mouth over my dick, her tongue licking the length of me as she swallows me whole. Xeno glares up at me, challenge and lust in his eyes. Yet, he still obeys.

"That's enough," I say, and even though I'm desperate to fuck her mouth until I come, I'm more desperate to see how far this can go.

Releasing me with a pop, Kid's cheeks pinken up, her nipples hardening as she awaits further instruction. "Kid, stay where you are for a moment. Xeno, sit on the bench."

Climbing to his feet, Xeno moves past me. Whether he intended to or not, the back of his hand brushes over my cock, and that brief touch is like an electric spark straight to the base of my spine.

Without even thinking about what I'm doing, I reach for the back of his neck, twist him around and slam my mouth against his in a quick, hard kiss.

"Oh, god," Kid moans, as she looks up at us both. I know it turns her on, and in turn that makes me feel good. Pretty fucking sure Xeno's enjoying it given he's rubbing his dick against mine.

"What the fuck was that?" I ask Xeno as he gives me a wicked smile.

"Accident," he shrugs, cocking a brow.

I cock my head to the side, sliding my thumb to the front of his throat, pressing a little on the groove just beneath his Adam's apple. "I think you're testing me. Are you testing me, Xeno?"

He doesn't reply.

"Very well," I say, sliding my palm over his chest, then lowering it towards his cock.

He smirks, thinking he knows what I'm going to do next. Only instead of gripping his dick and fisting him like I can see he wants me to do, I slap his dick with the back of my hand instead. Not hard enough to really hurt, but hard enough to remind him I'm in control.

"Fuck!" Xeno exclaims, his cock jerking, leaking precum.

"Sit. Down," I demand.

He sits.

"Widen your legs."

He does as I ask, spreading his legs, his cock resting against his abdomen. Thick veins curl up the side of his dick, the head a little darker, more a deep plum to my blush pink.

"Kid, I want you to suck Xeno's cock. I want you to give him the best fucking blow job you've given anyone, but the minute you feel him start to come, you stop."

Xeno's chest heaves as he glares up at me in challenge, and I'm just waiting for him to say something. Almost wanting him to. Instead, he turns his heated gaze back to Kid and watches her position herself between his legs.

Taking a seat next to Xeno on the bench, I fist my cock, squeezing it at the base as I watch Kid take Xeno in her mouth. He lets out a groan and reaches for her, but I drop my dick, grasping his wrist.

"I didn't say you could touch her."

His muscles tense, but he lowers his right hand and doesn't try to fight me as I place his other hand on my cock, and guide him to curl his fingers around me.

"Fuck," he groans as Kid deepthroats him, taking him all the way to the back of her throat, before sliding back up and repeating the action all over again.

"Look at how she sucks you off, Xeno. It feels good doesn't it?" I ask.

"Yes," he replies, his fingers flexing around the base of my shaft as he holds me in his palm, my hand wrapped around his.

"Every time she slides her mouth up and down your dick, I want you to mirror that movement on my cock with your fist. Got that?" I ask, removing my hand from his.

"Yes," he bites out, instantly sliding his palm up my cock in time with her mouth on his dick.

"That's it, fist me, Xeno. Feel how my dick hardens watching our girl suck you off," I say, turned on, fucking desperate to come. I won't though. I will only come deep inside my beautiful girl's pussy. Tonight that's mine.

When Xeno's hand movements become less controlled, I know he's close to coming, and fuck, part of me wants to let Kid continue so that I can come too, because fuck knows I'm close.

"Kid, stop!" I grind out, my chest heaving in time to Xeno's.

She immediately pulls off his dick, her tongue snaking out as she licks her lips. Xeno's dick falls against his abs, pre cum beading on the tip as she settles back onto her haunches.

"Fuck!" Xeno exclaims, his hand still fisting my dick.

"You can let me go now," I say, chuckling as I try to ease the racing of my heart. I look down at our girl, waiting patiently for further instruction. Xeno eases his fingers from around my cock, but not before sliding his thumb over my slit. "Motherfucker," I groan.

Now it's Xeno who's chuckling.

"I think it's time our girl was rewarded, don't you, Xeno?" I ask, rolling my head to the side as I give him a wink.

"Fuck, yes. What do you have in mind?"

Licking my lips I turn my attention back to Kid. "I want you to stand on the bench, Kid, legs either side of Xeno's thighs.

"Yes, Daddy," she replies, taking my hand as support, and stepping up onto the bench.

Xeno sits between the two shower heads and warm water

hits the tiled floor, steaming up the room around us. "What now, Dax?" he asks.

"I want you to use one hand to spread your pussy lips, Kid. Let us see how pretty and blush you are for us both," I continue.

"Like this?" she asks, using her pointer and ring finger to spread her pussy lips just like I asked.

"Just like that, Kid," I reply, fisting my cock and running my hand up and down my length just to ease some of the pressure, because fuck her pussy is good enough to eat.

"Christ," Xeno mutters, his hands still resting on his thighs, his fingers curled into his flesh as he forces himself not to touch her.

"Now play with your clit. Tease yourself for us," I instruct, loving how Xeno groans as Kid gently pulls back the hood of her clit and starts pleasuring herself inches away from his face.

She moans, her eyelids drooping as she continues to gently play with herself. She rocks a little, and I reach up grasping her hip to keep her steady.

"Let me taste her. Fuck, let me taste her."

"What do you say?" I ask.

"*Please*. Let me please taste her," he grinds out shifting forward, his mouth just centimetres away from her pussy.

"Good enough," I say, grinning as Xeno side-eyes me. "Kid, hold onto the bar with both hands," I say, urging her to reach up and hold onto the silver rail we had fixed into the wall above the showers. We use it to hang our toiletries, but tonight Kid's going to use it to keep herself upright whilst Xeno fucks her pussy with his tongue. "I think Xeno's hungry."

"Like this?" she asks, looking down at us both, her wet hair sticking to her breasts as she grips the bar tight. Her breath hitches as Xeno blows on her pussy. He'll pay for that later, but for now I'll let it slide.

"Just like that. Good girl," I praise her. "Xeno..." I prompt shifting forward, my fist pumping my dick. "You're free to touch her how you please. Make our girl come."

"Fuck, yes," he growls, reaching up and grabbing the back of her right thigh, slinging it over his shoulder as he buries his face in her cunt. There's no warning, no soft lick to tease her. He just goes in for the kill, ready to fucking destroy her pussy with a mind-blowing orgasm.

And I'm here for it.

"Xeno!" she cries out, her body shuddering as he laps at her without restraint. Her fingers tighten on the rail and she jerks against him, lost to his tongue and lips as he eats her out.

"Does that feel good, baby?" I ask, getting to my feet, moving to stand behind her.

"Yes. Yes, it feels good," she pants, her head dropping between her shoulders as she rocks against his face.

"Well, it's about to get a hell of a lot more intense, beautiful," I say, reaching between her legs and sliding two fingers inside of her tight hole.

"Oh fuck, oh fuck," she cries as I pump my fingers in and out of her, my thumb rimming her arsehole before pushing past the tight ring. She cries out, her arse cheeks reddening under Xeno's tight grip. She writhes against us both, panting. I know she's close, I can feel how her internal muscles tighten around my fingers.

Dropping lower, I replace my thumb with my tongue, rimming her arsehole. It's enough to set off her orgasm.

"I'm going to come. I'm going to come. I'm going to come," she repeats over and over, her body stiffening as she falls over the precipice, then relaxing as she jerks against Xeno's face.

Her hands slip from the bar, and I pull my fingers out of her, catching her with one arm and pulling her against my chest as she falls, limp in my arms. Xeno's dark eyes meet mine, and I know he's about ready to explode, just like I am.

"Take her to my bedroom," I order, releasing her to him.

He nods, ducking down and picking her up bridal style before carrying her out of the shower and to my bedroom down the hall. I turn off the shower, following close behind.

"On the bed. Now," I demand, water droplets running in rivulets over us all as he lays her down on the bed then looks at me for further instructions. "Tonight her pussy's mine."

He nods, swallowing hard as she blinks up at us both, relaxed from her orgasm. "I want you both," she whispers.

"I know, baby. And you'll get us both," I reply, crawling up the bed between her parted legs. Ducking down, I lick her glistening pussy, humming around the taste as she gasps and rolls her hips beneath me.

Slowly, I kiss my way up her body, pressing my lips against her stomach, and the underside of her breasts before sucking each nipple into my mouth. Her lips part as her spine arches.

"Dax, please," she says, forgetting herself.

I don't punish her for being so lost in the moment, instead I kiss her, spearing her lips with my tongue. We kiss, her hands coming up and grasping the back of my head as she wraps her legs behind my arse, pulling me against her. I feel the wet heat of her pussy lube my cock with the movement. Beside me, the bed dips as Xeno makes himself comfortable next to us. Pulling back, I look across at him. "Just wait, I promise I'll take care of you too."

He nods.

Turning my attention back to Kid, I look down at her. "Baby, I'm going to fuck you now," I say, before lining my dick up at her hole.

"Please, fuck me. Please just fuck me, Daddy," she replies, and I nearly lose my everloving mind as I slide into her with one hard thrust.

She cries out, her legs tightening around my arse as I slam into her over and over again, her cunt gripping me tight. "Fuck!" I grind out, losing my fucking grip on reality. I'm so turned on that an orgasm already begins to build at the base of my spine.

"Dax," Xeno grinds out next to us. "I can't fucking do this anymore."

Forcing myself to stop, I turn my head to the side. "You want in?" I ask him, knowing full well he does.

"Please, I'm going fucking crazy over here," he replies, his chest heaving as he mindlessly pumps his dick.

"I'm going to roll us both on our sides. You know what to do," I say, through gritted teeth, the tight clench of her pussy making me go fucking blind for a moment. I bring her leg up over my hip so Xeno has easier access. "There's lube in the top drawer. Use it," I instruct, flicking my gaze back to Kid who starts to move her hips against mine.

"Please," she begs. "Please just let me come."

"Baby, you're gonna come so hard for us. Just let Xeno get you ready first, okay?"

"Okay," she whispers, gasping when he slides his lube covered finger into her arse hole.

"Fuck. She's so tight," Xeno says, gently pumping his finger inside of her.

I kiss her, rocking into her gently this time. "Relax, baby. You know we'll take care of you."

"I know," she whimpers, gasping as Xeno adds another finger. "That feels so good. Fuck, you both feel so good."

Looking over at Xeno, I nod. "Take her."

Xeno slides the rest of the lube over his dick, then he lines his cock against her arse, pushing in slowly. My body stills as I feel the tip of his cock push past the tight ring, only a thin section of muscle separating us.

"Fuuuuck," Xeno exclaims, his hand grasping Kid's hip as he stills for a moment.

"You good, Kid?" I ask, pressing soft kisses against her lips as her chest heaves at the sensation of the two of us inside of her.

"I feel so... full," she cries as Xeno edges further in, his dick sliding inside of her.

"You feel so fucking perfect," Xeno replies, his lips finding the sensitive spot on her neck as he kisses and licks her there. Inch by inch he presses himself deeper, kissing her and whispering sweet words of encouragement as she takes him like a good girl.

"I'm gonna move now, baby. You ready?" I ask.

She nods. "Please. I just want to come. Make me come."

Meeting Xeno's gaze I nod, and right at that moment we

pull out a little then push back in slowly together, always with Kid's pleasure in mind.

"I can feel your dick rubbing against mine," I say, my whole body tensing with the need to come. Xeno smiles at me, a wicked glint in his eyes as he pulls back and slides in once again. I match him move for move as Kid whines between us, her little pants of pleasure making me fucking crazy.

It isn't long before my orgasm builds again. I can feel it gathering momentum as my balls tighten and my cock thickens. I press my lips against Kid's mouth, sucking on her tongue that she offers me, groaning around it as my eyes roll back in my head.

"Fuck, I'm gonna come," Xeno bites out, his movements losing that steady rhythm as he succumbs to his own mounting pleasure.

"Go easy," I warn him, fully aware that we need to keep control so as not to hurt Kid.

"I've got this," he grinds out, back to controlling his movements. I hold his gaze, telling him silently that he needs to be careful.

Our dicks rub against each other, that thin wall of muscle barely keeping us apart. The sensation is like nothing I've ever known and it turns me the fuck on knowing we're both responsible for Kid's orgasm as well as each others. When Xeno's eyes roll back in his head, and his mouth hangs open on a building cry, I raise my hand and slap him hard against his arse cheek.

"That's for disobeying me earlier," I say gruffly as he comes with a shattering roar, pumping his load into Kid.

And just like that, his orgasm sets off hers. Kid stiffens

between us, her internal muscles fisting me so tight, I nearly fucking pass out from the pleasure.

"Ahhhh," she screams, shaking and trembling between us as she comes, and just for a moment I'm lost in the tightening coil of my own pleasure as it bursts up my spine and spreads through my dick.

"Yes, fuck. Yes," I cry as I empty myself inside of her, my spine arching, my fingers gripping her breast as I come. Fuck, it goes on for ever, and I swear to fuck I'm afraid I've emptied my balls of semen when it's over.

"Jesus, that was... that was... fucking amazing," Xeno gasps, his body loosening, his muscles relaxing as his orgasm begins to fade.

Between us, Kid laughs. "I'm completely spent. In the best possible way."

"Fuck, Kid. Fuck," I reply, blinking back the black spots in my vision. "I almost fucking passed out."

"I think passing out sounds like a really good idea right about now," Xeno says, gently pulling out of Kid, as he wraps his arm around her and kisses her cheek. She reaches up to him, kissing him deeply, smiling as she pulls back.

"I love you," she whispers.

"I love you too," he replies, lifting his gaze to meet mine. "And you. I fucking love you too."

"Feelings mutual," I grin, sliding out of kid too, and pressing a kiss against her cheek. "Sleep?"

"Shouldn't I clean up first," she whispers. I'm pretty sure that's the last thing she should be doing right now.

"Baby, just sleep."

"Okay," she murmurs, snuggling between us, her body relaxing.

It isn't long until she's fast asleep, her soft breaths feathering against my skin, and for the first time in a long time I feel more like myself wrapped up in the arms of the people I love.

ELEVEN

Tell Me You Love Me

PEN

"WHAT'S THE MATTER?" I ask Lena the following night as she glares at Gray from the other side of the room.

"Are you *kidding*?" she counters, her voice rising with every word. "Gray is my new boss!"

"Yes," I reply, resting my hands on my desk in our office at Twisted Bullet. I daren't look at York who I know is grinning with amusement from his desk in the corner of the room. Pretty sure he's got a smug look on his face to boot. He warned me that there'd be fireworks, and that I should broach the subject with her on my own first, but I'd convinced myself she'd be happy about the fact we've offered the man she loves the managerial role at the club.

Talk about misjudging the situation.

"This is bullshit!" she shouts, folding her arms across her chest, her cheeks flush with rage.

"What is bullshit exactly? That we've offered Gray the management position or that we didn't tell you first?"

"Both," she snaps, nostrils flaring. "I had a right to know that *he* was going to be my boss." She points at Gray, but he simply watches her with an even expression. The man's an expert at hiding his emotions, and I know for a fact it irritates Lena. She's said as much on several occasions.

"We thought you'd be cool with it," York adds with a smirk. I shoot him a glare.

"Why would I be cool with it?" Lena screeches, her head snapping around as she narrows her eyes at York.

He swallows his smile, forcing a straight face. "Because you've known each other for years. Because you're friends," he offers with a shrug.

"We are *not* friends," Lena snaps, her hair whirling about her face as she whips her head back around and folds her arms across her chest.

"We're not?" Gray asks evenly, cocking his head to the side as he looks at her in that same intense, unreadable way of his. He's always been a closed book, and I know my sister, not getting a reaction out of him will drive her insane.

"You made that pretty clear not so long ago, or have you conveniently forgotten that particular conversation, *arsehole?*"

she counters with a scoff, this time focussing her ire on him. Gray barely reacts to her insult, which only serves to irritate her more. "Well, don't you have *anything* to say?"

Keeping his focus intensely fixed on hers, he replies calmly, "I remember what I said, Lena. Pretty sure being friends was the whole point of that conversation."

"That's not how it went down and you know it!" she shouts, losing her cool entirely now.

"I know what I said, and I know what I meant," he reiterates.

Lena laughs a little hysterically at that. "*That's* the whole point, Gray," she replies, firing his own words back at him. "What you say and what you actually mean are two entirely different things!"

"Woah, looks like you two need a minute to sort through your shit," York says, rising to his feet. "Titch, I could use a drink, you coming?"

"In a minute," I reply, giving him a stern glare as he smothers another laugh with a cough. He's enjoying this way too much. To be honest, you could cut the sexual tension with a knife. It's so obvious to everyone that the two are hopelessly in love with one another, but knowing that and facing it are two very different things. Gray obviously struggles with that, and Lena is clearly over it.

Narrowing her eyes at me, Lena shoots a look over her shoulder at York. "What's so damn funny? Do you find ruining my life amusing?"

York pinches his lips together, but there's no hiding the smile in his eyes. "That's a little dramatic, don't you think?"

Lena's nostrils flare. "Don't tell me I'm being dramatic. You don't know anything about this situation," she says, flicking her hand between the two of them.

"Pretty sure I've got a clue," York mumbles.

"York," I warn, shooting him another *shut the hell up* look.

"I'm just a little... shocked is all," York continues, trying to cover his tracks. "I thought you liked each other?"

"We don't," Lena bites out.

"*We do*," Gray responds simultaneously.

Lena gasps, and Gray swipes a hand through his dirty-blonde hair. It's the first time I've seen his guard drop and it's as unnerving for him as it is for Lena.

"What I meant was," he quickly corrects, "Is that we're *friends*. We can work together. This won't be a problem, I'll make sure of it."

"Oh you will, will you?" Lena protests, shaking her head. "And how do you propose to do that?"

Gray's eyes flicker with some unspoken emotion, but he grits his jaw, ripping his gaze away from Lena and looks at me. For the briefest of moments I see the conflict in his eyes, the uncertainty. Maybe he's having second thoughts about taking the job, or maybe he's beginning to realise that you can't run from your feelings forever.

"If you want to back out, we can find someone else for the job..." I say, letting my voice trail off as he considers my offer. I don't actually want him to back out, what I want is for him to take the job and make my sister happy. But I firmly believe this is something he's got to figure out for himself.

"No," he replies after a beat. "I *want* the job."

"Then I quit!" Lena explodes. Tears springing to her eyes that she furiously blinks back.

"Lena, you don't mean that," I say softly, glancing at York who's eying me then motioning towards the door.

Let's leave them to it, he mouths.

"I won't work with him. It's either him or me," Lena says stubbornly, drawing my attention back to her.

"Won't or can't?" I ask softly.

Lena swallows hard, then whispers, "Can't. I *can't* work with him."

Gray flinches and York pulls open the door to our office. "I think that's our cue to leave. Come on, Titch, I could use that drink."

"Yeah, me too," I agree, pushing up from my desk and swerving around the table. When I get to Lena who is chewing on her lip and trying her very best to keep her tears underwraps, I rest my hand on her arm, squeezing it gently. "Whatever you decide to do, I'll support you."

"You're choosing him over me?" she whispers, meeting my gaze.

I shake my head. "I love you. Remember everything I do is for your benefit. *Always.*"

Pressing my lips against her cheek, I look over at Gray. "It's about time you sort this out, don't you think?"

Gray's mouth drops open, but he slams it shut when Lena squares her shoulders, and tips her chin up, glaring at him. "There's nothing he has to say that I haven't already heard."

"Lena, be reasonable," I urge knowing that she's pushing

him away because he's done it one too many times to her. I get it. I really do.

"Why, so he can hide behind his morals and make us both miserable. I'd rather find somewhere else to work, thank you very much."

"Oh for fuck's sake," York snaps, grabbing my hand and pulling me through the open door and into the hallway beyond. "We're done here. Let them get on with it."

"What the heck, York?" I complain as he slams the door behind us both, slides the key in the lock, trapping them both inside.

"Call this an intervention," he says, smirking as Lena bangs on the door.

"Open the door right now!" she yells, the handle rattling as she tries in vain to open it. "This isn't funny!"

"It's not supposed to be, Lena," he replies, his smile widening when she fires back with a string of curse words.

"York, I'm not sure this is what I had in mind when I meant for them to sort this out," I say, pulling a face when I hear the low tones of Gray speaking. I can't make out his words, but I'm positive it isn't what Lena wants to hear when Lena starts shouting again.

"And you can piss off too, Gray!" she screeches.

I wince. "Sometimes I wonder how we're even related."

York lifts his brows. "You are joking, right? She's as stubborn and hot-headed as you are."

"I am *not* hot-headed," I retort.

"Pretty sure you've eviscerated each of us with your sharp tongue a few times over the years."

"I've done no such thing."

"Hmm," he comments, earning him a shove to the chest and a pointed glare. "Okay, so perhaps you deliver your words with a little more finesse than Lena does," he concedes.

"I really should talk to her about her delivery," I muse, wincing when she yells at Gray to intervene, and using a few choice swear words to hammer her point home.

There are more muffled words, and then the deep timbre of Gray's voice penetrates the thick wood of the door this time. "You should sit down, Lena," he says.

"I quit, remember?" she fires back. "So you can't tell me what to do!"

"Lena..." He sighs, and this time there's no mistaking the pain in his voice.

Shit.

"Maybe you should open the door," I say, pulling a face. "At this rate she might end up wringing his neck out of sheer frustration."

York grins, his eyes twinkling with mischief as he leans against the door, pocketing the keys. "I'm not letting them out until they've kissed and made up."

"We weren't going to interfere," I point out.

"If giving Gray the managerial job then telling him to sort this thing out between them isn't interfering, I don't know what is."

Blowing out a breath, I tap on the door and say, "Lena, Gray, you've got until closing to come to some kind of agreement."

"Agreement?" York sniggers. "This isn't a business deal, Titch."

"I'm well aware of that, York," I snipe back, instantly regretting my snappy tone. York just gives me a soft, loving smile, and I thank my lucky stars he loves me as much as he does. He knows I don't mean it, that I'm just stressing over my sister's happiness, or rather her *unhappiness*.

"That's in two hours, Pen!" Lena complains, her fist thumping against the door.

"I'm well aware."

"Pen! *Please*, just let me out. I can't do this again with him," Lena says, her voice cracking.

"Again?" York pulls a face.

"Shit, I should probably let them out," I whisper, having second thoughts.

"Pen, *please*," Lena begs.

"Maybe we misjudged this whole thing," I say, reaching for York's pocket where he stuffed the door keys.

He grabs my hand and shakes his head. "Trust me, we didn't."

I'm about to argue with York, and force him to pass me the keys when Gray speaks up. "I'm sorry to do this to you all, but I think you should open the door and find someone else for the job."

"Gray?" Lena whispers, and despite her protests I know she doesn't really want him to walk away from this position, or more importantly, her. What she wants is for Gray to admit he's in love with her, and her frustration and anger is because he refuses to do that.

"What are you going to do?" York asks, leaving me to decide my sister's fate.

"Something tells me if I open this door then Gray will walk away from Lena forever, and I'm not cool with that. It'll break her heart," I whisper.

"Okay then..." York replies, waiting for me to decide.

Pinching the bridge of my nose, I make a decision and say, "Gray, you're a good man. We all know that. You care about Lena as much as she cares about you, and I just want her to be happy. I don't care about anything else, do you understand me...?"

"Go on," York urges, as both Lena and Gray fall silent.

"Her happiness is my priority, and quite frankly she's miserable without you. So don't fuck this up, because you'll lose something far worse than your job if you do."

York chuckles. "Threatening his manhood, that'll do it."

"I was talking about *Lena*," I reply, pushing off the door.

"Of course you were," York counters, side-eying me as we head down the hallway and towards the main floor of the club, not sticking around to listen to any more demands from Lena to open the door. It's simple, they can sit in silence for the next couple of hours and not resolve a thing or they can hash this out once and for all.

"Not sure that it matters what I meant, I figured I made my point," I say with a shrug.

"Yeah, I reckon you did," he says, and when we reach the door, York blocks the way, wraps his arms around my waist and pulls me against his chest, dropping a sweet kiss against my lips.

"What was that for?" I ask when he pulls back and brushes his nose against mine.

"I love how you love the people in your life. You're the best person I know. Lena and Gray are lucky to have you interfering."

"I just hope they figure this out, because honestly, they'll be the lucky ones if they do."

"Damn straight," York says, checking his watch. "So what are we gonna do for the next two hours then?"

A smile pulls up my lips. "Oh, I can think of a thing or two."

"Yeah?" York grins, his hands sliding down my spine before grabbing my arse cheeks. "Shall we christen the broom cupboard? I reckon it could be fun."

I wrinkle my nose. "Eww, no thanks. Besides, I was actually talking about helping behind the bar given we're down two staff members."

"You want to work the bar?" York groans.

"Well you could grab a mop and bucket and clear up the vomit that lad has just chucked-up over the floor instead," I say, looking through the window of the door, and eying the drunken lad stumbling around in his own vomit.

"Urgh, fuck that. The bar it is."

"Thought as much," I chuckle.

Running up that Hill

YORK

"DRINK?" I ask Pen, waving goodbye to the last of the staff as they leave the club. It's pushing three in the morning and despite us both really enjoying working the bar, Pen looks exhausted. I should probably get to bed soon as well, even though I'm not feeling all that tired.

"Sparkling water, please," she replies, dropping onto the seat of one of the booths that circles the dance floor and pulling out her phone, presumably checking for a message from Lena.

"Coming right up," I reply, grabbing us both a drink from behind the bar.

"And some lemon," she adds.

"You don't need to ask. I know how you like it," I say with a hint of suggestiveness and a waggle of my brows, because, I'm sorry, she walked right into that one.

"You sure do," she agrees, smiling up at me as I set her drink down on the table and take a seat opposite her.

"Everything okay?"

Pen nods, lifting her eyes to meet mine. "Lena sent me a message."

"Yeah? What does it say?" I ask, taking a swig from my own glass of water.

"She said; *Tell York thanks.*"

I grin. "Must've worked out alright then?"

"I guess it must've," she grins, lifting the glass of water to her lips and taking a sip.

"So I'm guessing they kissed and made up? I wonder how that went down. Lena looked pretty pissed when she left earlier. Thought Gray was gonna start sobbing at one point. Not that there's anything wrong with a man showing his emotions, but we all know Gray is a closed book, so it took me by surprise. Anyway, did she give you any juicy details?"

Pen chuckles softly. "You really are a gossip, you know that right?"

"Not a gossip, per se. I just have a healthy appetite for wanting to know all the intricate details of the people I care about love lives. So, spill. Is she happy?"

"Pretty sure she's ecstatic," Pen replies, turning the phone around.

"Pretty sure they've just had sex," I laugh, grinning at the selfie Lena sent Pen. They both have mussed-up hair, broad grins and sex-glazed eyes.

Pen scrunches up her nose. "Not sure I need those thoughts in my head, thanks very much."

"Okay then, how about this? They've been playing twister all night long, and ended up getting so into it that they decided to up the stakes and add in a little strip poker."

"Definitely worse," she replies, clicking off her phone and resting it on the table between us. "What did you say to Gray anyway? I'm curious?"

"Just some advice, man-to-man," I reply, a little vaguely.

"Want to elaborate? Because whatever you said seems to have done the trick."

"I can't really remember, something about gravity," I mutter, skirting over the subject.

It's not that I don't want to tell Pen what I said, it's just that it was pretty intense, and I'm not normally that kind of guy. *Lighthearted-jokester* is my middle name, after all.

"*Gravity?*" She cocks her head to the side, a curious expression on her face.

"Yeah, something along those lines."

"No jokes then?" she asks, pressing the matter.

"I *can* be serious, you know," I say, meeting her eyes. "I'm not just the funniest man on the planet. I do have as much depth as the others."

Reaching for me across the table, Pen grasps my hand. "I know you do. Don't think all we see is a joker. That's part of who you are, not all of who you are. You have so much depth, York. So much emotional intelligence. I love you for all that you are. Tonight you made two people very happy, and I'm so grateful."

"Grateful enough to dance with me?" I ask, grinning.

"Now?"

"We have the whole dance floor to ourselves," I point out.

"As much as I want to, I'm super tired. I don't know what's up with me lately, but I'm bloody exhausted," she replies, wincing a little.

"Covering Lena and Gray's shift on top of all the recent overtime is going to have that effect. We've all been lighting the candle at both ends," I say, feeling the opposite of tired, but sympathising nevertheless.

Truth be known, I'm feeling strangely energised. Maybe it's because not so long ago I was forced to lie in bed and got plenty of rest, or maybe it's knowing I had a hand at getting Lena and Gray together, or perhaps it's because all this recent dancing has lit the passion within me again and all I want to do is move my feet.

"Yeah, that's a total one-off. Now they've got things sorted we can ease off properly just like we've planned. I'm looking forward to spending more time together," she replies, stifling a yawn, apologising with her eyes. "Maybe after the performance we can book a holiday or something? I could totally spend a week or so sipping margaritas on a white sandy beach some-where hot recovering with a whole dose of sex and yummy food."

"Sounds like a really good fucking plan to me," I agree, picking up my phone and flipping through my music playlist, an idea forming. "These past few days rehearsing has felt like I've been running up that hill, so I could use a few days at the beach."

"Running up what hill? You don't run, York," Pen asks, too tired to catch on.

Sliding out from the table, I bluetooth the song with the same name to the club's sound system, then place my phone on the table and step back onto the dance floor. I waggle my brows as the beat drops.

Pen laughs. "Oh, *that* hill?"

"What other hill is there?" I reply, my feet tapping against the hardwood floor as I sing along with Kate Bush. "It doesn't hurt me...yeah, yeah, yeah, yeaaaahhhh!"

Pen laughs louder as I throw my arms wide, and proceed to sing at the top of my lungs, enjoying the thrum of music as it rises up through my feet, sparking this energy within me.

"From now on I think everyone should call me Cupid," I announce suddenly.

"You're incorrigible," Pen shouts over the music, shaking her head as she watches me.

"Well, it's either that or Fred, because I think I've got my Astaire back."

Pen chuckles, leaning her chin on her hand as her eyes follow me around the dance floor, glazing over with memories as I perform for her.

The last time I danced to this song was with Pen at Stardom Academy. Back then we were still enemies, or at least that's how it felt until the teacher called us up to dance. But that day she'd shown me the truth of heart. In front of everyone she'd bled her pain and heartache into her steps, showing me how she truly felt towards me, how devastated she was for all the pain and heartache between us.

Now I want to show her how *happy* she makes me. How much joy she's given me over the years. How, without her, nothing in this world would feel right.

Pen is my once in a lifetime love. She's *my* force of gravity. Just like Lena is to Gray.

Finding that kind of love is special. Christ, not everyone gets to find the kind of love I share for my four best mates either. I'm a lucky bastard, there's no denying it. And maybe it's these feelings, this realisation, that gives me this sudden, overwhelming need to dance.

Without thinking, I move my feet in a series of rhythm turns across the floor, ending up at the far side where I dance on the spot to the beat of the song. I feel this energy burning inside of me as my feet move with lightning speed. I might not be wearing my tap shoes, but for me tap dancing isn't really about the sound my toe and heel caps make when they hit the floor. It's about what it feels like to express myself with a dance that matches my energy, that is a representation of who I am as a person.

My recent illness from the flu might've knocked me out for a while, but I'm back with a vengeance now. Flying across the dance floor, I tap out a series of steps and turns that have me grinning from ear to ear. Spinning and twirling, my arms mirroring the movements of my feet, I feel like Fred Astaire, an entertainer, a legend, someone who gave endless joy to those who watched him dance. But I'm nothing without my very own Ginger Rogers, so I dance towards Pen, stupidly happy as she gets to her feet and slides out of the booth.

"You sure?" I ask her, my chest heaving as the song we both know so well comes to an end.

"What's one dance?" she replies, picking up my phone and flipping through the playlist.

"Seriously, we can go home. I'm good now. Got all that excess energy out. I'll sleep like a log."

Pen shakes her head, then presses play. Another familiar song plays out over the speakers, and I throw back my head and laugh.

"Thought you might appreciate that," Pen says playfully.

"*Shut Up and Dance With Me?*" I question, the biggest, goofiest grin spreading across my face as she pushes past me and skips to the centre of the dance floor, turning to face me just as the lead singer belts out that infamous line.

"Forever," she replies.

"And always."

Then we dance. Not tap. Not contemporary. Not lyrical. Not hip-hop.

We simply move our bodies, jumping to the beat like a couple of carefree kids. We laugh and smile. We groove it out, pulling stupid faces as we pretend to play air guitar. We grab each other's hands and twirl on the dance floor, the room spinning around us, all whilst we sing at the top of our lungs.

It's fucking incredible.

This right here, is us. Me and Pen. This is the *us* when we're alone together.

This energy. This vibrancy. This exuberance.

Sure we can have serious conversations, we make love, and we fuck. But the heart of *our* love, mine and Pen's, is pure *joy*. It's the happy beat to our steps. It's our eyes sparkling with tears of laughter. It's the fast pulse of two breathless hearts in love. It's the adrenaline rush of high energy. It's our sense of fun. It's that glow, the one that comes from the inside out, just like she's glowing now as she jumps up and down, her loose hair whipping around her face, her cheeks flush with happiness, her pink lips parting with a smile as she sings, her eyes dazzling with laughter.

She's breathtaking.

I still, my chest heaving as I watch her throw away all the physical confines we tend to wrap ourselves up in. It's human nature to keep our bodies in check, to move with structure and purpose in a way that is socially acceptable. Even as dancers we follow a series of steps, steps that can be named, that have their place in a performance.

But right now, there's no rhyme or rhythm to her movements, and if someone who wasn't familiar with Pen's ability to dance were to walk into the club right now, they'd assume she had no formal dance training, that she was just a woman dancing like no one was watching, without inhibition or restraint. She dances messily, happily, with a goofy expression, and a smile on her face.

And somehow, the freedom in her movements, the way she's given herself up to the joy of the moment causes this sudden wave of love to flood through my veins. It sparkles and crackles, filling me with wonder, a sense of deep satisfaction, and utter, blissful contentment.

When the music stops, and Pen looks at me from the other side of the dance floor, her body loose, her eyes smiling,, I do what any sane man in love would do, I stride over to her, pull her into my arms, and kiss her senseless.

"What was *that*?" she exclaims when I pull back and grin down at her, feeling that rush of euphoria. "That was..." Pressing her fingers to her lips, she looks up at me in wonder this time. "That was a *really* good kiss. I felt it everywhere."

"Told you, I'm basically Cupid. That was an arrow straight to the heart. I am also what you call a man of many talents," I quip, but I see the wonder in her eyes. Pen felt that ceaseless, undying love we have for one another. I know it's that way for her and the others too, and I'm okay with that because if anyone has the capacity to love more than one person as deeply as she does me, it's Pen. "Pretty sure that was our souls tying the knot," I add with a smirk.

"Either that or there's something in the water," she agrees with another tender press of her lips against mine.

"Well, whatever it was, if we could bottle that feeling and sell it, I'm sure we'd become billionaires overnight. Imagine becoming rich from love."

"I'm *already* rich from love," she replies, wrapping her arm around my back and hugging me closer. "I'm the richest woman alive. I'm so lucky."

"This *is* true," I agree. Reluctant to let her go, but knowing we really should close up, I pull back. "Let's go home, yeah?"

"Not before you tell me what you said to Gray. I've got to know."

"It's not that big of a deal."

"York, spit it out," she urges.

"Alright," I respond, then cupping her cheek, I look into the eyes of the woman who has stolen my heart and say, "I just told him the truth as I know it."

"And what's that?"

I lower my lips to hers, pressing a kiss against her mouth before continuing. "I said that not everyone gets lucky enough to find their once in a lifetime love. That the way Gray feels for Lena is a force of gravity. There's no fighting it. In fact, it's impossible to live without. Fuck knows I tried for three long years to do that..."

At first Pen doesn't say anything, and I feel heat creep up my cheeks from embarrassment. "You think what I said is corny...?"

She shakes her head emphatically. "No! God, no. I think... I think what you said is *beautiful*."

"Well, that's a relief," I reply, blowing out a breath.

"It's pretty bloody romantic, York," she says, rising on her tiptoes to plant a soft kiss against my lips. "I like this side of you."

"That's not all I said," I say, pulling a face.

"Oh yeah? What else?"

"I told Gray not to be a fucking idiot and to go and claim his woman," I explain with a rueful grin.

"Okay, so that's a little more caveman," she laughs.

"*Caveman*?" I smirk, tipping my head to the side in thought.

"I'm happy to take on that title too. Do you think I could pull it off, Pen? Being a caveman, I mean."

"York!" she warns, knowing the moment our eyes meet what I'm about to do, Backing away from me, she holds her hands up. "Don't you dare–"

"Man must claim woman," I say, bashing my fists against my chest as she turns on her heel and runs. I chase after her, catching her near the door where I swoop her into my arms. "Mine," I add for good measure as laughter bursts free from her lips, swelling both of our hearts with joy.

Family Affair

PEN

"IT'S FULL-ON TONIGHT," Zayn mutters, on high alert as he pulls out my chair a few nights later and searches the crowd at Tales for any threats.

Everywhere we look there are men and women from rival gangs, all here to watch two men beat each other to a pulp. In any other setting this would be a recipe for disaster but Tales is unique in that respect. Firstly, no weapons are allowed in the club, and if a fight were to break out, the security team circling the walkways above our heads would put an end to any violence with one well-placed bullet between the eyes. No warning. No second chances. Secondly, no one fucks with Beast and Grim, at least not since Malik Brov tried to, and that didn't end too well for him.

"Mate, we've got shit covered," Beast says, squeezing Zayn's shoulder before redirecting his attention back to Lena. "I don't know what you did to put a smile on Gray's face, sweetheart, but I'm sure happy you did. You know, I ain't seen him this happy for a long fucking time."

Right now Gray's standing at the bar chatting with Eastern and Sonny, two of Asia's men, as well as Dax and Xeno, and there's no denying his happiness. He's like a different man.

"I'm pretty sure I know exactly what Lena did to put a smile on Gray's face," York jokes, winking at Lena whilst Beast starts handing out the drinks he brought over from the bar.

Even beneath the dim lighting of the club, I can see how Lena's cheeks flush crimson. Reaching over, I give her hand a squeeze in sympathy. "He'll tire of it eventually," I whisper.

She gives me a withering look that tells me she doesn't believe that for one second.

"I think you'll find that talent lies with Christy," Leon pipes up, slinging his arm over the back of Christy's chair. She's busy talking in hushed tones with Asia on her left.

"What's my talent?" Christy asks, looking at Leon—one of her partners—who leans in and presses a kiss against her cheek.

"Knowing what Lena did to put a smile on Gray's face," Jakub replies for him, almost bored.

His lack of expression when conversing has always been unnerving, even after all these years of knowing him. Still, I can't fault his love for Christy, and if he provides her what she needs out of a relationship, then who am I to judge?

"On this occasion, I don't think we need Christy's skills to get insight into what's made Gray so happy," Asia grins, taking her cocktail from Beast with a smile. "The guy has most definitely had his cake and eaten it."

"Not you too," Lena groans, reaching for her own drink and knocking back a healthy mouthful.

"Hey, I'm just stating a fact. We've all got eyes."

"Can we all just stop hyperfocusing on mine and Gray's relationship? You all must lead such terribly boring lives to have so much interest in our sex life."

"You do realise I have four boyfriends, right?" Asia counters lightheartedly.

"Yeah, and I heard a rota's on the cards because your vagina can't hack the regular pounding it's been getting," Lena throws back.

York practically chokes on his drink, and Zayn laughs until I elbow him in the side. I groan internally, Asia is going to think I've been talking about her behind her back, and I wasn't. Lena caught me chatting to Grim about the conversation we all had together at her house, and questioned me about it afterwards. There was nothing catty in it, just merely me discussing what it's like having four boyfriends, and how much of a juggle it can be.

"A rota?" Camden asks, quiet until now. Like Zayn he's been keeping an eye on the criminals surrounding us, but this conversation has certainly helped to refocus his attention.

"That was private!" Asia accuses, flicking her gaze between

me and Lena, before throwing Camden, her boyfriend, a sheepish look.

"Yeah, and so is my and Gray's sex life," Lena retorts, her brows lifting in challenge.

Asia pulls a face, suitably chastised. "You've got a point. Sorry, Lena."

"So, a rota?" Camden questions, his turquoise eyes glinting with amusement as he drops a kiss to Asia's temple. "Want to elaborate?"

"It's just a thought," Asia shrugs. "Pen mentioned it."

"Oh yeah?" Camden looks over at me, then across to Zayn on my right. "You have a rota?"

"Seems to work for us," he replies with a shrug like it's no big deal, because it isn't.

Camden nods as his eyes meet Leon's across the table. "Do *you* have a rota?"

Leon shakes his head. "No. We fuck together," he deadpans.

"You don't *ever* want to have time alone with Christy?" Asia asks, her curiosity peaked.

"We do spend time alone with Christy, but not to *make love*," Jakub corrects Leon, his thumb rubbing across Christy's knuckles as he speaks. "That we prefer to do together."

"You know the thought of another man's hands on my woman is enough to send me psycho," Beast says, shaking his head. "Fuck that."

"Send you psycho? Beast, you already *are* a psycho," York points out. "A loveable one, granted, but a psycho nevertheless."

"If anyone were to touch Grim, their hands would be cut off

and shoved up their arse before they could even blink," Beast continues, a scowl forming on his face.

"That's... *very specific*," Lena comments, brows lifting.

"I mean I'd probably cut his dick off and feed it to him first, so there's that," he replies with a shrug.

Lena shudders. "Ew, gross."

"Okay, Beast, I think we've gathered you're not into sharing," York grins. "Moving on."

"I can't help it if you motherfuckers turned this conversation upside down. You know I was actually trying to be supportive, Lena. No harm intended when I started this conversation. It's not my fault that dicksplash lowered the tone."

"Supportive? You're about as supportive as a wet paper bag," Lena retorts, but despite her words, her tone is lighthearted, and she leans over and briefly gives Beast's hand a gentle squeeze. We all know despite Beast's predilection for violence towards his enemies, he is fiercely protective, loyal and supportive of the ones he loves.

"You wound me," Beast replies, putting his hand over his heart in mock hurt. "But seriously, Lena, we're all just excited to see you both so happy. You know how Gray gets when he's all broody and shit, and for the last year or so he's been like a thug without his weapon."

"Shouldn't that be a *bear with a sore head*?" York asks.

"Same difference," Beast shrugs. "Anyhow, we're all glad Gray finally pulled his finger out of his arse and made you his."

Lena can't help the small smile that graces her lips. "I know. I just wish everyone would stop making such a big deal out of it."

"Fair enough, sweetheart. We hear you loud and clear, don't we, York?" Beast asks, giving him a pointed look. "No more winding Lena up."

He holds his hands up in defeat. "Fuck, fine. Spoil my fun, why don't you."

"What fun?" Konrad asks, pulling out the chair next to Leon and taking a seat. "Are we taking on some of these cunts you've got here tonight?"

"Woah! Calm down, Mr Mask," Beast says, holding his hands up and giving Konrad a look. "You know the rules of the club. No fighting unless it's in the cage."

Konrad rolls his eyes. "Then set me up. I'm in the mood for a good brawl."

"You'll do no such thing," Christy chastises, turning her attention to Beast. "Put any of my men in the cage, and you'll have me to deal with."

Beast pulls a face, mumbling something indistinct under his breath.

"Christy, a good fight never hurt anyone," Konrad says, smirking when she throws him a glare.

Like Jakub and Leon, Konrad's dressed in an expensive tailored suit made of the finest black wool money can buy. Incredibly handsome even with the scar running down his cheek, Konrad is as beautiful as he is deadly. With the Brov name as their legacy, they come from old money, money that's been bathed in a long history of bloodshed. Pretty sure most of the criminals in attendance have heard of The Masks, their namesake, and I'd bet that most of them are too afraid to cross them, which is another reason why Zayn needs to relax. We're sitting at a table with powerful people. Between Asia and her men, who've grown up scrappy and helped her take out her dad, the King, The Masks who have a fierce reputation and a streak of violence even Christy can't quite tame, Beast who is known to cut the hearts out of his enemies and is married to the toughest woman in the criminal underground scene, and of course my own men who once had a reputation of their own, I think we're good.

"In answer to your earlier question, Konrad, we were just admiring Lena's ability to put a smile on Gray's face," York deadpans, and I can see his need to slide in another quip, but he refrains when I glare at him in warning.

"Ah, so that's why he's so... *smiley*," Konrad retorts as if that word is offensive.

"Nothing wrong with being happy, mate," Beast says, patting Lena on the shoulder.

Konrad considers Beast's words, eying Lena. "The love of a good woman can do that to a man,"

"Don't we all know it," Beast agrees good-naturedly, as Konrad turns to his brother Jakub.

"You've been cracking smiles *and* mirrors with your love-sick grin ever since Christy tamed our wild hearts, isn't that right, Jakub?"

"You actually smile?" Camden blurts out, saying what we're all thinking.

For a moment we all hold our breath, waiting to see how he'll respond. Jakub's never been a banter kind of guy so when he replies, "I think you'll find it's *your* ugly as fuck face that's been cracking all the mirrors, Kon," we all fall about laughing. Even Jakub grins. "And for the record, I *do* smile."

"Glad that's been cleared up," Beast says with a chuckle. "Well, as much as I've enjoyed the chit-chat, I've got to check in on our fighters. Make sure they're ready to go. Ford's been keeping them company with Grim whilst I do the rounds. Catch you later?"

He winks at Jakub, who gives him a brief dip of his head before wandering off.

As the group continues to chat and joke around, the noise levels rise until I can barely hear myself think. Feeling a headache coming on, coupled with the same tiredness I've been feeling for a few days now, I rest my hand on Zayn"s thigh to get his attention.

"I'm just going to wish Clancy and the girls good luck before their performance."

"You want me to come?" he asks, his gaze flicking around the warehouse still looking out for danger, a habit I don't think he'll ever break, especially not when it comes to protecting me.

"No. Stay. I won't be long," I reply, plastering on a smile. If he comes with me I might not be able to hide that I'm feeling off, and it'll only worry him.

Sensing my discomfort, Christy stands, catching my eye with a soft smile. "I'll come with you. I need to speak with Grim before she kicks off the fight anyway."

Zayn, satisfied that I'm not walking across the warehouse on my own, nods. "See you in a minute?"

"Give me five before you send out the search party," I tease, dropping a kiss to his cheek, before turning on my heel.

The noise levels drop as soon as we push through the door and head down the corridor towards Grim's office, only to rise again when we get closer to the dressing room. The girls have always been a little raucous, and normally I'm happy to join in with all the fun. But tonight I wince, rubbing at the sudden sharp pain in my temple, maybe this wasn't the best idea after all.

"You alright, Pen? You look a bit off-colour," Christy asks, guiding me to a stop. She studies me with her strange eyes, and I feel my skin cover in goosebumps like it does sometimes in her presence.

"I'm fine. Seriously. Just work catching up on me."

"You sure?"

I cock my head to the side. "I'm not sure if you're asking me that question because you *haven't* seen something in my future, or you're asking me that question because you have, and you're trying to work out if I know something that you already do."

Christy scrunches up her nose. "This is just a concerned friend. No visions, I swear."

"Then as a concerned friend, you wouldn't mind grabbing me a couple of headache pills from Grim's office, right? She keeps a stash in the top drawer of her desk. I'm not sure I can face the girls without at least trying to get rid of this headache first."

"You can come with me. I'm sure Grim would be glad to see you."

"I'm actually desperate for a pee. Be there in a minute?"

"Sure thing," Christy replies as I push open the door to the ladies, and she carries on to Grim's office.

Breathing a sigh of relief at the quiet, I head into the stall to relieve myself. I don't hurry to unlock the door once I'm done, instead, I flip down the toilet seat and sit down. The pain in my head thumps and I draw in a couple of breaths to try and deal with it, which only seems to bring on a sudden bout of nausea. I slam my hand over my mouth, trying not to retch.

Fuck, this is what happened to York when he started to get sick. I bet he's given me the damn flu.

When I hear the door to the toilet open, I force myself to my feet, pulling open the door as I say, "Thank goodness, I really need those headache tablets," stopping in my tracks when I come face to face with Cynthia, and not Christy.

"Hello, Pen, how are you?" she asks, throwing me a sweet smile, her soft Irish lilt oddly soothing.

"Oh hey, I didn't know you were coming. Grim said that Faith hasn't been well," I reply, giving her a brief hug, and hoping I don't throw up all over her. Cynthia is married to the Deana-dhe, the three Irish criminals who helped us deal with an issue we had a few years back, and they live off the coast of Ireland.

"She's much better actually. That nasty virus took a while to clear out of her system. I didn't think she'd enjoy the journey so soon after feeling so poorly, so her great Uncle Connall agreed to look after her for us."

"I wondered where he was tonight," I say, turning on the faucet to wash my hands.

"He was more than happy to spend the weekend doting on her."

"Well, it's really nice to see you here," I add, shaking out the excess water, and patting my forehead, relishing the cool liquid against my skin. Fuck, I look really pale.

"It's good to be here..." Cyn replies, her voice trailing off as she watches me. "How's York? Is he feeling better?"

"So much better, thanks. That tincture you sent did him wonders. Literally the next day after taking it he was up and out of bed. You're a wonder," I say, patting my face with a paper cloth, and doing my best not to run back into the stall and throw up my dinner.

"Pen," Cynthia says, resting her hand on my arm. "Are you feeling okay?"

"Just a headache, Christy went to grab me some tablets," I reply, turning to face her and plastering on another smile. I don't know why I don't mention that I feel sick too. I guess I don't want anyone fussing over me. Plus we have a show to perform in just over a week, and I do not need the guys forcing me to rest. I *need* this performance. It's important to me, to us. "Me and the guys have been burning the candles at both ends for a while."

Cyn nods, her eyes grazing over my face as she regards me. "Work hard and play hard?"

"No, just work hard, work hard," I say. "Well, up until recently anyway. We've actually stepped off the gas a little, and handed over the management of Twisted Bullet to Gray, and are getting a performance together for a dance competition we're holding at the club next week."

"I see," she replies, her eyes still searching mine.

"We'd love you and the guys to come, by the way."

"Wouldn't miss it. That's another reason why we're here.

Connall is going to bring Faith over in a few days. She'll be so happy to see Iris, so it's a win-win..."

"What?" I ask, feeling a little unnerved by her intense gaze.

Her eyes drop from my face to my body and back up again, and I can't help feeling a little bit like some kind of specimen under a microscope.

"Pen, I think maybe–"

"Sorry, Pen, I got chatting and I–" Christy stops in the doorway, then lets out a squeal of delight. "Cynthia! You're here, what the hell?" she says, before wrapping her arms around her best friend and squeezing her tight.

"Of course I'm here," she says, eying me with concern. "Arden's fighting tonight and I wasn't about to let him get all busted up without me here to fix him up afterwards."

"*He's* the one fighting?" Christy exclaims, her mouth popping open in shock. "I did *not* see that coming."

"Then I guess you didn't see who he's fighting against either?" Cyn replies, pulling a face. "I thought maybe he would've told you by now."

"Who would've told me what?"

Cynthia bites on her lip. "Shit."

"Wait... What do you mean?" Christy asks carefully.

"Jakub is Arden's opponent in the cage."

"No way!" I exclaim, my headache and nausea momentarily forgotten. "I thought they were friends. What are they doing going head-to-head?"

"I'm going to kill him!" Christy seethes.

Cynthia gives her a sympathetic look. "Believe me, I had plenty to say to Arden over this, but you know how they get.

Jakub challenged him and he's not one for backing down in a fight. They're both stubborn to a fault, and way too prideful for their own good."

"But that was over six months ago and they were both drunk! I thought they'd forgotten all about it. I certainly did."

"Apparently not," Cynthia replies, glancing at me, her eyes flicking with concern when I swallow down another wave of nausea.

Feeling my cheeks flush as a sudden wave of dizziness comes over me, I pretend to adjust my hair in the mirror. At this point I'm not sure if it's the headache that is making me feel sick, or if I really do have the flu. Either way, it's not fun.

"Do you have those headache pills?" I ask, tucking my hair behind my ear.

"Oh shit, yes. Here you go, Pen," she says, handing them to me alongside a bottle of water.

"Thanks," I mumble, throwing a couple back whilst Christy continues with her tirade.

"You know I think I'm losing my touch," she cries, throwing her hands up in the air. "What good is it having a *gift*, if it doesn't work when you need it to?"

"Must be frustrating," I say, trying to appease her rising temper. The Masks might be fierce, but I wouldn't want to get on the wrong side of Christy, she's got way too much Grim in her not to be just as formidable. Hell, she tamed men no one thought could be tamed. It takes an exceedingly strong woman to do that.

"Wait a minute, why didn't *you* say anything?" Christy asks, turning her ire on Cynthia.

She winces. "I only found out myself yesterday, and when I spoke to Grim she asked me not to tell you, not because she wanted to hide it from you but because she knew as well as I that neither of us would be able to stop them. You *know* what they're like. At least being here I can make sure they get the best care after they finish pulverising each other like two foolish school children."

"Whatever happened to sisterhood?" Christy bites out. "Grim should've told me."

"Grim probably figured the same thing as Cynthia. Better let them fight it out here than some other dinghy club, right? Besides, if something really bad was going to happen, I'm sure you'd have seen it," I offer, regretting my words the second they leave my mouth.

"It doesn't work like that!" she says with frustration. "You know what, I'm going to murder Jakub but not before I murder my sister first!"

Striding to the door, Chisty yanks it open before storming off down the hallway.

"Not sure I'd like to be in Grim's shoes right now," I say, hearing Christy hollering at Grim.

"She's very strong willed, that's for sure," Cynthia says, laughing softly.

"Aren't you worried they'll kill each other?" I ask. "All bets are off in the cage. We *all* know that."

Cynthia shakes her head. "I trust them both not to take it too far."

I give her a look that tells her without words that I'm not sure I believe that given their history.

"Trust me, if they wanted to kill each other, they've had ample opportunities over the years. Believe it or not, they're friends."

"You certainly know them best," I acknowledge. "I guess we should head back out there? Clancy and the girls will be performing soon. I don't want to miss the show."

Cynthia nods, but when I reach for the door, hauling it open she says, "Pen?"

"Yes?"

"I think maybe you're—"

But her sentence is cut short when Clancy appears in the doorway, throwing her arms around me in a tight embrace. "There you are! Zayn's been looking for you, the guy's about to have a coronary."

"I've not been gone that long," I sigh into her curls.

Clancy chuckles. "Doesn't stop him from worrying though."

"I'm afraid the worrying is going to get a whole lot worse," Cynthia mutters behind me.

Before I'm able to ask her what she meant by that, light-headedness comes over me once again but this time black spots prick my vision.

"I don't feel so..." I mutter, the end of my sentence lost to unconsciousness as my legs give way beneath me.

FOURTEEN

The Feels

PEN

"PEN, CAN YOU HEAR ME?"

Zayn's face comes into view, worried and tense. He breathes out a relieved sigh as my eyes flutter open. "Thank fuck," he murmurs, squeezing my hand tight.

"What happened?" I query groggily, pushing upright with the help of Zayn, his arm sliding around my back as he eases me against the armrest of the sofa I'm lying on.

"Easy now," Cynthia says, placing a glass of water on the

side table as she drops to her knees beside me. "Just give your body a moment to adjust. No sudden movements, okay?"

"I'm in Clancy's changing room," I reply uselessly, the faint thud of music and the roar of the audience penetrating the walls as Clancy and her dance troupe bring the house down.

"You fainted in her arms, luckily Zayn was just down the corridor and rushed to help. He brought you here."

"But I'm missing the show." I move to get up, but Zayn shakes his head, pressing his hand gently against my shoulder.

"Don't even think about it, Pen. You're staying put."

"But—"

"No buts. You're clearly not well. Why didn't you say anything to us? We wouldn't have come tonight had we known," he says, scraping a hand through his hair as he looks at me worriedly.

"I was feeling fine before we arrived. Seriously, I'm as surprised as you are that I passed out."

"So do you want to tell us what happened?" Cynthia asks, pressing the back of her hand against my forehead.

"Are you checking for a temperature?" Zayn asks.

"I am, and she's good where that's concerned," Cynthia confirms.

"That's something I suppose," Zayn says. "What do you think is wrong?"

"Let's hear what Pen has to say first." Cynthia turns her attention back to me as she hands me the glass of water. "You mentioned to me just before you passed out that you've been feeling tired lately."

"We've *all* been tired lately. Just working too hard, I guess?" I offer, taking a sip of water.

"Okay. Anything else? It'll help if you can tell me about any other out of the ordinary symptoms you might've been having recently."

"The headache, of course," I add.

"You have a headache?" Zayn asks, resting his hand on my thigh, his thumb swirling circles on my jean clad skin.

"Well it's a little less painful now. More of a dull ache."

"When did that come on?" Cynthia queries, her pretty grey eyes assessing me.

"When we were all sitting and chatting around the table waiting for Clancy and the girls to perform. It just got a little too loud, so I went to find some headache pills."

"You said you were going to wish Clancy luck before the show. Not that you had a headache," Zayn says, frowning. "Why didn't you say something?"

"It's just a headache," I reply.

"Clearly not, Pen."

"I didn't think I was going to pass out, Zayn."

He puffs out a breath. "I know, fuck. It's just, you don't get sick. This is freaking me out a little."

"Please don't. It's going to be bad enough when the others find out. Especially Xeno, I don't want this to make him spiral. I'm fine."

"No one needs to freak out," Cynthia says, smiling kindly. "Let's just go over everything. Anything else aside from the headache, feeling tired lately, and this fainting episode?"

"Shouldn't you be with your guys? Arden will be fighting

Jakub soon and they'll need you afterwards," I say, trying to move the conversation away from me.

"Arden's fighting Jakub?" Zayn questions. "I haven't seen Lorcan or Carrick tonight."

"They're with Grim and Ford right now. They couldn't exactly keep the fight a surprise with them wandering around the club," Cynthia explains, before resting her hand on my arm. "It'll be a while before they need me. Besides I'm not here to watch the fight, just to clear them up after."

"You're really very calm about this whole thing," I say. "When Dax got in the cage with Beast I was a bundle of nerves."

"I guess it's just not in my nature to panic. Now, is there anything else you want to share, Pen?" Cynthia repeats, steering the conversation back to me.

"I think I might have caught York's flu or something. I've been feeling off for a little while now, and the headache made me want to throw up," I reluctantly inform her.

"You've felt nauseous too?" Zayn asks, swiping a hand over his face, a habit of his when he's feeling frustrated with me, and is trying to figure out how to say something without it turning into an argument.

"Yes. I remember York felt like that with the flu. The virus really knocked him out. Faith was poorly recently as well so there's obviously something going around, right?"

Zayn and Cynthia exchange looks. "Do you have a sore throat? A cough? Congestion?" Cynthia questions, grasping my wrist whilst looking at her watch.

"Are you checking her pulse?"

Cynthia nods. Zayn shifts uncomfortably as we both wait

for her to count my heart rate. When she releases my wrist, she grins, and that reaction throws me a little. It seems odd given the circumstances.

"So, do you have a sore throat, a cough or congestion?"

I frown. "No, come to think of it, I don't."

"It's not the flu then?" Zayn questions.

"No, I don't believe it's the flu."

Zayn swipes a hand through his hair. "Then what's going on?"

Cynthia stands, brushing her hands over her ankle length skirt. "I do have one question to ask before I give you my opinion on what's happening here."

"Okay, so what's the question?" Zayn says, flicking his gaze to me briefly. I can see he's as confused as I am. Confused and concerned.

Cynthia turns her attention back to me. "When was your–"

"Where is she?" Xeno shouts, the door crashing open as Dax and York rush in behind him.

I can feel their concern like a wall of bricks crashing down, and I brace myself for the impact. Xeno's gaze snaps to me on the couch. "What the fuck happened?" he demands, his voice sharp with worry.

"Pen fainted," Zayn explains, climbing to his feet. "She hasn't been feeling well."

Xeno strides over and kneels in front of me, taking my hand. "Are you okay?"

"I'm fine," I assure him, my voice barely above a whisper. "Just a little tired."

"You don't look fine," he counters, his gaze scanning my face.

"How long have you been feeling unwell?" Dax asks, slightly calmer than Xeno, but only just.

I look up at him, feeling like I'm causing so much unnecessary drama. "It's nothing really. I think it's just a culmination of working too hard. I'm sorry to panic you all. I honestly feel okay now. Really."

"Kid, stop making light of this. You don't just faint for no reason," Dax says, his voice laced with concern.

"We should take you to the hospital," York adds, his expression serious. "They can take some blood or something. Do some tests?"

"I'm sure it's nothing," I protest weakly, but they're already discussing who should grab the car and who should let our friends know what's happening. "Honestly. We've all been reacting differently to working too hard. This is just how my body is handling it. I'm positive it will get better with a good night's rest. Please, I don't need to go to the hospital."

"This isn't up for debate, Titch. You're sick. We don't know what's going on, and we love you. You're going," York says firmly.

"Well, I think I can help you there," Cynthia says gently.

"We appreciate your offer to drive her, but you're needed here for Arden and Jakub. We'll take her," Zayn says, glancing over at York. "Do you want to bring the car around back so Pen doesn't have to walk through the club? I'm sure she could do without the audience."

"I wasn't offering to drive Pen to the hospital," Cynthia explains, glancing over at me, her eyes twinkling with mirth. "Pen doesn't need a hospital right now."

"With all due respect," Xeno says, standing, "I'd feel better if she had some blood tests run, or whatever the hell needs to happen to find out what's going on, and that can only be done at a hospital."

"Oh, I'd definitely think an appointment with a doctor will be needed to confirm my suspicions, but that can wait until Monday. Pen isn't ill–"

"She just fainted," Zayn reminds her.

"She did. But she's not ill," Cynthia presses, looking between my four guys, clearly not in the least bit worried about whatever's going on with me. "I believe she's *pregnant*."

The room falls silent as Cynthia's words sink in.

Pregnant? Me? *What?*

"No way. I can't be," I blurt out, the thought is almost too overwhelming to process.

"You definitely can," Cynthia says with a chuckle.

"But I..." My voice trails off as I look around at the faces of the people I love more than anything in this world. "Surely not?"

Cynthia chuckles, her soft Irish lilt warm and full of love. "Would it be such a bad thing if you were?" she asks softly.

"No it wouldn't, but... I... but..." I look up at the guys who are all stuck in some kind of shocked limbo. "I'm going to be a mum?"

"I'm pretty certain," she replies.

"*How* can you be certain?" I ask, because right now none of my guys seem able to speak. They're all staring at me like I've grown another head. Which I suppose–if what Cyn is saying is true–technically I have.

"The only way to be certain is to take a pregnancy test, but given the description of your symptoms, and..."

"And?" I ask, swallowing hard, because my men still remain strangely quiet. Forcing myself not to look at any of them, I keep my focus on Cynthia.

"And, I have a feel for this kind of thing."

"A feel?" I frown, taking a huge gulp of water because suddenly my throat is parched. "I'm not sure it's wise to trust a feeling when we're talking about me growing a baby."

Cynthia frowns, considering my words. "I wouldn't have said anything if I wasn't positive."

"So you truly think I'm pregnant?"

"Christy isn't the only one who is often referred to as a witch," she explains with a soft laugh, but when I don't react with anything other than shock, she crouches down beside me, takes the glass of water from my hand, placing it back on the side table, then presses her hand to my tummy. "There are the more obvious signs of early pregnancy of course: the fainting, the nausea, the headaches, the fatigue you've been feeling. Those things happen because your body is changing and adjusting to the growing foetus. Your body will be producing more of the hormone progesterone which can contribute to the fatigue you've been experiencing as well as the other symptoms. You may have been peeing more and this is because the body's blood supply increases and your kidneys have to work harder to filter the blood and remove the extra waste."

"I have been going to the toilet more," I admit, "But I just thought that was because I've made a conscious effort to drink more fluids during our rehearsals for the show next week."

My gaze drops from her face to her hand pressed against my belly. "You said you have a feeling about this kind of thing?"

"Women in pregnancy have an inner glow about them," she explains.

"So I look like some kind of human lightbulb?" I reply, shaking my head in disbelief.

"It's far more subtle than that, but the second you stepped out of the stall I noticed it."

"An inner glow? I thought you were staring at me because I looked like shit," I whisper, still unnerved that none of the guys have moved an inch let alone spoken a word. They're clearly in shock.

"You look utterly beautiful, Pen," she reassures me.

"But wait, you had your period last month, right?" Zayn finally says, seemingly snapping out of whatever trance the others are still under. Of my four men, he always knows when I'm due on my period, and is always there with a hug and a box of chocolates when I need it.

"Zayn's right, I did. So I *can't* be pregnant."

"How was the flow? Lighter than normal?" Cynthia asks me.

"Come to think of it, yes much lighter..."

"Some women have what is called implantation bleeding. It normally happens about six to twelve days after the egg has been fertilised, and can often be mistaken for a period as it happens around the same time you would normally expect it."

"I'm pregnant?" I whisper, my own hand sliding under Cynthia's as I stare at my belly.

"I strongly believe so, but if you need reassurance I suggest you buy a pregnancy test and make an appointment with your doctor as soon as you can," Cynthia replies, squeezing my hand briefly before getting to her feet, stepping back to give us space.

Tears prick my eyes and I look up at my men, all four of whom are still remaining freakishly quiet. "We're going to have a baby," I repeat, feeling the truth of that sit in the air around us.

"Holy shit. Holy shit, Pen!!" Zayn gasps suddenly, his eyes locked onto mine as he drops to his knees and embraces me tightly.

"We're going to have a baby," I repeat, a happy sob escaping my lips as we hug each other tightly.

"This is the best news!" Zayn exclaims, his laughter and joy triggering something in the others until one by one they each react to the news.

York is next to snap out of his trance, fist pumping the air, he cries, "I'm going to be a dad!" Then he grabs Dax's shoulders, giving him a little shake. "*We're* gonna be dads, Dax!"

"Kid, this is... This is fucking incredible!" Dax says, throwing his arms around York and slapping him on the back before nudging Zayn out of the way and giving me a hug too. His lips meet my ear, and he says, "Kid, I fucking love you."

"All the more reason to go to the hospital," Xeno adds, and my eyes meet his over Dax's shoulder. He looks absolutely terrified, and I know it's not because he doesn't want to be a dad, but because he'll already be head over heels in love with the tiny foetus inside of me, and equally as terrified of losing it.

Shifting position, I push to my feet, allowing Dax and Zayn to help me stand. I feel completely fine, but I allow them this after giving them such a shock. Before I can reach Xeno, York pulls me into his arms, his tear-soaked laughter tugging at my heart.

"You are the most incredible woman, Pen Scott, and you're going to be the most perfect mum. I can't wait to be a dad."

"I can't wait for us to be parents either," I reply, cupping his cheek and pressing my lips against his. He gives me another quick hug before letting me go to Xeno.

"Xeno?" I question gently.

"This is..." he mumbles, searching my face as I reach up and cup his cheeks.

"This is the most wonderful thing to ever happen to us. Don't be afraid."

"But I *am* afraid," he admits, dropping his gaze to my stomach, his fingers pressing gently against it.

"We'll work through this together. I'm okay. We'll be okay," I say, pressing my hand against his, holding it against my stomach relishing the warmth as his fingers rub gently over my skin.

"We're going to have a baby," he whispers, and when his eyes meet mine they're brimming with tears.

"Yes we are," I nod, laughing as he hauls me against his chest and Dax, York and Zayn all pile in until I'm squashed between them in a huge group hug.

"You might want to give her space to breathe," Cynthia laughs. "Oxygen is terribly important for mother and child."

They all step back, grinning stupidly as Cynthia steps towards me, taking both my hands in hers.

"If you're okay with it. I'll pop over to see you before the performance next week. I've got some stuff you can take that will help with your symptoms and will also help promote a healthy pregnancy. I'll ask Connall to bring it with him when he comes with Faith."

"Thank you, I'd appreciate that," I reply, hugging her to me.

"Oh no, there'll be no performance now," Xeno says, shaking his head as we pull apart.

"Why ever not?" I reply, frowning as the others exchange looks.

"You're pregnant."

"Yes, I'm pregnant. I'm not sick, Xeno. Dancing isn't going to hurt the baby, is it?" I ask, looking to Cynthia for reassurance.

"At this stage, absolutely not. Might get a bit trickier in the final trimester. Believe me, carrying another human life tends to get a bit cumbersome especially if, like me, you're prone to birthing giants. At that point I'd recommend gentle exercise, lots of stretching to keep supple and a *slow* dance or two." she suggests.

"See," I say, relieved that it won't affect our performance next week.

When Xeno opens his mouth to protest, I shake my head. "We're going ahead. I need this, Xeno. We *all* do."

"Just keep your fluids up, eat regular healthy meals, and rest when you need to," Cynthia advises. "There's no need to stop doing what you love, just be sensible about it."

"Are you sure this is okay?" Dax asks, chewing on the inside of his cheek.

Cynthia rests her hand on his arm, squeezing gently. "Women have been carrying babies and kicking arse since the beginning of time. We're not fragile."

"That's fair," he acknowledges before wrapping his arm around my shoulder and pressing a kiss against my head. "Shall we get out of here, Kid?"

"Would you mind? I just want to go home, let the news sink in," I say before looking back at Cynthia. "Will you do me a favour and let us tell everyone when we're ready?"

Cynthia grins. "Your secret's safe with me. I'll make your excuses."

"Thank you. Truly," I reply.

"See you soon," she says, hugging me briefly before pulling open the door and stepping out into the hallway.

The second she's gone I place my hand over my stomach, this sudden well of emotion bubbling up my chest as one by one the loves of my life place their hand over mine.

"I already love this baby so much," I whisper, choking up.

"Forever," Xeno adds, with this fierce kind of love burning in his eyes.

"And always," we all respond, just as fiercely.

FIFTEEN

Make You Feel My Love

ZAYN

"HOW MUCH LONGER?" Xeno asks, pacing back and forth in the kitchen as the rest of us hover over the thin white stick on the countertop. Right now the little window that will either say *pregnant* or *not pregnant* remains stubbornly blank.

"It's only been a minute," York says, eyes wide with excitement as he looks over at me. "Two more minutes to go, yeah?"

"The instructions said we should wait the full three minutes."

"Fuck, not sure if I can take the wait," Dax says, chewing on his fingernail as Pen leans into my side, her arms wrapped around my waist. "This is the worst kind of torture."

"What if Cynthia was wrong?" she asks. "I'm already in love with this baby. I don't think I'll be able to take it if I find out I'm not actually pregnant."

"She's not wrong," I say, turning Pen in my arms and cupping her cheeks in my palms. "You're carrying our baby. I know it."

"But what if she is?" Pen insists, blinking up at me, her eyes welling with tears. They spill over her lashes, and I gently wipe them away with the pads of my thumbs.

"Then we make a baby. Tonight. Right now. If that test is negative, we will make love until you are so full of our cum, there isn't a possibility that you're not pregnant by the end of the damn night."

Pen laughs softly. "It doesn't work like that. There's only a small window of opportunity in a woman's cycle that pregnancy can occur."

"Then we stay in the bedroom until that time. We will eat, sleep and fuck over and over again," Xeno says, striding over to us both. I step back, giving him some room as he hugs her close. "Whatever it takes, we'll have our family."

"I'm down for that," York says, grinning widely. "Second best thing to having a baby is making one."

"Dax?" I question, needing to know he's on board too, that if this test is negative, then we put a smile back on Pen's face, whatever it takes.

"There's nothing in this world that would stop me," he agrees, jumping when the timer on his mobile goes off. He snatches up the pregnancy test, fisting it. "Fuck. It's time."

All eyes are on the white stick gripped in his hand. "Are you going to tell us the result?" I ask, blowing out a nervous breath.

"Just give me a second," he replies, clearing his throat.

"Jesus fuck, Dax," York snaps, scraping a hand over his face as he stares at Dax's clenched fist.

"Dax, please?" Pen whispers as Xeno hauls her against his chest, his voice stolen as we wait.

"Okay, fuck. Here goes," Dax replies, his fingers unfurling as he looks at our future resting there in his palm. Seconds pass, the silence only broken by a sob escaping his lips. When he looks up, the undeniable truth is written all over his face.

Cynthia was right.

She's pregnant.

With tears dripping over his lashes he nods once, his gaze burning into Pen with an intense, undying love. "Come here, Kid," he says, holding his arms wide.

She walks right into them, her happy sobs making unfamiliar tears well in my own eyes as he folds himself around her, pressing kisses into her hair. "Fuck, I love you. I love you so damn much," he says.

Xeno approaches them, his voice thick and unsteady with emotion. "Can I see?"

Dax nods, and their eyes meet as he holds out the test. A fierce kind of love passes between them as Xeno takes it, lips parting slightly as he releases a breath, before silently passing it to me.

Right there in bold is our happy future.

Pregnant.

"This is the best fucking news," York says, smiling broadly as he takes the test from my hands and stares at it in wonder. "This kid is going to be *so loved.*"

Without hesitation, I pull him into my arms, holding my best friend as we both contemplate how our lives are going to change, and how fucking lucky we are for it.

"So what now?" York asks, swiping at his eyes.

"We should make an appointment with the doctors," Xeno says, reaching for his mobile phone, and tapping in the number.

"Mate, it's ten o'clock at night on a Saturday. The doctor's office won't be open until Monday morning," Dax reminds him.

"Shit, of course," he smiles ruefully, swiping a shaking hand through his hair. "Does anyone else feel completely overwhelmed?"

"Yes, but so happy," Pen adds, stepping out from Dax's embrace and taking Xeno's hands in hers, kissing his knuckles. "I'm so happy, Xeno."

"Me too, my love. Me too," Xeno replies, "Doesn't mean I'm not scared shitless though. I'm fucking terrified."

"I'm terrified too," Dax admits. "Terrified and excited."

"I third that," York adds, shifting from one foot to the other, his emotions overflowing.

"Zayn?" Pen asks, looking at me.

"Of course I feel the same. This is a huge deal. We're bringing another human soul into this world, and that is a massive responsibility," I say, trying to find the right words to articulate how I feel.

"How the hell do people do this?" York asks, scrubbing a hand over his face. "I'm already feeling protective over our child and the little nugget hasn't even been born yet."

"Nugget?" Pen laughs.

"Yeah, our precious little nugget," York says with a shrug.

"We learn as we go along," I reply.

Dax scrapes a hand over his face. "What if we fuck up?"

"Not if, but when," I say, with a small laugh. "We're going to fuck up. We're going to make mistakes, but I also know that we'll learn from them. Together. We'll support each other, we'll guide each other, we'll learn together so that we can be the best dads this kid could wish for."

"But what if I'm–" Dax's jaw grits, and I know what he's finding difficult to say. We all do.

"Never, Dax. You won't ever be like your dad, just like I will never be like my mother," Pen says vehemently. "You are good. You are kind. You are thoughtful. You are not your father."

He nods, swallowing hard. "You're right, I'm nothing like him."

"We all have our own baggage, our own trauma, but that doesn't define us," I add, understanding his fears, feeling my own swell inside of me. "But we're our own men, and I know without a shadow of a doubt that we'll be fucking amazing dads. This kid will feel our love every day of its life. There's nothing we wouldn't do to make our little nugget happy. That I know for certain."

"Of course you will," Pen cries, throwing herself into my arms and kissing me. "You'll make an amazing dad to our baby girl. You *all* will."

"Girl?" Xeno questions, tipping his head to the side.

"Just call it a hunch," Pen replies, smiling softly. A smile that soon turns into a yawn.

"Maybe you should get to bed?" I suggest. "It's been a long day."

"I think I'd like a bath first, if that's okay? Then I wouldn't mind a good eight hours of sleep."

"Of course it's okay. Come on, I'll run it for you," I say.

Pen hugs each of the guys in turn, then we head out of the kitchen. Less than five minutes later the bath is filled with warm water and Pen's favourite rose bath oil. I dip my hand into the water, checking the temperature one last time before calling out to Pen.

"It's ready," I say.

"Thank you for this," Pen says, stepping naked into the bathroom, her hair piled up on her head in a messy bun. Maybe it's all in my mind, but I think I see that glow Cynthia was talking about. It's behind her eyes, in the flush of her cheeks, the warmth of her smile. It's in the rise and fall of her chest, and the pink blush of her lips.

"Anything for you," I reply, taking her hand as she steps into the bath.

"This feels amazing," she sighs, lowering herself into the water.

Taking a seat on the chair next to the tub, we sit in peaceful silence as Pen hums to herself, rubbing body wash into her skin. When she's satisfied that she's clean, Pen lays back against the porcelain tub and closes her eyes with a soft, contented sigh. She doesn't ask me to leave, and I remain seated next to her enjoying her proximity without the need to fill the silence.

For the most part, our relationship has been built on deep conversations where we spend hours talking about both the big and the little things. Tonight, however, we are both content to sit in each other's company without the need to speak. There's a freedom in that silence, a deep understanding of each other. It suits me just fine because it allows me a moment to gather my thoughts.

Dipping my hand into the water, I study the contours and curves of the woman I love. Her face is free from make-up, her dark lashes feathering against the tops of her cheeks as she rests. Her skin is clear and her cheeks rosy, matching the colour of her lips. As my gaze slowly drops, I watch the gentle rise and fall of her chest as the water laps at her breasts. They seem a little fuller somehow, and as my gaze roams I can't help but notice the slight roundness of her belly. Not a bump per se, because it's too early for that, but a thickening I guess.

"Hello, little nugget, I'm one of your daddies," I whisper, kissing my hand and leaning forward so that I can press it to her tummy, imagining the tiny life growing inside her womb, safe and warm.

Pen's eyes flicker open as she looks up at me. Smiling softly, she says, "I know we've talked about this before but I just want to reiterate that as far as I'm concerned you're all her father no matter whose DNA runs in her veins."

"I agree," I reply, bending over Pen and dropping a kiss to her lips. "We've always said that if you were ever to fall pregnant that none of us would want a paternity test. The only reason we would request one is if it were needed for a medical emergency, but other than that we all know from experience that blood doesn't make you a dad, love does."

"That's beautiful."

"Only because it's true," I murmur, lowering my lips to hers in a gentle kiss.

She kisses me back, her mouth parting as she tenderly strokes her tongue against mine, and as much as I want to fall into this kiss, to haul her into my arms, take her to bed and make love to her, I have to physically force myself not to. Right now what she needs most of all is sleep, and that's what she'll get.

"Can I ask you to do something for me, Zayn?" Pen asks when I reluctantly pull back, removing my hand from her stomach.

"Anything."

"I don't want to be treated with kid gloves. Today, I saw this fierce protectiveness in all of you, and I understand why you feel that way, but it'll drive me crazy if I'm treated like I'm breakable. I'm not. I'm pregnant. If this body has the strength to grow a baby, to carry a life, it's strong enough to do all the things it did before falling pregnant, and I need to be able to do that."

"I think York and Dax can be talked around," I say, understanding where she's coming from. "But Xeno...?" I wince.

"Will have you to guide him," she finishes, rising out of the water. Taking my proffered hand, she steps onto the bath mat, and allows me to wrap a towel around her shoulders. "Tonight I'm going to get a good night's sleep. Tomorrow we go back to rehearsing. We have a performance in a week's time and I refuse to cancel. No arguments, okay?"

"You're the boss," I say, pressing a kiss against her head.

"Damn straight," she replies, a joyful smile spreading across her face. "And when this baby comes, I'll be a *mum*."

SIXTEEN

Say You Won't Let Go

PEN

STANDING ALONE in the middle of our dance studio, wearing nothing but my white cotton underwear, I stare at my reflection in the row of mirrors before me. My hair hangs loose over my shoulders, as spots of colour sit high on my cheeks. My eyes are bright from a rested sleep, and my lips are parted on a contented breath as I rest my hands on my stomach, fingers feathering over my skin.

I see it.

That glow.

Just like Cynthia had said.

My happiness seeps from the inside out. It's buried deep inside my womb, a tiny beating heart within a tiny forming body.

My baby. *Our* baby.

Our precious little nugget.

"I love you so much," I whisper, dropping my gaze to my stomach, feeling infinitely stronger for carrying our precious cargo despite how tired I've been feeling these past few weeks.

There's a strength in knowing what my body is creating, and I know that I can deal with more sickness and fatigue, more headaches and lightheadedness knowing what it's all for. My fingertips brush over my abdomen as I stare at my reflection, both stunned and happy that I'm carrying this new life.

"You'll be so loved. So adored by so many people. You have four dads who will protect and love you as fiercely as they do me. Together we will teach you what it means to be happy. Truly, deeply, joyously happy," I say vehemently. "You will never need to fear us. I will *never* hurt you. Not ever, sweet baby. I cannot wait to hold you in my arms, to sing you lullabies, to make you smile, and laugh. I can't wait to teach you how to talk, to walk, to *dance.*"

I laugh then, happy tears pricking my eyes at the thought.

"For now, little nugget, I'll dance with you encased safely in my womb, and through our shared blood, and the beats of my heart you will know what it means to find your true joy in life." With one last glimpse at myself in the mirror, I say, "Play *Say You Won't Let Go* by James Arthur."

As the guitar intro begins, I close my eyes, swaying my body to the beat. I don't think about the steps, I just feel the music as it guides me to move. With no other thought in my head other than wanting to dance, I rise up onto the balls of my feet, twirling slowly in a circle, my arms floating at my side just like I remember doing when I was a child imitating a prima ballerina.

The lyrics soon join the music as James Arthur's soulful voice sings about two kids experiencing their first, undeniable stirrings of love. It reminds me of that night I stepped into 15 Jackson street, meeting the Breakers for the very first time, how fate had brought me to their door, and how over time, we formed a deep and everlasting love.

As I sway to the rhythm, my thoughts wander to all the things that I want to teach my child, and the wonderful experiences I hope to share with them. I know that they will grow up to be brave, kind, and full of adventure. I pray that they never lose sight of their dreams and most of all, I want them to find the same soul-deep love that their fathers and I share with each other.

With those thoughts brimming inside of me, I glide across the floor as I spin and twirl like a dandelion seed blown across a field, just like those wishes I'd made on a childish breath. And even though my little nugget is too small for me to feel, I imagine her dancing within me, our hearts beating in perfect sync.

Throwing my arms wide, I run then jump into a split leap, floating through the air momentarily, the studio blurring around me as I'm transported to another place, a place where I'm lost in the magic of the music and my dreams for the future.

Landing on the warm wood, I rock on my feet, imagining

that I'm holding a beautiful baby girl with dark curly hair in my arms. She's smiling up at me as I stare down at her, her perfect rosebud mouth parted on a soft breath.

Then as my arms fall away, I take a few steps forward, my hand reaching out to the side as I look down at the sweet, innocent smile of a toddler sliding her palm into mine. With each step, that child grows into a small child then a headstrong teenager who breaks away from the love of her parents to find out who she is. Performing a pirouette, I imagine her life unfurling around me like images in a zoetrope. With every turn she grows from a toddler, to a child, to a teenager into a confident young woman travelling the world, experiencing all it has to offer. I see her experiencing the hills and valleys of what it means to fall in love. I see her pursuing her own dreams and building her own family as she finds her place in the world. With every pirouette she blossoms into a fiercely independent, passionate woman with her whole future waiting for her.

A little breathless, my steps falter, and I swear I see the ghost of my grown up daughter staring right back at me. A mirror image in so many ways. She smiles, and I lift my hand, cupping her ghostly cheek.

"Tiny?"

Behind me Xeno rests his hand on my shoulder, and the moment of magic dissipates. Our daughter disappears, but instead of feeling bereft, I only feel utter contentment and joy as I focus on the men I love as they stand behind me.

"You were somewhere else there for a moment. Are you okay?" he asks, pressing his lips against my bare shoulder.

I meet his gaze in the mirror, my heart tightening with love as I look from him to Dax, to York then Zayn. All four of them are still in their sleepwear, bare-chested, hair mussed up from sleep, completely relaxed, utterly beautiful, and wholly mine.

"I just needed to... dance," I say, placing my hand over Xeno's as he rests it on my stomach. "Can we join you?" Zayn asks, stepping in front of me, his hands resting on my hips as I lean my head back against Xeno's chest and look up at him.

"Of course," I whisper as they look at each other above my head, an unspoken agreement passing between them.

Zayn steps closer as my free hand travels up his scarred chest, the tiny silver slashes of healed skin a constant reminder of the trauma he's been through. All those knife fights he was forced to partake in because his uncle was a cruel bastard who ruled the Skins with an iron fist. Thank god that's all in the past now.

With one hand pressed against Xeno's on my stomach and the other wrapped in Zayn's over his heart, the three of us begin to dance. I'm caught between the two of them, held in their warmth, connected by our touch as we move together, gently swaying our hips. Beside us, York and Dax watch on. They don't try to intervene, they simply watch and wait, knowing that my time to dance with them will come soon. We have a rhythm, the five of us, a way of existing that encourages all of us to be ourselves without judgement or criticism. We take turns leading and supporting as needed, both in how we dance, and how we choose to live our lives.

It's what I love most about us as a family unit. There is grace, understanding, and a deep unyielding love for one another that cannot be broken no matter what life throws at us.

I may be the centre of this family, but the four of them are the cornerstones. Without each other we'd crumble.

"Last night whilst you were sleeping, we talked," Zayn says, releasing my hip, and twirling me in their arms so that I face Xeno now.

"What about?" I ask, as Xeno holds one of my hands in his, his arm wrapped around my back as we fall into the sultry rhythm of bachata. I feel Zayn at my back, his hands resting back on my hips, following our steps.

"Everything. Our roles as fathers, providers, lovers," Xeno explains.

"How we divide our time with you and the baby, how we want to spend it together as a family," Zayn adds, pressing his lips against my ear, kissing me gently.

"And what did you decide?" I ask, as Zayn steps back and York takes his place.

I feel the heat of his chest seep into my skin as he towers over me and says, "That we will all take an equal share in our role as a father. That we will be conscious of each other's needs, that we will have open communication at all times," York explains, sliding his arm between us as he hauls me back against his chest and Xeno releases me from his hold with a gentle kiss to my lips.

"We will make sure your needs are met," Dax adds, replacing Xeno as he cups my cheeks, his thumbs brushing over my skin. "In *every* way. If you want to dance throughout your pregnancy–so long as it's cleared by your doctor–you will. If you want to stop working at the club and fill this flat with dozens of children, you can," he continues with a soft laugh. "If you want to keep working and prefer to hand the reins over to one of us as a stay at home dad, you can do that too. Whatever you want, we'll work together to make sure you get it."

I grin up at Dax, pressing a kiss against his lips. "Sounds like you all had a really good conversation."

"We want to be the best men we can be for you, and for our baby," he replies, serious now.

"You will be. You're *already* proving to me what amazing dads you're going to be," I reply.

"But we also want to know what you want, Kid. What you need from us," York adds, as I turn in his arms, my hands smoothing up his chest and around his neck as I look up at him, his bright blue eyes glowing with love and a whole dose of lust, making my breath catch.

"What I need from you right now or in the future?" I ask, cocking my head to the side.

He smiles down at me, understanding the subtle hints of my body as my nipples peak, and I press closer to him, acutely aware of my own arousal.

"Tell us what you need, now and in the future."

"In the future I want everything you all want. Understanding, compromise, laughter, love, a happy family," I say.

"And now, Titch?" he asks, his fingers trailing down my spine, his touch making my breath hitch with need.

"Right now I want you to make love to me. All of you," I reply before slamming my lips against his in a heated, heartfelt kiss.

SEVENTEEN

Sexual Healing

YORK

TITCH STANDS in the centre of her bedroom, the four of us surrounding her in a semi-circle. Her arms hang loosely by her side as she looks between us. "I'm not breakable, you know. You can touch me," she says, smiling gently.

"Not gonna lie, I'm kind of worried I'll hurt the baby," Dax says, running a hand over his head.

"What, with your monster cock?" I joke, shoving him on the arm.

"I mean—" he shrugs, looking sheepish as he shifts his gaze to his dick.

"He's got a point," Zayn says, glancing at the huge bulge in Dax's joggers. "Not sure I want our daughter eyeing that thing."

"Hey, not sure I want her eyeing yours either," Dax retorts with a smirk.

Xeno chuckles, rolling his eyes. "I don't know much about pregnancy—which by the way I intend to rectify as soon as the books I've ordered have been delivered—but I do know our baby is well protected in Pen's womb."

"*You've* ordered books?" I ask, glancing at Xeno.

He nods. "Don't sound so surprised. We need to read up on all the changes that are going to take place in Tiny's body and all the things she's going to need from us to support that."

"Hey, fair play, mate. I'll study them with you," I say, grinning. "I'm excited."

Titch laughs softly. "Number one, I have everything I need right here in this room, though I do appreciate you making the effort to learn about what pregnant women go through."

"You might be the one responsible for growing a life, but we're responsible for making sure you're taken care of in order to do that," Xeno says.

"Thank you, that means a lot," Titch whispers, pressing a kiss against Xeno's cheek before turning her attention to Dax. "Number two. You're not going to hurt the baby, but if it makes you feel any better, we can go slow?"

He grins. "I can do slow and steady."

"Is that a promise?" she asks, biting on her lip suggestively.

"It sure is," he replies, groaning as she reaches for his cock, rubbing his length over his joggers.

"Keep doing that, Kid, and there'll be nothing slow about it," he chuckles, cupping her face and pressing a kiss against her lips before pulling back and looking between the three of us. "Tonight is all about Kid. What she wants, she gets. Agreed?"

"Agreed," we all reply in unison.

"So what do you want, Pen?" Zayn asks, his heated gaze roving all over her body. "Because right about now I'm ready to give you the fucking world just to get a taste of your lips."

"That's an awful lot," she replies, stepping towards him, a sensual smile pulling up her lips. "But for now, you naked is a good start." Reaching for the waistband of his joggers, she gently snaps the band against his abs.

"That I can do," he smirks, pushing his joggers over his thighs, and kicking them off. He fists his dick, completely relaxed in our presence. "Now what?"

Titch steps towards him, her fingertips running down his chest and abs until she reaches for his balls, her palm cupping them gently.

"Now you *all* get undressed," she orders, never taking her eyes off of Zayn as she fondles his balls and he fists his dick. Then with her free hand, she reaches up and pulls his head towards her, "Kiss me, Zayn."

Without a moment's hesitation he wraps his arms around her waist and hauls her up into his arms, planting an unforgiving kiss against her lips. She moans into his mouth, her legs wrapped tightly around his back as she melts into him.

"Fuck, Pen. I need you so much," he grinds out as she presses her pussy against his abs and kisses him messily, all lips and tongue and passion. "I want to taste you," he adds, and she gasps when he reaches up and fists her hair, tugging on it so he can trail his lips across her jaw and down her neck.

"God, yes," she hisses, arching her back and winding her hands around his neck begging for more as his mouth finds her nipple, sucking it roughly.

"I need you all," she moans, losing herself in Zayn's arms, but wanting us too.

"And you've got us all," Xeno replies, pulling off his pyjama bottoms, his erection bobbing with the movement.

With arousal coursing through our veins, the rest of us strip away our inhibitions alongside our clothing until we stand before each other totally exposed. My gaze flits from the hard plains of Dax's tattooed chest, to Zayn's perfect fucking arse and Xeno's beautiful arms. There's no denying they turn me on too, that I've always felt an attraction towards the four of them, that's been blatantly obvious over the years, but that's never gotten in the way of my absolute devotion to Titch.

She's our queen, and the centre of our universe. Her power over us is so strong that I always feel myself being inexorably pulled into her orbit when we're together, loving each other like this. My desire for her intoxicates me as it always does. She turns me on so fucking much, and tonight there's something infinitely deeper, something wilder, more potent between us than ever before. I can feel their energy, Xeno's, Dax's and Zayn's. I can feel their need and love for Titch.

It's huge. Powerful.

Sure, I might enjoy giving head, and fisting my best friends' cocks until they come, but it's always been Titch first. Always. No one else sets my soul alight like she does, no one else makes my heart swell with love and joy like Titch.

I love her so fucking much.

And I love this family we've built, the five of us.

"Put her down, Zayn," I say, pressing an affectionate kiss against the curve of his neck to get his attention. My cock rests against the crack of his arse, and I can't help but rock my hips against him, craving human contact, and the love we all share for each other.

Titch's gaze meets mine as she leans forward and kisses me over Zayn's shoulder. "I love you," she says.

"I love you too, Titch," I reply against her lips, before licking up Zayn's neck and biting on his ear knowing it'll turn both her and him the fuck on.

She grins, as Zayn releases his hold on her and she steps out of his arms. "Seeing as you're all naked, I think I should join you."

Wrapping my arms around Zayn's chest, and continuing to trail kisses across his shoulder and up his neck, I watch as Titch reaches behind her back to unfasten her bra, allowing it to slide down her arms and to the floor. Licking her lips her gaze flickers between us as she slowly brings her hands up over her stomach towards her breasts.

"They feel different already," she says, gently cupping them.

"They hurt?" Xeno asks, frowning.

"Just a little tender," she admits, dropping her hands as she slides her fingers under the waistband of her knickers and slowly pushes them over her hips. As the fabric puddles at her feet, she steps out of them, revealing her beautiful body to us all.

"What will make them feel better?" I ask, still holding Zayn in my arms.

She meets my heated gaze, understanding my intention. "Watching you fist Zayn might help to take my mind off it."

Zayn chuckles, placing his hand over mine and guiding it towards his cock. "Consider it done."

"Like this?" I question, fisting him as my gaze drops from her pert breasts to the darker areola of her nipples, and slowly falls to the curve of her hips and stomach. Fuck she's beautiful, and not one of us can take our eyes off of her.

"Just like that," she whispers, her gaze fixed on me jerking off Zayn in firm, even strokes.

"Fuck," he mutters, swelling in my hands.

"What else is different, Kid?" Dax asks, leisurely pumping his cock as he watches her, fucking enraptured.

"I'm more sensitive here," she says, her breath hitching as she slides her hand lower, stopping just short of her pussy before falling away.

"How much more sensitive?" I ask, fucking desperate to touch her.

"I could come with the slightest touch," she replies as I release Zayn and step in front of her, running the pad of my finger gently down her neck, circling her nipples but not touching them, then lower still, pausing just above her mound.

Titch stares up at me, her eyes glinting with arousal and lust as I cup her cheek, and run my thumb over her bottom lip. She opens her mouth slightly to suck my thumb inside, tonguing it, reminding me what it feels like when she sucks my cock.

"Are you really that sensitive?" I ask as I slide my index finger lower, touching the line of soft curls at the top of her heat, then dip lower until I find her clit. My gaze flicks to hers briefly, and a small gasp escapes her lips as I play with her clit. I barely put any pressure against it, revelling in the wet heat flooding her pussy, and the way her eyes roll to the back of her head.

"That feels... ah... so... *good*," she murmurs breathlessly.

"Fuck, you really are extra sensitive," I say, before lowering myself to my knees in front of her, her lips parting on a soft moan as I press my tongue against her clit and taste her.

"York!" she cries, her hands instantly fisting my hair, needing something to hold onto as I flatten my tongue against her clit and grip her hips to keep her steady.

"Come on my tongue," I mutter against her pussy, licking and flicking her clit.

"Oh god," she cries as I keep up the pressure. "It's too sensitive!" But as she tries to wriggle away, I hold her tighter, sucking on her clit until she begins to jerk and shake and cry out my name. In my periphery I see Dax step up behind her, supporting her body as she writhes against my face.

"That's it, baby, use him. Ride his face whilst you come," he encourages gruffly.

"York! Fuck, York! I'm coming. I'm coming," she cries, her fingers pulling on the strands of my hair as I lift her legs off the floor and place them over my shoulders.

Elevated like that she's able to rock her hips against my face and I'm able to slide two fingers into her pussy, moving them in a come hither fashion until she releases on a scream, coming in my mouth, her internal muscles pulsating around my fingers.

"Oh my god. That was intense," she breathes after a minute or so, her legs shaking as I place her gently back on the floor, and rise upwards.

Her cheeks are flush as I kiss her, letting her taste herself on my tongue. "Hold that thought," I say, glancing at Dax who nods.

"On the bed, Kid," he demands softly, taking her hand and guiding her to the bed. Positioning himself against the headboard, he pats the mattress between his legs. "Come sit here."

She crawls towards him, giving Xeno, Zayn and me a fucking beautiful view of her peachy arse and the glistening slit of her cunt.

"Fuck," Zayn mutters, glancing over at me, his dick leaking precum.

"She's so fucking beautiful, no?" I say, because it's not a question, more of a statement.

"She's perfect," Xeno agrees, stalking towards her, his knee pressing against the mattress as she settles herself between Dax's legs, her back resting against his chest. "What do you want to happen now?" he asks, as Dax trails his fingers gently up and down the centre of her chest, and Xeno settles on his haunches at the foot of the bed.

Titch looks between the three of us before resting her hand over Dax's and guiding it to her breast. "I want to show Dax that he won't hurt the baby whilst I sit on his cock and he plays with my tits."

"Fuck, yes. Whatever you want. We got you," Dax groans,

cupping her jaw and dragging her head to the side so he can kiss her deeply.

"What else?" I ask, my dick throbbing as I watch Dax gently cup her breast, his thick tattooed fingers in stark contrast to her creamy skin.

"I want Xeno to lick my pussy whilst Dax fucks me," she says, drawing back from Dax's lips.

"Nothing will stop me from tasting your pretty cunt," Xeno agrees, eyes flaring with lust.

"And what about us?" Zayn asks. He's gripping his dick, his thumb smoothing beads of precum over the head of his cock, a feral look in his eyes.

"I want you to fist Xeno's cock whilst he eats me out. I want to come watching Xeno come all over your hand," she says, addressing Zayn then looking over at me. "And I want you to put your dick in my mouth so I can taste your orgasm on my tongue."

"Fuck, Titch, that's hot," I say, moving around the bed so I can position myself next to her.

Zayn hesitates, not because he doesn't want to do as Titch has asked, it's not as if he hasn't done it before, but I bet it's because he's wondering who's going to get *him* off. Can't say I blame him.

Titch picks up on Zayn's hesitation, and checks in with him. "Are you okay with that?"

"Pen, you know I am. What you want, you get. Besides, I'm pretty fucking sure Xeno has been looking forward to me fisting his dick again, right?" he replies, cocky as fuck.

Xeno glances over his shoulder, arching an eyebrow at Zayn,

though I hear the amusement and love in his voice when he says, "I think it's you who's been looking forward to it more."

Zayn stalks towards Xeno, grasping his face in his hands, then says, "Your pleasure is my pleasure... Is *our* pleasure," before pressing a hot-as-fuck kiss against his lips.

Xeno doesn't pull away, instead he kisses Zayn back, gripping his head with one hand, whilst pumping his cock with the other until I clear my throat with a chuckle.

"What about Zayn, who's getting him off?" I ask, stroking my cock languidly, curious what she has in mind for my best mate.

"When we've all come," Titch says, making eye contact with Zayn. "I'll reward you with my pussy for being so patient. I want you to replace Dax's cock and fuck a third orgasm out of me."

Zayn grins, letting Xeno go with one last gentle kiss, before climbing on the bed behind him. "Well, when you put it like that..."

"You know what, I think we need some music for this," I say, smirking. "Play *Sexual Healing* by Marvin Gaye."

The guys chuckle at my choice of music, but that laughter falls away as the music begins to play and Titch shifts forward onto her knees, resting her hands against Dax's thick thighs, giving him a perfect view of her pussy.

"Fuck, Kid. I'm so fucking turned on," he says as she adjusts her position, straddling him reverse cowgirl style.

Kneeling, she looks over her shoulder at Dax, and says, "I need you to guide your cock inside of me, can you do that, my love?"

"Baby, I'm ready," he replies gruffly, fisting the base of his dick as Titch slowly lowers herself over his length until she's pressed flush against his pelvis. "Fuuuuuuckkk," he cries, his fingers curling into her hip as he drops his forehead against her shoulder and centres himself.

"Jesus, fuck, Titch," I groan, squeezing my dick, knowing how good she must feel fisting his cock.

With her chest heaving, she manoeuvres herself so that she's leaning back against Dax's chest, still joined together. He groans with the movement, his tattooed hand sliding up her chest as he cups her tit, rolling the nipple with his finger.

"Xeno, come here," Titch breathes, her hands resting on her thighs, the engorged nub of her clit needing his immediate attention. She rocks her hips, the base of Dax's veiny cock slipping in and out of her an inch or so as she moves.

"Look at how Dax spreads her wide," Zayn says, as Xeno lowers his mouth to Titch's clit and sucks it into his mouth. "Taking you so good."

She cries out, Dax groans, and Xeno slides his knees apart, arse up in the air as he gives Zayn access to his cock, bobbing between his legs.

"Fuck her pussy with your dick, Dax. Take her for us." Zayn demands, before spitting into his hand and reaching between Xeno's legs, fisting his dick.

Xeno jerks, lapping at Titch's clit as he rocks into Zayn's hand.

"That's it, use that talented mouth to get her off," Dax adds with a groan as he starts undulating his hips. "Suck on our girl's clit, and while you're at it, make sure you slide that talented tongue of yours over the base of my cock, like a good boy."

"Fuck, Dax," I say, my dick aching to be sucked. "This is fucking turning me on. Pretty sure I can be a good boy too."

"Mate, you're already a good boy waiting patiently for Kid to suck your cock," Dax grinds out, his tattooed hand reaching for my dick as he guides me towards Titch. "Open wide, Kid. I wanna see York fuck your mouth with his cock whilst I fuck your pussy with mine."

"Damn," Zayn mutters, pumping Xeno's dick with his hand, twisting his fist to add more friction.

Titch cries out, her cheeks flush as Xeno laps at her pussy and the base of Dax's cock, and I slide my dick between her parted lips. She looks up at me, her eyes hooded with lust as I gently fuck her mouth. Sucking around my dick she allows me to set the pace, unable to move her head much given her position.

"Look at you. Look at how we love you," I say, my balls tingling with an oncoming orgasm. "Spread wide, and filled with Dax's cock as my dick slides in and out of your perfect mouth."

"Yes, baby. You take me so well," Dax groans. "Always so fucking wet for me, for us. Xeno is being such a good boy licking your clit, tasting your pleasure on my cock."

"Yeah, he's a greedy fuck," Zayn adds, "Feasting on your pussy whilst I fist his huge cock in my hands. He can't get enough of my hand bringing him to orgasm."

Titch makes a garbled noise, humming around my dick,

turned on by our dirty words, by our shared love. When my dick hits the back of her throat, I grip the headboard to steady myself.

"Shit, I'm so fucking close, Titch. So fucking close watching you get touched, licked and fucked by my best friends," I groan.

Reaching up she grips my dick, flicking her tongue up against the underside of my cock, and I can't help but moan as her soft lips wrap around the head, her tongue flicking over the veins bulging beneath the skin of my dick. With each stroke, my insides coil with pleasure, heat building at the base of my spine as she sucks and fists me at the same time.

"That's it, baby, take my cock like a good girl," Dax says, rocking into her. "Suck York off until he's pumping his cum down your throat."

My focus hones in on Dax sliding in and out of Titch's tight cunt, his abdomen rippling as he fucks her with deep, slow strokes, making me crazy with fucking desire. My balls feel heavy, my heart races as her eyes glaze over and she sucks me good.

"Fuck, just like that, Titch," I cry as she hollows out her cheeks and sucks hard, sending me over the edge, my breathing harsh and ragged as I stiffen, blowing my load into her mouth. She licks up every last drop of my cum, only releasing my cock when I'm clean. My heart is practically beating out of my chest. "Jesus, Titch. Fuck."

"I'm so close," she cries in response, grabbing Xeno's hair, jerking against him, eyes wide with lust and surprise as she comes suddenly with a guttural cry.

"Fuck. Yes. Fuck, Kid!" Dax yells, pumping into her,

coming with her too, his body shuddering against hers as they both reach their climaxes in perfect synchronicity.

Whilst the three of us breathe heavily through the lingering after effects of our orgasms, Xeno pulls back, forcefully removes Zayn's hand, twists to face him, and says, "Suck me off. Do it, right the fuck now!"

"Bossy," Zayn smirks, but takes Xeno's cock in his mouth without resistance, deep-throating him until he comes with a wild cry that reverberates throughout the room.

"Fuck me!" I groan, collapsing on the bed beside Titch who is still trembling from her orgasm, her fingers curled into Dax's thighs as she drags in deep, steadying breaths.

"That was... fucking amazing," Xeno lies back onto the bed beside me, chest heaving, a wicked smile on his face as his own orgasm ebbs away.

"We're not done yet," Zayn says, swiping the back of his hand against his mouth. He reaches for Titch, lifting her chin to meet his gaze. "Now it's my turn to love on you."

Kneeling on the bed between Dax's parted legs, Zayn gently lifts Titch off Dax's cock. He groans, his dick falling to his abs, covered in their combined cum.

"Love me good," Titch whispers, straddling Zayn's thighs with her legs.

"Forever and always," he replies, grabbing her arse and hauling her against his chest, sliding her on his cock in one gentle thrust. Holding her to him for a moment, his mouth searches for hers and the kiss tenderly, her hands twined in his hair, his arms wrapped around her back.

Slowly, Titch begins to move her hips, moaning in pleasure,

her arms and legs wrapping around Zayn as she grinds against him. I can see the slippery wetness of her arousal, and Dax's cum glistening between them as Zayn fucks her.

"Look at what you do to us, Pen. Look at how you please us with your beautiful body, and how you love us with your generous heart," Zayn murmurs, cupping her face and pressing kisses against her flushed cheeks. "You are our everything. I fucking love you so much it hurts."

"And I love you," she declares, kissing him with lips and tongue, with passion and love until she's jerking and shaking, her third orgasm breaking through her body as she cries out his name.

Later that night when they guys are all back in their own bedrooms, I stand in the doorway of Titch's room, leaning against the doorframe as she speaks in low tones with Lena. Her hair is tied back in a loose ponytail, her phone propped between her ear and shoulder as she takes a sip from a mug of tea. She's laughing, so fucking happy, and my heart swells inside my chest at the love I feel for her and our unborn child.

I wait until she's clicked off the call before stepping into her room.

"Hey, you're still awake," I say.

She turns to face me. "Lena called. She wanted to check in on me, make sure I was okay after my *stomach bug*," she says with a soft laugh.

"And what did you tell her?"

"I said that I was feeling much better. That you've all taken really good care of me."

"All that *sexual healing*, eh?" I laugh.

She grins. "Exactly."

"You don't want to tell Lena yet?"

"No. Not quite yet. Not until I've seen the doctor tomorrow and chatted with Cynthia."

"That's fair…" My voice trails off as I drop to my knees at her feet.

She turns to face me, brushing an unruly strand of hair out of my eyes. "What is it?"

"You're the love of my life, Titch," I say, feeling choked up suddenly.

"As you are mine," she replies, cupping my cheek and studying my face. "Why so serious all of a sudden?"

I shrug my shoulders. "This is huge isn't it?"

"It is," she agrees, gently stroking her thumb over my stubble.

"I'm so happy, but fucking petrified at the same time," I admit.

She tips her head to the side. "You know what, I'm not scared."

"You're not?"

She shakes her head. "No, because I have you all, and we have each other. There's nothing we can't face together. We've already proven that over and over again."

Blowing out an even breath I nod. "You're right…" Shuffling on my feet, I stand, sliding my hands into my jogger pockets.

"What?" she questions, rising with me.

"Can I sleep with you tonight? No sex, just sleep," I add.

"Of course you can." Taking my hand in hers she guides me

to the bed, then slides under the covers. "Come here," she adds, patting the mattress.

Slipping in beside her, she turns away from me and grabs my hand placing it over her stomach as I spoon her. "This is our future, York," she whispers.

"I know. Crazy huh? It doesn't feel all that long ago when we were kids trying to figure out our place in the world. Not to mention the fact that you didn't even know the meaning behind the saying, *tickle her pickle.*"

She swats at me, laughing. "I was innocent back then. You all corrupted me."

I nuzzle into her neck, kissing her. "Damn straight. Now look at us about to become parents."

"It's pretty surreal for sure," she agrees.

"You know I'm not sure I'm going to be able to cope when the time comes for our little girl to find the loves of her life. I'm already ready to kill the little shits who try it on."

"York," Titch chuckles. "Let's just take this one day at a time, okay?"

"That's good advice," I mutter, curling around her with a smile on my lips and love in my heart, excited for tomorrow to begin.

EIGHTEEN

Count on Me

PEN

"GOSH, IT'S HOT TODAY," Cynthia says, settling down beside me on the picnic blanket in Abney Park a few days later. She hands me a paper cup of homemade lemonade, and I sip on the cool liquid, enjoying the sweetness followed by the sharp tang.

"It really is warm for late September," I agree, my bare feet digging into the freshly cut grass.

A warm breeze lifts my hair and I feel a deep sense of peace and happiness watching my friends entertain their children a little ways over. Grim and Beast, and Cynthia's three husbands, Arden, Lorcan and Carrick are playing catch with Iris and Faith who are two years apart in age. They're laughing and messing around in carefree abandon. Looking at them you'd never suspect they're five of the most respected *and* feared gangsters in Europe, they just look like any other family enjoying an afternoon at the park.

"It's not how many men it takes to change a light bulb, but how many it takes to cook on a barbeque," Cynthia jokes as she points at my men arguing over the best way to cook the meat.

I giggle. "They've been squabbling for the last ten minutes. By the time they've got the meat cooked through, we'll have passed out from starvation."

"Speaking of passing out," Cynthia says, lowering her voice as she looks over at me from beneath her long brown hair. "How have things been these past few days?"

"Okay. I've been getting more nauseous, but other than that no fainting spells. My guys have made sure I'm kept well fed and watered," I laugh, rubbing my belly over my cotton summer dress. "At least I'm not showing just yet, any roundness can be passed off as a food baby until I'm ready to tell everyone the real reason why I've suddenly started filling out."

"So you've confirmed the pregnancy?" she asks, leaning in closer. I get a waft of fresh lavender and find myself breathing in her scent. My sense of smell is so much more sensitive these days.

"I'm officially eight weeks pregnant," I say with a smile.

Cynthia grins, her smile transforming her pretty face into a beautiful one. Before I met Cynthia for the first time a few years back, I was really intrigued by her story. Daughter of the late Niall O'Farrell, Ireland's answer to Al Capone, she witnessed her mother's murder as a small child and became mute from the trauma. It wasn't until years later she found her voice in the castle of her childhood friends The Masks, then ended up falling in love with The Deana-dhe after they called in a debt she owed them. Her life, and love story, is as complicated as the rest of ours. I guess where we're all concerned, there was no easy path to true love.

"You know I loved being pregnant with Faith. It was such an easy pregnancy..." Her smile drops as she stares over at her little girl. She's the spitting image of Cynthia, with the same mid-brown hair and sweet smile.

"You okay?" I ask, reaching for her hand and squeezing it gently as she swipes at her eyes.

"Sorry, please excuse me," she sniffles. "I'm feeling a little emotional today for some reason."

"Hey, it's okay. You're amongst friends."

She sighs, giving my hand a squeeze back. "Sometimes I just wish life had turned out differently for my friend. She was a good woman. So strong."

"Your friend who Faith is named after?" I ask tentatively. It's the first time she's opened up about Faith, to me anyways.

She nods. "Yes, that's right. I wanted to honour her memory by naming our child after her. It seemed the right thing to do. In our daughter, I get to see a life lived, not one taken so brutally."

"I can't imagine how painful that was. I'm so sorry."

Cynthia gives me a soft smile. "Me too..."

Her voice trails off and I give her a moment to gather

herself, refusing to pry further. I know a little about Cynthia's ordeal with the Skulls from Grim. She told me how Cynthia's friend Faith, who was also kidnapped by the Skulls, passed away at the hands of those animals. Her men, the Deana-dhe, alongside The Masks, Beast and her uncle Connall rescued Cynthia from them a few years back, taking out the entire gang in one afternoon. That story has become something of an urban legend amongst the criminal underground. No one knows the full details of what happened, apart from the people involved, and it's probably best it stays that way.

"Anyway, back to happier things. How's the sex?"

I choke on my lemonade, laughing when Cynthia grins at me. "Pretty insane, actually. I feel perpetually turned on."

"Pretty sure that's what I miss the most about being pregnant, that and the wild dreams. Wait until you wake up orgasming, that's quite the experience," she says, giggling.

"Really? Wow," I reply, shaking my head at the thought.

"Especially when you're not actually dreaming about the men you love..." Her voice trails off as she smirks, looking over at Arden, Lorcan and Carrick who are currently getting beaten up by a four and a five year old, Grim and Beast encouraging them.

"Wait, *Beast?*" I ask, wide-eyed.

Cynthia shakes her head. "No. Grim."

I gasp, and we both fall about laughing. Eventually I contain myself enough to say, "Well, she *is* hot."

"Really, really hot," Cynthia agrees right at the moment Grim makes eye contact. She waves, and we both wave back holding in our giggles.

"Is Lena not coming today? I heard her and Gray are an item now," Cynthia asks.

"They were invited..." I smile over at her, letting her fill in the gaps.

"Ah, the honeymoon period. Totally get it."

"I'm so glad they've finally connected. Gives me some peace of mind to know she has someone that's all for her. He's a good guy."

"I agree," Cynthia nods, and then holds her finger up, as though remembering something. "Oh, before I forget, I had Connall bring some of my tinctures and teas over with him," she says rummaging in her bag. She lays two small bottles on the blanket and two hessian bags, pointing to each one in turn. "This bottle contains alfalfa, borage, dandelion, nettles, red clover and yellow dock. It's super nourishing for the body and rich in vitamins and minerals, including iron," she explains, picking up the small green bottle, labelled *Wellness*.

"How do I take it?" I ask, taking it from her.

"Two drops under your tongue in the morning," she replies. "Super simple."

"Okay, perfect. Thank you. And what's this for?" I ask, picking up the next bottle. It's a dark brown, and labelled *Sleep Easy*.

"To aid sleep," she smiles.

"That would make sense given the label," I grin. "Is this what they call *baby brain?*"

"Yeah, expect a lot of that."

"Fabulous. So I'm gonna need help with sleep too then, because right now all I feel like doing is sleeping."

"Afraid so. You start off exhausted from your body doing this miraculous thing and you end up exhausted from carrying that miraculous baby within you, which always manages to press a body part against your bladder. The amount of times I nearly peed myself."

I wrinkle my nose, holding in a laugh. "Oh christ."

"Towards the end of pregnancy the baby pushes on the bladder *a lot* more," Cynthia continues, "So you get up a million times in the night to relieve yourself. Not to mention it gets pretty uncomfortable sleeping with another human growing inside you, especially if you end up carrying a huge baby who wants to rearrange your organs for most of the night. Anyway, this tincture should help you get a few hours of sleep at least."

"You're not selling this whole pregnancy to me," I whisper under my breath, laughing.

She pulls a face. "I guess it's the body's way of preparing us for motherhood. You'll be getting up several times in the night with your newborn, but at least this tincture will help you get some rest before the baby comes."

"And what's in the hessian bags?"

Cynthia picks up the first bag. "Just a simple peppermint tea in this one. Great for nausea and preventing vomiting, and perfectly safe to drink throughout your pregnancy."

"Ooh perfect, thank you."

"And this one," Cynthia says, picking up the second hessian bag, passing it to me, "Is raspberry leaf tea. I recommend you start drinking this during your third trimester. No more than one cup a day."

"What does it do?" I ask, impressed by Cynthia's vast

knowledge. I mean, I shouldn't be surprised, she invented a drug called Diamonds that alters the mind's perception and heightens sex with zero side effects, but still.

"It's been known to help reduce pain during labour, improves contractions, helps balance postpartum hormones, and has a high mineral count which helps to bring in breast milk for most women. All the good stuff."

"Wow. This is really nice of you. Thank you," I say, my eyes welling with tears as I pop the items in my bag and out of sight of prying eyes. My tears trickle over my lashes, and I give her a wobbly smile. "Oh my goodness. I'm so sorry it's all the hormones."

"Believe me, I totally get it. But you might want to wipe those tears away, looks like the smell of meat cooking has attracted the hunters," Cynthia laughs as her men stride towards us.

Lorcan has Faith propped on his shoulders, and Grim and Beast follow behind with Iris swinging between them. Arden and Carrick take up the rear, laughing at something as they approach.

"That smells delicious," Arden says with a grin, wincing a little when his top lip starts to weep a little blood. He plonks down on the picnic blanket and drops a kiss to Cynthia's lips as the others ask my guys if they can help with anything. "Hey, you okay my love?" he asks her.

"I'm perfect. But it looks like you need some more ointment on that lip," she replies, licking the droplet of blood from her lips, and giving him a look that can only be interpreted as sexual.

"Ah, it's no bother," he replies, waving away her concerns before focussing on me. "And how are you, Pen? Are you feeling better after the other night? Cyn said you had some kind of stomach bug."

"Much, thanks for asking," I reply, shifting awkwardly as he gives me an intense look. The first time I met him in Tom O'Brien's pub when I was with Beast he'd made me feel super uncomfortable, not because I thought he was a pervert or anything, far from it. More because he had this mysterious, almost otherworldly way about him, just like Lorcan and Carrick, the other two members of the Deana-dhe, do. Even to this day the three men are cloaked in mystery.

Though now I know them better, they're a little less otherworldly and a lot more human.

"What about you? Apparently Jakub gave you a run for your money," I counter, trying to manoeuvre the conversation onto safer ground.

"That he did. He might be a skinny fucker, but he don't half pack a punch," Beast pipes up as he strides towards us with Carrick, carrying a huge makeshift ice bucket filled with alcohol between them.

"Jakub's hardly skinny," Cynthia retorts.

"Well in comparison to me he is," Beast shrugs, dumping the ice bucket next to us and grabbing a beer, chucking one to Arden who catches it.

"*Everyone* is skinny in comparison to you," Carrick remarks, nudging him with his elbow, his dark hair falling into his eyes with the motion. "You're a fecking *beast* after all."

"What can I say? I'm more than most can handle."

"Except for Grim. We all know she has you well and truly under her thumb, big boy," York says, giving him a wink as he passes him by with a tray of sizzling meat and sets it on the bench next to us.

"Damn straight," Grim interjects, looking down at me whilst Iris wriggles in her arms. "Would you take Iris for a sec, I need to give Christy a call. She said she'd be here half an hour ago."

"They've probably got her trussed up somewhere," Arden mutters under his breath, and I hold in a laugh at the look Grim gives him. The Deana-dhe aren't the only ones with a reputation. Let's just say The Masks, and Christy, have certain sexual preferences that don't align with the average couple.

"Urgh, please, I do *not* need that visual," Grim says, pulling a face as she passes Iris to me.

"Hey darling," I say, settling Iris on my lap. "I think we should change the subject, don't you? Innocent ears and all that?"

She smiles up at me, completely oblivious to the very adult conversation going on around her. "Auntie Pen-Pen. You look pretty. I like your yellow dress."

"She sure does," Dax says, dropping down behind me, pressing a kiss to my cheek, before patting Iris on her bouncy curls. "Would you like a drink, Kid?"

"Cynthia got me one thanks," I reply, picking up my paper cup that Iris snatches from me and guzzles down. Smacking her lips when she finishes.

"I hope that didn't have any alcohol in it," Beast asks, eying Iris.

"Nope, just homemade lemonade," I say, pressing my finger against the tip of Iris's nose, "With *lots* of sugar."

Lorcan snorts, settling Faith on the blanket too. "Good luck when that sugar rush hits," he says from beneath his baseball cap as he leans over to kiss Cynthia.

"You too mate, you too," Beast replies, jerking his chin towards Faith who's currently tipping back huge mouthfuls of the same drink, stolen from her mother.

"Ah feck!" he exclaims, grasping the cup, but it's too late, she's already finished it.

"Foooooooood!" Faith grins, her nose lifting in the air as she sniffs.

Jumping up out of my lap, Iris rushes over to her dad, grabbing the burger that he'd only just placed in a bun. "I'm hungry!" she exclaims.

"Don't you want Ketchup, sweetheart?" Beast asks, as she snags another burger and runs back to Faith, handing it to her. They sit side-by-side, giggling and whispering under their breaths. "I'll take that as a no then," he grins, shaking his head.

"Pretty sure those two are going to be a handful when they hit their teenage years," Zayn says, handing me a hotdog and smirking in amusement. I give him a smile in thanks, taking a bite.

"When they're older? They're *already* a handful," Beast scoffs, then groans.

"I'm not being funny," York pipes up, his mouth filled with food, "But they've got the genes of you fuc–"

"York!" I warn, eyeing the girls.

"You... *feckers?*" he smirks. "Pretty sure this is karma."

"Didn't anyone ever tell you not to speak with your mouth full?" Carrick questions with a chuckle.

"What can I say, I was practically brought up by those three," York retorts, looking between his best friends. "Not exactly the best influences."

"Err, rude," Zayn replies in mock offence.

York laughs. "Love you, mate."

Zayn shakes his head, eyes smiling. "Yeah, yeah."

"Ah, fuc– *fecking* hell," Beast groans.

"What?" Xeno asks, following Beast's line of sight.

"Two of my worst nightmares have just arrived," he grumbles, just as Grim finishes her call to Christy and we all turn towards the direction he's looking.

Approaching us from the other side of the park are Asia and her partners: Camden, Sonny, Eastern and Ford, as well as Asia's younger brother, Sebastian and George. It's Sebastian and George who are currently Beast's worst nightmare. Which is completely unfair, they're good kids who Iris happens to be completely enamoured with. I guess that's the point.

"Beast, they're family! Stop being so protective," Grim warns, rolling her eyes.

"Georgie! Sebby!" Iris squeals, jumping to her feet and dropping her half eaten burger as soon as she notices Sebastian and George. They're both tweens but clearly Iris doesn't care about the age difference given the way she happily takes their hands, grinning.

"They're a bad influence," Beast mutters.

"Oh for shit's sake, stop being so ridiculous. They're *children*."

Lorcan snorts. "And children grow up to be adults."

"My point exactly!" Beast agrees, throwing Grim a, *I told you so,* look.

"Do *not* encourage him," Grim warns, getting to her feet. "He's being completely irrational."

"Hey everyone," Asia says as we all exchange pleasantries and she and her guys sit with us.

"Where's Christy and The Masks?" Camden asks, throwing a welcoming nod to us all, and Grim and her half-brother Ford exchange hugs.

"They're going to catch up with us all at the Twisted Bullet this weekend. Christy's feeling a little... under the weather," Grim explains, throwing me a look. "She thinks she might've picked up Pen's bug."

Cynthia and I exchange looks, and I smother a smile.

"Which is basically code for *we're too busy shagging to hang out,*" Ford says, winking at his half-sister Grim when she throws a sandwich at his head.

We all burst into laughter, eagerly digging into the food, and as we all fall into conversations, I lean back against Dax's chest, content to soak up the atmosphere and listen to the music from the radio playing in the background. As the afternoon wears on and Sebastian and George entertain Iris and Faith, the conversation turns to more interesting topics. Grim, Ford, and Cynthia's men are arguing over who they think is the best boxer of all time. My guys are talking to Asia and Camden about commissioning an art piece for Chastity nightclub whilst Cynthia is deep in conversation with Eastern and Sonny about the benefits of herbal medicine. Meanwhile, Beast is keeping a watchful eye on Sebastian and George as they play with Faith and Iris.

It's only when the sun starts to dip beyond the line of trees, the sky turning a dusky pink and deep orange that we all start thinking about heading home.

"Time for bed, I think," Beast says, picking up a sleepy Iris and settling her in his lap.

"I'm not tired!" Iris complains, rubbing her eyes and yawning.

"But you *do* look pretty tired," Sebastian comments, his dark brown eyes warming with a sweet smile as he looks at her. "Maybe you should listen to your dad, eh? He knows best."

Beast's brows raise and Grim chuckles. "See, a *good* influence," she whispers, pressing a kiss against Sebastian's cheek, who flushes a deep red at the attention.

Beside him George rolls his eyes. "What a suck-up," he mutters, earning him a dig to the ribs from Sebastian. They start squabbling, and Eastern rises to his feet, glaring at them both.

"Over here, now," he says sternly, taking them to one side whilst he reminds them how he expects them to behave around friends and family.

"Well, I guess we should be heading back to Connall's too," Cynthia says, her arms wrapping around Faith, who is also sleepy and sun-kissed from her afternoon playing in the park. "We've enjoyed ourselves. Thank you for inviting us."

"Short of sounding sappy as fuck," Beast says with a rueful smile, "I think I can safely say we've all enjoyed today too. You're good people. I mean that."

A murmur of agreement goes around the group, and as we

start slowly packing up a familiar song begins to play on the radio. Arden catches my eye, the same strange look on his face he had the night Xeno, York and I danced for him in a private performance at Tales nightclub. Back then we weren't friends, and were coerced into doing it in exchange for information. Today, things are very different. Funny how time, perspective, and mutual affection for the same group of people can change things.

He gives me a knowing smile then says, "Don't think I ever told you how beautiful you were dancing together. It was quite a performance."

"I hope you aren't flirting with my missus," York jokes.

"No. I mean it sincerely. You were *all* incredible."

"Thanks," I mumble, not sure where he's going with this.

"Hey, what performance?" Asia asks, unaware of the story behind what happened. It's not something I've ever talked to her about.

"Pen, Xeno and York danced to this song for me and the guys a few years back," Arden explains, referring to Lorcan and Carrick who were there too.

"I didn't know that. I'd love to see it," Asia says, looking between us. She leans against Sonny, his blonde hair picking up the fading evening light.

"Yeah, man. I'd like to see it too," he adds.

Xeno glances over at me. "I'm not sure that's a good idea."

"It was a long time ago," I say, feeling my face flush with memory. I remember the night vividly. We were under the influence of drugs when we danced to this song and it was an intense experience, one that ended up with me making love to

York and Xeno right there in the gym at Tales. Thankfully, the Deana-dhe were decent enough not to stay for that part.

"Oh, come on. We'd love to see it," Asia persists.

Beast clears his throat. Aside from the Deana-dhe, and Dax and Zayn, he's one of the only other people here that knew what went on in that room given he was guarding the door when it took place. "Don't suppose you remember it all that well. Wasn't it improvised?" he says, trying to give us a way out.

"It was," I agree, even though every single step is burned into my memory.

"Dance! Dance! Dance!" Faith and Iris sing-song together, their childish exuberance endearing.

I swear if I didn't know they weren't related, and a year apart in age, I'd assume they were twins. They have a habit of ending each other's sentences and blurting out the same thing right at the same time.

"Sebastian and George would love to see it too," Eastern adds, his hands resting on their shoulders. "They've heard all about your skills as dancers and are desperate to watch you perform."

Xeno sighs, clearly torn as he looks over at me. "Tiny?"

"Only if York is okay with it too," I reply, looking over at York who shrugs and nods his assent.

"Sure, why not? I think I remember the steps..." He winks, his voice trailing off as he smiles over at me. By the look on his face, I'm pretty sure he's remembering what happened after we stopped dancing that night just like I am.

"Okay then... My love," Xeno says, offering me his hand.

"You've got this beautiful," Dax says, pressing a kiss against my bare shoulder as I slip my hand into Xeno's and he guides me to an open spot in the field. The grass is soft and warm beneath my bare feet, and as the fading light douses us all in a soft glow, York steps up behind me, placing his hands on my hips.

"Ready?" Xeno asks.

I nod, then with a gentle brush of his lips against mine, we begin to dance.

NINETEEN

Waves

XENO

THE SUBTLE NOTES of *Waves* by Dean Lewis float through the speaker, filling the air around us with powerful memories of that night. Just like back then, the three of us are swept up in the current of the music, and the need to move swells inside of me in a rising tide of emotion.

Moving my body in gentle waves, I hold my arms out in front of me, undulating them like tendrils of seaweed drifting and dancing in a warm ocean stream.

Next to me, Tiny and York slip into their own memories as

the music plays, dancing solo just like we had that night when we'd been taken over by the music and the magic of the drug the Deana-dhe had given us to heighten our emotions and perception.

It's amazing how the music playing now takes us back to those same intense feelings so easily. It's like slipping into a welcome dream, and I feel the pull of those memories wash over me as I move, dancing in a current of memories with two of the four people I love more than life itself.

I close my eyes briefly and I'm transported back to that moment when I was high on the hallucinogenic drug, simply compelled to move. I can almost feel the salty water embracing me just like I'd felt back then. I'd been weightless, a mythical creature soaring through the depths of an endless expanse of blue. Today is no different.

Turning in a pirouette, I allow myself the freedom to embrace what I'm feeling and just go with it. I'm driven by instinct rather than conscious thought. The memories of that night come alive and I allow them to merge with the present, moving my body in a way that feels natural, right. My arms flare wide as I dance, performing powerful leaps, turns and spins with a grace and poise I haven't felt before. I'm not a natural lyrical dancer, but there's something about this memory, this song, that enables me to embrace this style as well as Dax and Tiny can.

My body ignites as a hand brushes my arm and thigh, a reminder that I'm not dancing alone. There's a beautiful simplicity to the way we dance with each other, a rise and fall, a gracefulness and knowing. We've been together for so long now, every movement is natural, effortless as we move around each other. We know each other so well we can predict the next movement, reacting instinctively to every turn and dip as we circle one another. There's an unspoken understanding, a knowing, as we dance that is as magical as it is skilled.

Before, when the music began to swell, I'd felt a heavy weight on my heart due to my love for Tiny and the fear her brother would take her away from us. But now he's gone, and I can breathe again. Here in this park with friends and family, we are liberated. I no longer feel the same acute suffocation. We are free to dance, to laugh, to love without limits.

We have formed bonds with these people here today. Powerful alliances built on friendship and loyalty. We're safe to dance free and unencumbered in their presence. We can share a piece of our souls, of our shared history knowing that we'll never be judged, but supported.

"Titch?" I hear York question, drawing my feet to a standstill as I watch his warm fingertips follow the path of Tiny's sudden tears, her emotions overwhelming her in the moment.

Outwardly sharing the same emotions I feel coursing in my veins. My breath hitches, my chest heaving as I watch the droplets slowly track their way down her cheeks. York tenderly traces them with his fingers, before crushing Tiny to his chest, swaying together. God how he loves her.

"We're here. We're with you," he says, and something inside of me breaks free.

A fiery surge of love blooms outwards from my chest and I bolt towards them both, enveloped in the memory of that night and the raging emotions that tore through my veins, just as they do now. York catches my movement, and just like before, he dips Tiny backwards, arching over her as she folds backwards. Spinning my body to the side, I soar through the air, flipping over his back only to tumble away, propelled by my own momentum as I continue to dance around them both.

Out of the corner of my eye, I catch a glimpse of York and Tiny as he lifts her up, her legs encircling him as they spin with wild abandon. She throws her head back, and releases a joyous cry as her hair flies out around her in a halo of deep mahogany, the dying embers of the sun highlighting her hair with gold. I hold my breath, caught by her beauty, and her trust in him.

Her faith in us even through the dark times has never wavered. She is, and will always be the centre of our world, so deeply treasured, loved with every part of us.

Letting go of York's arms, trusting him to keep her safe, Tiny leans back and throws her hands above her head. Fear catches in my throat, but it's forgotten the moment I register our friends cheering and clapping, in awe of our performance. Their approval washes away my fear like a soothing salve, feeling their love and friendship is a balm to my fear, and as the music cascades around us I look over to Dax and Zayn, who are watching us with pride. Forgoing the rest of my steps from that night in favour of new ones, I motion them over.

Getting to their feet, they move towards us, picking up the feel of the dance and interpreting it in their own way. Dax, of course, is better equipped for this style than Zayn, York and me, and he approaches us in a series of barrel leaps that has everyone on their feet, roaring in support.

When the three of us reach York and Tiny, she's back on her

feet held in his arms as they sway together. Her cheeks are flush, and happiness shines out of her eyes like a beacon as she turns and holds out her arms towards me.

"Come here," she whispers, her smile breaking my heart and reassembling it all at the same time.

"It didn't seem right not to include them" I say, brushing my lips against hers as York steps back and I take his place, twirling her beneath my arms before letting her go to Dax who snakes his arm around her waist and lifts her off the ground, turning on the spot.

More cheers. More whistles and claps.

"That was stunning," he says, as she steps lightly to the ground, leaning up to press her lips against his before pirouetting into Zayn's arms, the skirt of her yellow sundress lifting up to show her lean legs and white cotton knickers. Desire stirs inside of me just like it always does.

Swiftly ducking down, Zayn catches her at the waist, and with incredible strength, lifts her up in the air above him as she arches gracefully over his head, her carefree laughter bubbling up her chest in this sweet moment of pure joy.

Slowly lowering her to the ground, he wraps his arms around her, swaying from side to side as he kisses along her shoulder, and right at that moment I feel the truth of who we are. In this field amongst friends we dance as a powerful, unified force. The ebb and flow of our bond moves our feet and synchronises our steps. There isn't a moment when we're not joined in some way. A touch of a hand, arms folding around each other, fingers sliding over bare skin as we lift Tiny, then fall into step, moving in sequence and harmony.

We're carried by the song, the motion, the indescribable way we can predict each other's moves. It's as though a spell has been cast. Our love, friendship, passion and hope for the future stirred up in the warm late summer air around us, creating an unexplainable feeling of power and strength witnessed by our friends. That magic takes over, carrying us away into memories we've shared together. Right here in Abney Park we become so much more than the sum of our parts.

We evolve from broken kids into adults who found love, affection and home in each other.

As the music comes to an end, the sun has almost set, and twilight wraps us all up in its comforting embrace. We pause, catching our breaths and basking in the afterglow of our dance, our friends looking on. It's hard to believe that just a few years ago we were just a group of strangers thrown together by circumstance. Now we're bonded together through hardship and turmoil, love and kinship, brotherhood and loyalty.

Tiny slides her hand into mine, and we walk slowly back to the group. Arden is the first to approach us, and he reaches out, shaking my hand. As his fingers wrap around mine, I feel him slip something into my palm. Pulling me to him he wraps a hand around my back, whispering in my ear.

"She's going to be beautiful."

My eyes meet his and understanding passes between us. "Thank you," I reply.

Later when we're back home, I pull out the piece of folded paper he gave me, unfolding it, and find myself staring into the eyes of a small child, her curly dark hair and bright green eyes so very similar to mine.

TWENTY

No Diggity

PEN

"I'M SO PROUD OF YOU!" Asia says, her eyes bright with happiness and pride as George and Sebastian step off the stage. It's glassy and smooth, a flat plain of black. The glare of the stage lights reflecting from the polished floor making it look like a sheet of obsidian.

It's the afternoon of the competition and Ivan and Rose's troupe have just finished their final dress rehearsal before the big night. The atmosphere in the club is electric as the competing troupes mill around, waiting for their chance to rehearse. To our left, one group of dancers are wearing sparkly leotards, their faces hidden behind a spray of body glitter as they get ready to take to the stage.

In every booth and corner of the club, competitors are chatting excitedly, their ages ranging from ten years old, right up to an incredible dancer in her mid-sixties. Some of the dancers are stretching, others are practising their moves, but what really strikes me the most is the supportive vibe between everyone. It's a far cry from my early days at Stardom Academy when I was treated like an outcast by some of the pupils simply because I hadn't had any formal dance training. Now here I am hosting a dance competition, in a club that I own with the loves of my life, who I'm going to perform with in less than a few hours

Funny how life turns out.

"That was the best I've ever seen you dance!"Asia exclaims as the boys push their way through the waiting dancers, grinning widely.

"You were amazing!" I add, as they beam up at us both.

"Thanks," George and Sebastian reply, smothered by their sister as she pulls them in for a hug.

Tears prick her eyes as she says, "You were incredible!"

"Are you *crying*?" George asks, wrinkling his nose. "Jeez, sis. Get a grip."

"I am *not* crying," Asia retorts, swiping at her eyes. "I'm just so proud of you both."

"Thanks, Asia," Sebastian says, shuffling awkwardly on his feet, totally at that age where he's young enough to appreciate a hug, but wanting to be old enough not to need one.

"Go on. Go and grab a drink. You both deserve a nice tall

glass of something fizzy and sugary," she says, pointing to the bar where York, Xeno, Gray and Lena are serving drinks to the dancers. Dax and Zayn are checking in with the crew who're working the music and stage lights.

"You mean I can have vodka and coke?" Sebastian throws a grin over his shoulder as he and George head to the bar.

"Absolutely not. You're thirteen, not eighteen!" Asia yells, giving him a warning look.

He just laughs and she shakes her head, rolling her eyes. "Teenagers."

"Good luck with that. I know what I was like at his age," I say.

"You and me both," Asia replies, turning to face me as she grabs my hands and squeezes them tightly. "You know what?" she asks.

"What?" I laugh as she beams at me, her love for her younger brothers shining through every pore.

"When I introduced Sebastian and George to Rose and Ivan, I never thought that they'd be interested in pursuing ballet. They've both been such incredible role models, and I'm so glad they've found something they love. I saw just how much they love dance when they watched you and the guys at the park. They were enraptured. Seriously. We all were."

"Thank you," I reply, hugging her. "But just so you know, *you're* an incredible role model, Asia. You *and* your guys."

She laughs, shaking her head. "It wasn't all that long ago I was sent to a reform school because I was a *difficult kid*," she says, using her fingers to make air quotes. "I wasn't seen as anything other than a mouthy, obnoxious kid from a broken home who'd never amount to anything and who'd probably end up a junky like her mother."

"And you proved them wrong. You're a trained physiotherapist and an incredible artist. Not to mention the fact you've provided your brothers with a loving, safe home. You've taken care of them. They're a credit to you."

"Not sure Beast thinks so. Pretty sure he thinks they're little thugs," Asia says, smiling ruefully.

"Firstly Beast *is* a thug," I laugh, "And he's *also* a great father. He's a little protective of Iris, that's all."

"I know. I don't envy the person who falls for her. Beast is going to be the *worst* father-in-law."

"He really, really is," I agree, my attention drawn to Clancy as she enters the club, her grin wide as she waves over to us both.

"Pen, Asia! Hey, ladies," she calls.

"Hi, Clancy. You're about four hours too early. We don't officially open until eight o'clock," I remind her, grinning as she hugs me then Asia, her curly red hair bouncing around her face as she gesticulates widely.

"Oh my god, the energy in here is insane. I can't bloody wait to see all the performances later," she says, her enthusiasm catching as she glances around the club.

"It is, isn't it? I don't ever remember rehearsals at the Academy having this vibe."

"That's because we were surrounded by stuck up bitches. River and Lola aside," she winks.

"Aren't they here with you?" I ask.

"They're coming later. I didn't want to overwhelm Luka—I

mean Ivan—with all three of us fangirling," she replies, pulling a face.

"Ah, so you're not here to see me then?" I ask with a grin.

She pulls a face. "I mean, I love you and all, but he's kind of my hero, so..." Her attention turns to Asia as she bites her lip and tries to contain her excitement.

Asia laughs. "Give me a second. I'll bring Rose and Ivan over."

Clancy squeals, clapping her hands.

"You so need to chill," Asia says, giving her a stern look whilst holding back a smile. "Remember he's a very private person."

"Okay, shit. You're right. Fuck. How do I look?" she asks, swiping her hands over her pretty red dress, nervous suddenly.

Asia lifts a brow. "It goes without saying, you look hot, Clancy, but Ivan only has eyes for one woman and that's Rose."

Clancy bursts out laughing. "Don't worry, I'm not going to jump his bones or anything... not unless he wants me too."

"Girl!" Asia warns with a shake of her head. "You're taken."

"That's true." She grins. "Speaking of which, where are your guys?"

"Having dinner with the Freeds, they'll be here for the start of the show."

"Awesome..."

Her reply dies on her tongue, eyes widening as she hones in on her idol making his way over to us with his partner Rose. I met her other men, Anton and Erik, earlier in the day when they dropped the pair off. They hadn't stuck around for the rehearsal, electing to come later.

Rose seems really nice, and her men too, if not a little reserved. There's nothing wrong with that. I like the confident calm her men seem to exude, and maybe that comes from being rich as fuck, or maybe it's because they don't need to be the centre of attention, and are entirely self-assured. Asia met them when she became Rose's physiotherapist a few years back, and they've been friends ever since.

"Hey, guys!" Asia smiles. "That was fucking epic!"

"Thank you. Sebastian and George are becoming quite the ballerinas" Luka, or should I say Ivan, replies with a controlled smile. He flicks his gaze to mine, then to Clancy who's barely containing her excitement.

He's the epitome of tall, dark and handsome. Throw in beautiful poise ingrained in him from dancing ballet, and an incredible physique, it's no wonder Clancy is salivating over him. Rose's other men aren't hard on the eyes either, one with dark blonde hair and a stoic expression, the other with auburn hair pulled in a man bun on top of his head. They make a gorgeous trio. Of course Rose is stunning too. Asia says that all three of them have demons, and pasts cloaked in mystery. That they're real life Heathcliffe's in their own way. What is it about men and their demons that make them so dangerously attractive?

"So, Alicia, is this your friend that you wanted to introduce me to?" Ivan asks, holding his hand out to Clancy and drawing me out of my reverie.

"Alicia?" I question, eying Asia as she waves her hand in the air and mutters. "My actual name."

"Pretty," I mutter under my breath, smothering the smile at her snort.

Clancy takes his hand, shaking it, her cheeks flaming red. "Hi!" she squeaks.

I don't think I've ever seen her so tongue tied, it's adorable.

"Yes, this is our friend Clancy. She's a dancer too, and works for Grim and Beast at their club Tales as their lead choreographer. Pen and Clancy went to Stardom Academy together."

"Ah, Stardom Academy. Madame Tuillard has been trying to get me to take a class there for some time. I hear it's very good," he replies.

"It would've been soooo much better had you taught whilst we were there," Clancy blurts out. Her eyes widening at how flirtatious that sounded. She looks at Rose, pulling a face. "I'm not normally this..."

"Flirtatious?" Asia finishes, smothering a smile. "Yes, she is. Don't worry though, she means nothing by it. You'll get used to it."

"I'm so sorry. I'm just a little lost for words, and when I get nervous I blurt out stupid shit. I have a boyfriend and a girl-friend who I adore. They're not here right now, but they will be later. River and I attended Stardom Academy with Pen and her guys. Best friends ever since. Pretty sure I've propositioned Pen and her guys several times over the years. Not because I actually want to have sex with them, but because I'm..." Clancy babbles on, her mouth running away with her.

"*Flirtatious?*" Ivan finishes for her, his smile turning into a full blown grin.

"Shit! What must you think of me? Can we start over, please? I swear this is just nerves."

Rose laughs, wrapping her arms around Ivan's waist, as he tucks her petite frame into his side. "That's quite alright. Ivan makes me tongue tied on a regular basis."

"Darling, I think it's you who does that to me," he replies, amusement playing on the edge of his lips.

Pretty sure Clancy melts into a puddle at that remark.

"Well, as lovely as this chat has been, Rose and I want to go over the routine one more time with the troupe," Ivan says, smiling at Clancy. "It was very nice to meet you."

"Oh the pleasure is all mine," Clancy retorts, then slams her mouth shut, cheeks flaming a deep red like her hair.

Rose and Ivan chuckle, and Asia shakes her head. "See you all later?"

"Indeed," Ivan says, before turning his attention to me. "Pen, I understand you and your men are performing tonight?"

"That's right," I reply.

"Well, as the saying goes, *break a leg!*"

I grin. "You too."

With that Rose and Ivan wander off, and Clancy turns slowly on her feet, her eyes wide with horror. "OH. MY. GOD. Kill me now."

"You were fine," I laugh.

"I was very much *not* fine. I practically jumped his bones. The poor man must think I'm a freak, and his partner, Rose... Oh my goodness, if someone flirted like that with my loves, I'd lose my shit. How does she stay so composed?"

"Rose is very secure in her relationship," Asia says, with a shrug. "Those men adore her."

Clancy frowns. "Are you saying I'm not secure in my relationship with River and Lola?"

Asia throws her arm over Clancy's shoulder. "I think you need a drink, one with less fizz and sugar, and a shit load of alcohol. Come on," she says, throwing a look over her shoulder. "You coming?"

"I'm going to watch the next troupe's rehearsal. You go ahead. I'll be over in a minute," I reply.

"Sure thing."

As Asia and Clancy wander off I soak up the atmosphere, my mind wandering back to the first time I performed with my Breakers at Rocks nightclub back when we were kids. It seems both like yesterday and a lifetime ago. Drawing in a deep breath, I let the memories of that night wash over me. The sweat on my skin, the adrenaline coursing through my veins, the roar of the crowd as we danced. Those were the days when we were fearless, when we believed we could conquer the world, one breakdance move at a time. As I'm lost in my thoughts, someone taps me on the shoulder. I turn around to see Zayn holding a glass of sparkling water.

"Thought you might be thirsty," he says, handing it to me.

"Thanks," I reply, taking a sip.

"You okay? You looked deep in thought there." Zayn says, his arm wrapping around me as the next troupe gets into their positions.

"Just thinking about the first time we performed together," I reply, leaning back against his chest. "We had so much fun didn't we?"

"The best," he replies, his voice trailing off as *No Diggity* sung by Blackstreet, Dr Dre and Queen Pen begins to play. A group of breakers step up onto the stage and rip up the dance floor to the roars and approval of the crowd.

"They're really good," I remark, starting to groove to the music, Zayn's body instinctively moving with mine.

"An appropriate song don't you think," he chuckles, pressing a hot kiss against the curve of my neck. "You were always *our* queen, Pen."

"Were?" I joke back.

"Are! You *are* our queen, Pen, and tonight you'll be the queen of that stage once again, just like you were when we were kids."

TWENTY-ONE

No Ordinary

PEN

"YOU READY, PEN?" Zayn asks, his hand pressing against the base of my spine as we wait at the side of the stage for our cue. "I don't think any of us have felt this nervous, or this excited to perform for a while."

Just like Xeno, Dax and York, who are gathered on the other side of the stage waiting to start, he's bare-chested and oozing masculinity. Like them he's wearing black cargo trousers and trainers, his beautiful tattoos on display. I turn to face him and press my hand against the smooth plains of his chest, absent-mindedly stroking his silvery scars.

"I'm *so* ready to perform again," I reply, biting on my lip as I look up at him and see the surge of pride and love in his eyes that soon turns heated as his gaze slides downwards.

"Did I tell you that you look incredible?" he asks, tugging on a tendril of hair that has fallen free from beneath the black bowler hat I'm wearing.

"About a hundred times already," I reply with a grin.

"You really are shining from the inside out," he muses, his hand cupping my face as his thumb hovers over my red lipstick. "All I want to do right now is smudge this lipstick with my mouth."

"That can wait until after," I say, parting my lips, and licking the tip of his thumb.

"Fuck, Pen. Shall we just sack this off and go fuck in the office?" he groans, dropping his hand and adjusting his cock.

"Absolutely not."

Taking my hand in his, he traces his fingers over the new tattoo inked into the delicate skin of my wrist. It's a four pointed star, each point representing my men, the internal star, our unborn child. A child I know in my heart is a little girl.

"I love this so much," he says, understanding its significance.

"Me too. Beast did a great job."

Zayn chuckles. "Not sure he felt the love whilst we were glaring at him the whole time he touched your skin."

"Poor Beast. I ask him for a favour and he gets the third degree."

"What can I say, you're *our* girl, Pen."

"With everything I am..." I reply, my voice trailing off as Gray takes to the stage, and announces our surprise performance.

The crowd erupts into a frenzy of cheers, whistles and feet stamping that has the hairs on my arms rising and my nipples peaking beneath my black leotard in excitement. Zayn's eyebrow hitches, noticing.

"I'm not sure I'm comfortable with all those eyes on you in that outfit."

"It's a leotard, Zayn. Not underwear."

"Yeah, but you're wearing it with that hot-as-fuck cherry red lipstick and it's making it difficult to concentrate. What if I fuck up because I'm too busy imagining you naked beneath me with that colour smeared across your face from my cock and my kisses?"

I laugh, whispering, "Well, you'd better get over that real quick, because we're about to go on stage."

As if right on cue, Gray strides off the stage and the lights go out, making it fall into complete darkness. As the audience quietens, their excitement lowering to a murmur, I walk across the sleek black floor, my ballet slippered feet nothing but a wisp of noise. Zayn follows behind me, bringing with him our one and only prop, a wooden chair, which he places on the stage.

"Thank you," I whisper, straddling it, my forearms pressed against the rail of the chair with my hands crossed over one another.

"Good luck, my love," he murmurs in response before going to join Xeno, Dax, and York who are all standing in the shadows.

Taking a deep breath, I close my eyes as *No Ordinary* by Labrinth begins to play, and the spotlight gradually pushes back the darkness around me, highlighting me in its warm embrace.

Time seems to stand still as I blink open my eyes and stare out into the audience, their faces now cast in darkness and shadow.

The beat of the music flows through me, the opening verse washing over me as tingles rush up and down my spine. We went through so many songs before we chose this one. Were we going back to our roots and choosing a hip hop tune? Did we want something more instrumental? Or something more joyous and upbeat? In the end, this song was the perfect fit.

Because, ultimately, there's nothing ordinary about our love.

What we feel for each other is *extraordinary*. It's unconditional, deeply spiritual. Like the song suggests we are devoted to each other, to our *shared* love.

Love... That magical four letter word.

There really isn't any other word as powerful. It's an indescribable feeling to love and be loved. It's an emotion that has tied us together and made us believe that anything is possible so long as we have each other. With love we *do* have a reason. We have a home, a life built on friendship and a passion for dance. We have each other to lean on, to believe in for the rest of our lives. And now, growing inside of me is our future, our happily ever after.

A slow smile pulls up my lips, a feeling of deep peace settling inside of me as I begin to dance. Lifting my hands into the air, I sway my body from side to side, my hands twirling above my head as though reaching for the stars that we were all so desperate to grab hold of as kids.

We wanted a better life for ourselves. We wanted to be free of the pain we lived through, be that from abusive parents, cruel family members or our own internal struggles.

We each had a longing for more.

We were broken kids tired of life kicking us down.

Tired of being battered and bruised.

We wanted something more. Something worthwhile. Something that belonged to *us*.

And now we have it... Each other.

Behind me, Zayn is first to step out of the shadows and into the pool of light, just like he had that day all those years ago in the playground where we first met. He reaches for my wrists still held up in the air and guides my hands around his neck, his palms feathering over my skin as he slides them down my arms in one sensual stroke, resting just below my breasts and holding me there. I rock my hips on the seat, kicking my legs out in a wide split as he lifts me upwards and back so I can slide them together, my toes dragging across the shiny, opaque floor.

For the briefest of moments, his head dips and he swipes his lips across my ear and whispers, "I fucking love you." Then as rehearsed, I let go of his neck as he spins me in my arms and I drop back in the chair, legs opening as he steps between them.

A look passes between us. One I don't think I will ever forget. There's a tenderness in his gaze, utter devotion, and an unending, heart-clenching love. With one sharp nod, he grins, my pulse rate climbing as he grips the back of the chair, kisses me roughly, then presses the toe of his right foot on the seat between my crotch, the left on the rail and launches into a summersault over my head, taking my boiler hat with him. The crowd roars in appreciation as my hair tumbles out around my shoulders in a waterfall of sleek waves, and I let out a light laugh, joy rising up like effervescent bubbles in my chest.

The cheers continue as Zayn performs a series of somersaults into the shadows and York simultaneously slides into the pool of light on his knees, jumping up as his torso gently bumps against my shins. Taking his proffered hand, he pulls me to his side, as we transition into a series of tap steps that remind me of the old black and white musicals we used to watch curled up on the beat-up sofa in the basement of 15 Jackson street.

With our hands joined, feet moving like lightning, dancing with York is such a joyous upbeat experience as we synchronise our steps, practised over and over again these past couple of weeks. My smile spreads wide as we dance and York twirls me in his arms, dipping me backwards. With a quick kiss to my lips, he releases me and jumps up onto the chair, placing his foot on the rail and tipping it forward. The momentum takes him to the floor and once again the crowd cheers as he bends down and picks up the chair and dances out of sight.

The spotlight widens, illuminating the stage with a blinding intensity as Dax explodes into view with a barrelled calypso leap that propels him across the stage in a blur of graceful motion. As he stands up from a perfect barrel roll, the audience explodes once more. I don't need to see them to know they're all on their feet, unable to contain their excitement at the sheer magnificence of his entrance. The applause only intensifies when he takes my hand and I spin on the balls of my feet as he swirls around me, two electrifying forces orbiting each other.

The energy in the room is palpable, and I can sense the raw emotion emanating from Dax as he pulls me against his chest, wraps his arm around my back, lifting me. I kick out my legs, spinning with him as my hair flies out behind me, weightless, free.

It's a wondrous moment, and I'm filled with so much pride and love for this man who has saved me in so many ways. As his steps begin to slow, my toes find purchase on the floor, and with a heaving chest, I reach up and kiss him.

"I'm so proud of you," I whisper against his mouth.

He grins, his hand flying to his chest, his fingers curling into a fist as he beats his chest, thumping in time to the rhythm of our hearts as he disappears backwards into the shadows.

Moments later Xeno appears, stalking me with a slow, sensual sway of his hips. His ability to dance bachata sends chills up and down my spine. Biting on my lip, I turn away from him, close my eyes, and sway my hips in time to the music. In his hand he grips hold of a length of black silk, and slides it over my eyes, tying it behind my head.

Dropping his lips to my ear, he says, "Now dance with me," before sliding his fingers down my spine and resting his hand on my hip. With one gentle push, he guides me and I lift

up onto the balls of my feet, twisting to face him.

My breath hitches as Xeno slides his thigh between my legs, and he delicately traces the contours of my spine. His strong hand intertwines with mine, and I place my other on his chest feeling the steady thump of his beautiful, loving heart.

We move together in a sensual dance that ignites a fire deep within me. With each smooth, passionate step, our hips sway and brush against one another, and I'm left feeling completely under his command, utterly enthralled by his ability to make me feel like the only woman to ever exist. In Xeno's arms, I am his one and only.

As the music builds to its crescendo, Xeno's lips crash down on mine, his tongue exploring my mouth with such a fierce intensity my knees feel weak from pure bliss. If it wasn't for the sudden uproarious applause from the audience I would've lost myself to his kiss. As it is, he pulls off the silk tie and we part, breathless, smiling, as the whole stage is awash in a shower of rainbow coloured stars that rain down from the heavens. They twinkle and glitter, catching the light as York, Dax and Zayn join us. Falling to step with the loves of my life, we dance, our movements synchronised, our hearts beating as one as we move in a series of twists and turns, kicking up the stars, dancing amongst them. No longer in shadow, no longer held back by our past trauma, we dance with blissful abandon, our hearts full to the brim with an extraordinary love.

When the music finally comes to an end, we embrace in a circle of love and deep understanding, our connection so strong it seems almost tangible. Stars glitter in our hair, cascading over the opaque floor turning it into a brilliant, midnight sky.

"We did it," I exclaim, the thunderous applause from the crowd growing louder in a crescendo of sound.

"Together," Dax says, eyes brimming with tears of joy.

"And always," we all reply in unison.

YOU BELONG

LATER THAT EVENING after the contestants have left, we're gathered in the club, toasting a successful event with our closest friends. Surrounded by family, I take a second to look around the room, to absorb this moment and imprint it in my memory.

Sitting by my side are my soulmates, Xeno, Dax, York and Zayn. The loves of my life, the reason for everything I do. Together they've made me the happiest woman alive. Without them I wouldn't be where I am today, whole, happy, complete.

Opposite us sits my little sister Lena and her boyfriend Gray. Happy, content, utterly in love. I can rest easy now knowing she has a love like mine, that she has someone of her own, to grow old with, to love for the rest of her days.

Beside them are Grim and Beast. Two of the most brutal, savage and *kindest* people I know. Their friendship has given the five of us a family we never had. They helped us to put an end to a lifetime of abuse from my older brother, and without them, I doubt any of us would be alive to tell the tale. I'm so damn grateful to both of them. They're deep in conversation with Malakai and Connie, people I don't know as well as the others at this table, but welcomed into our extended family nevertheless. Malakai was instrumental at helping Asia and her men when they needed it, and because of that, and their love for Grim and Beast, they will always have a place at our table.

A familiar laugh draws my attention away, and my gaze falls

to Clancy, River and Lola, three of my closest friends. Their energy, love and devotion to each other is a reminder that love isn't restricted to just a man and a woman, that it can be shared and nurtured in *any* way. Next to them are Rose, Ivan, Anton and Erik, two of them dancers, one a classical musician and the other an artist. Despite only meeting them for the first time properly tonight, I already know they'll become firm friends.

Feeling someone staring, my gaze catches Asia's, a woman who has lived through and survived her own trauma. Our background, and her love story with her own men is a similar one to ours, and I feel a deep connection to them because of it.

"You okay?" she mouths, understanding flickering in her gaze as we both soak up the loving atmosphere, one neither of us experienced as children growing up in homes filled with addiction and abuse.

I nod giving her a smile as I relax into York's side. He wraps his arm around me and chats with Hudson Freed, a man who, alongside his brothers, Max and Bryce, and their wife Louisa, welcomed us into their home, giving us a safe place to stay when we needed it the most.

Huddled together at the end of the table are Christy and Cynthia, two women brought together in unusual circumstances. Surrounded by their men, The Masks and the Deanadhe, their love for each other and those brutal, mysterious men is something to behold. I admire them all for their devotion to each other, for their ability to put aside past differences and to forgive when so many other people would only continue the cycle of hate. Their friendship is a lesson to all of us.

Shifting in my seat, I pick up my glass of non-alcoholic

champagne, and stand. All eyes turn to me as I say, "I want to make a toast." Silence descends and I let out a tiny laugh, overcome with emotion as I clear my throat. "I honestly don't know where to start…"

"We're all ears, sweetheart," Beast says, winking up at me, whilst York takes my hand and squeezes it in support. I grin, then take a deep soothing breath before I begin.

"When I was a kid the only true joy I felt was when I danced. It enabled me to express my emotions I'd buried deep, *deep* down inside of me. It gave me an outlet for my frustration, my anger, my fear. It gave me hope when everything felt so utterly hopeless."

"Oh, Pen," Lena whispers, her eyes welling with tears.

"That's not to say you didn't give me joy, Lena. I love you more than anything," I add. She blinks at me through her tears, nodding in understanding.

My gaze drifts to the stage where Iris, Faith, Sebastian and George are playing together. Their budding friendship, fuelling the words and love I so desperately want to share. "Then I met the Breakers." I smile, looking between my men in turn. "We built a friendship on our shared love for dance. With every step and every routine, we grew closer and closer. I will never, ever forget that night you all welcomed a broken and scared girl into your lives. I love you more than I can ever express."

"We love you," they say in unison.

Blinking back the tears, I continue, "Circumstance tore us apart, and honestly those three years without you all in my life were the hardest I've ever had to endure. But in the end, we found each other again through dance. We healed past hurts, and fell more deeply in love. You are my forever and always."

"Damn girl, way to make us all fucking cry," Clancy says, weeping.

"These past five years since rekindling our love, we've built a life together, businesses, a family. We've found friends that love us, who are loyal and kind, and so very, very appreciated," I say, looking at each of the groups in turn. "That abused and broken girl I once was never believed that this kind of happiness, this kind of *love* could exist. I only ever knew pain, abandonment, loss and fear. I longed for more than that. I was a kid in the gutter who dreamed of reaching the stars." My voice cracks, and I take a fortifying sip of my drink, my smile wavering as tears blur my eyes. "Yet, here I am surrounded by the best people I know. So I want to raise a toast, to you my dear friends, and to the loves of my life, for showing me that good does exist in the world, that love is so much stronger than hate."

"Here, here," Hudson agrees, raising his glass, alongside the rest of my friends who I now call family.

"To friendship, and love," I add.

"To friendship and love," everyone repeats.

"And lastly," I say, placing my drink on the table and resting my hand over my belly, stroking my fingers over the life growing inside of me. "That kid I once was dreamed of dancing amongst the stars, and despite all that she'd been through she knew deep down inside that things would one day get better. She had *hope* for her future."

"Pen, are you..." Grim's voice trails off as I meet her gaze and grin.

"Now, standing here, I understand that what I truly wanted wasn't fame, or a life dancing on stage. It was all of you. *You* are my stars, you are the bold, bright, effervescent light within the darkness. And now as we prepare to bring a new life into this world," I say, beaming at each of my men in turn, "I know that she will grow wrapped up in the same love, supported by you all, our friends and family. She will be treasured for all that she is, and she will know what it means to be truly loved, wholeheartedly and completely. So here's to the stars, and to the futures we create for ourselves and for our children. May they be bright, and full of love, just like this moment right here. Cheers to us. Cheers to Star, our little girl..."

PEN

SEVEN AND A HALF MONTHS LATER.

"REMEMBER TO BREATHE, PEN," Zayn encourages, gripping my hand as the most bone-shattering, body-splitting contraction takes over me again.

"Don't tell me to breathe, Zayn Bernard!" I screech, the pain forcing this ungodly sound to rise up and out of my throat as another contraction takes hold. Through pain-glazed eyes, I glare at him. "This is all *your* fault!"

Zayn grimaces. "Well, I'm pretty sure it's one of ours," he mutters, then cries out as I grip his hand so tightly I'm *pretty sure* I've broken several of his fingers.

Not that I have any sympathy whatsoever, because this pain trumps all pain, *ever*. Either Grim and Cynthia have the pain thresholds of ancient goddesses, or they're fucking liars.

It doesn't hurt *my arse*.

"It's time to push, Kid," Dax says, his voice a gruff caress, as he holds my other hand and takes my bone-shattering squeeze like a champ.

My midwife, Janice, a middle-aged no nonsense type, gives him a soft smile, before looking up from between my legs and fixing me with her stare. "Dax is right. It's time to push, Penelope."

"Don't give him flirty smiles! This is as much his fucking fault as the others!" I shout.

"I wasn't–" she begins, and I feel a tiny bit of remorse for being so rude, until the contraction worsens and then I forget the fact I'm being a royal bitch, and let out a stream of nonsensical swear words that Beast would be proud of.

"Don't mind, Kid. She's not herself," Dax interjects, hiding a smile as he winks at Janice.

She flushes a deep shade of pink that tells me this is the first time she's met a woman with four partners. It's certainly the first time that many birthing partners have been allowed in the labour room, that's for sure. But I wasn't prepared to do this without all of them by my side, so here we are.

"Now then, Penelope, no swearing," she admonishes.

If I wasn't too busy pushing our baby out of my clearly too small vagina, I'd tell her where to shove it. As it is, I'm suddenly overtaken by this primal need to bare down and push with all my might.

Chin to chest, my feet pressed into the mattress, I push with everything I have. I can practically feel blood vessels popping in my eyeballs from the strain.

Damn, this is *hard*.

"That's it, keep pushing down into your bottom, just like that. Chin to chest. Baby's head is crowning. You're doing so well, Penelope," Janice croons, ducking back between my legs to get a good eyeful.

"Pen. She prefers, Pen," York interjects, looking over Janice's shoulder, eyes widening like saucers as he promptly averts his gaze from between my legs. "Damn, that's...*Fuck...*"

His words trail off as he turns puce and stumbles back a few paces, smacking into Xeno who's done nothing but pace up and down the room the entire time. For a fleeting moment I think York is either going to pass out or puke. Neither of which are ideal.

"York, are you alright?" Xeno asks as the contraction subsides, and I draw in a deep, steadying breath. "You don't look too good."

"York is fine!" I snap, pinning my gaze on Xeno who's finally stopped pacing, and is currently guiding York backwards to the chair in the corner of the room. If I had the energy to look at the floor I'm certain there'd be a three foot gulley carved out of the concrete. "I'm the one who isn't fine!"

"Tiny, you're doing so well," Xeno encourages, eyeing me warily, before glancing at Dax for reassurance, fear blazing across his face.

"This is all *totally* normal," Dax soothes.

"Totally normal," Janice agrees. "A perfect textbook birth. Mum and baby are doing so well."

"If you call *this* doing well..." I mutter, dropping my head back onto the pillow, sweat pouring down my brow.

"Don't worry, mate. Kid has got this," Dax says, then turns his attention back to me. "You *have* got this, Kid."

"I bloody haven't!" I reply, tears welling in my eyes and spilling over my lashes. "I need drugs. Just give me an epidural. Sod what I said about a natural, drug-free birth. I need an epidural right the fuck now."

"Maybe we should give her what she needs," York says weakly, drawing in deep breaths himself.

Janice pats my leg. "It's too late for an epidural, I'm afraid. This baby will be here soon. I promise."

Xeno rests his hand on York's shoulder and gives me a watery smile. "See, you're nearly there. You can do this, my love."

Janice straightens up, glancing over her shoulder at Xeno before checking the monitor that's recording both mine and our little girl's heartbeat. "Just a few more contractions."

"A *few* more?" I sob, tears streaming down my face as I feel another bastard contraction tightening my belly in a vice-like grip. "We've been at this for hours... I *can't* do this anymore."

"Yes, you can!" Zayn and Dax reply simultaneously, resolute in their belief in me.

I'm not so bloody certain. I'm exhausted beyond anything I've ever felt before. Utterly and completely spent.

"Can't I have a caesarean?" I stutter out, pain wrapping around my middle as my belly goes rock hard once again. I swear there are no lamaze classes that prepare you for this kind of pain. Throughout my pregnancy I was convinced I'd breeze through labour like one of those incredible earth mums who meditate and breathe through the pain like a goddamn champ. I was fucking wrong. I'm a screaming, sweaty, swearing mess, and about as far from an earth mother as one person can get.

"I'm afraid not, Penelop–*Pen*," Janice says, correcting herself. "It's too late for that now. Baby's coming. This time I need you to really push with all your might, then when I tell you to pant, you pant okay."

Right on cue, Dax and Zayn start panting, and if I weren't in so much pain, I'd laugh at how ridiculous they both look. Ridiculous *and* cute. That thought is soon overtaken by another body crushing contraction.

"OH. MY. GOD!" I scream, as I automatically put my chin to my chest, and curl my spine, baring down with one almighty scream that I'm sure is scaring all the other mothers and their partners in the other labour rooms on this ward.

"Pen, I need you to remember your breathing. Stop pushing and pant for me, the baby's head is coming. The worst part is almost over," Janice instructs, as she reaches between my legs. I'm so numb down there, I have no idea what she's doing.

Panting, I look to Dax and Zayn for reassurance, but both of them are looking between my legs. A sob escapes Dax's lips and tears spring into Zayn's eyes.

"It's really happening," York mutters, craning around Janice to look at our baby emerging from my beaten up vagina. If my head wasn't filled with the rushing pulse of my heartbeat, I could've sworn he then says, "Look how the head twists. It's like something out of the Exorcist movie..."

Xeno swats him, hissing, "Shut up, man. Tiny does not need to hear that shit."

"What did York just say?" I ask between pants. "Am I birthing a demon?"

"No, shit! No!" Dax shakes his head, pressing a kiss to my temple. "You are giving birth to the most beautiful, incredible, little girl. York is just freaking out right now. He'll be okay once the baby is here."

"I think I'm going to pass out," York mutters in response.

"Oh god," I pant. "He's going to pass out!"

"Xeno, keep an eye on York," Zayn demands, then squeezes my hand, drawing my attention back to him. "And you keep focussed on me, okay?"

"Keep panting, Pen. The head is almost out," Janice orders.

"I'm... scared," I reply between short, sharp pants, more tears trembling on my lashes as I feel her head emerge.

"Don't be scared, we're here. We've got you," Zayn adds fiercely, stroking my hand, then croaks, "The baby's head is out, Pen. She's so fucking beautiful."

"Do you want to feel the baby's head?" Janice asks me as I meet her gaze in a momentary reprieve from the pain.

"I can do that?" I stutter out, my whole body shaking with adrenaline.

"Sure you can. Help Pen sit forward," she instructs Dax and

Zayn, who each wrap an arm around my back, gently helping me up. "Now reach between your legs."

With shaking hands, I reach downwards. Janice gently takes my hand, and my fingers graze across a soft head, tiny strands of hair covering her scalp.

"She has hair," I say, choking on the words as Dax and Zayn settle me backwards.

"So much hair," Dax agrees, smiling through his tears.

But I have no time to settle in that moment as more pain begins to build. Instead, I kind of fall into myself, the pain is still intense, but knowing she's almost here, and knowing I have a responsibility to bring her safely into the world, I draw on the last reserves of my strength, determined to give birth to our little girl.

"Okay, the next contraction is coming," Janice says, the determination in her features matching the determination in my heart.

I nod, conserving all my energy for one last almighty push.

"It's time to push, Pen. Give it everything you've got, and your little girl will be here."

Chin to chest, my hands gripping Zayn's and Dax's, I press my eyes shut, take a deep breath, then bare down with all might.

I ignore the pain. I ignore the fear.

I push with all that I am, ready to see our little girl.

So ready to hold her in my arms.

I'm vaguely aware of Janice telling me to keep going, of Zayn giving me words of encouragement, of Dax's soft sobs, of Xeno holding York upright as he passes out. But I'm so much more aware of the strength I have despite the exhaustion, the love I feel despite the pain, and it's with that strength and that love that I do what women around the world do every second of every day, I give birth to the most precious gift of all.

Sobs erupt from my throat as Janice lifts up my blood and mucus-smeared little girl and places her against my chest. She screams loudly, her tiny little fists bunched, her perfect little face scrunched up in anger as Janice grins, and all my men sob with me. Even York is back on his feet, supported by Xeno as they approach the bed.

"She's here. She's finally here," I cry, clutching her to me, pressing my lips against her soft head as love blossoms inside my heart. It's wild, this love. Pure. It's the kind of love my mother should've felt for me. The kind of love that is endless and everlasting. The kind of love I share with my Breakers as they gather around us.

I look at each of them in turn, words failing me as her bleating cries abate and she nuzzles against my chest, knowing instinctively that I am hers as much as she is ours. And it doesn't matter that none of us can form any words, because I know they feel the same way I do, that they feel as deeply as I do. I see it in their eyes, in the tears streaming down their faces, in their smiles, in their utter devotion to us both and to each other.

"Forever," Xeno eventually says, his voice cracking with emotion.

"And always," we reply in unison.

The End...

FORCE OF GRAVITY

Remember Lena and Gray? You do? Good, because here's some super angsty, extra spicy, bonus content for you.

Simply sign up to my newsletter to grab your FREE short story.

Https://beapaige.co.uk/newsletter/

**Please note: to get the FREE book you must sign up to my newsletter (don't worry if you're already signed up, any duplicates will be deleted). You can always opt-out of my newsletter once you've downloaded.

ACKNOWLEDGMENTS

In 2019, I began writing Freestyle. I had no idea whether anyone would want to read about dancers, especially gangsters who could dance. All I knew is that I wanted to write a love story that I hadn't seen before (to my knowledge).

I wanted to read about all the exciting, sensual, upbeat, joyous dance that I'd seen in movies like Step Up, Dirty Dancing, Strictly Ballroom, Take the Lead, Flashdance, Feel the Beat, Magic Mike (you get the picture). I wanted to immerse myself in a love story that revolved around the beauty of dance, and the way it can convey emotion and feeling so incredibly well, just like all those movies I have loved to watch over the years.

It wasn't hard to think up Pen and her Breakers, they came to me easily, forming in my mind as I began to mentally imagine their story. I knew they were special the moment they danced across my imagination. Five tough kids, a little broken, but with a bond that felt incredibly special even before I sat down at my desk to write.

And then I had to write the first dance scene. I had no problem seeing every step in my head. It was like a movie playing in my mind, so incredibly clear, but *how* could I portray that on paper when dance is such a visual art form?

I can tell you, music helped. I'm not sure if this is a 'me' thing, or everyone is like this, but whenever I listen to music, I see a story in my head, actual images, and more often than not words flow in conjunction with the visuals. I write to music always. I invent scenes based on songs. This was never more apparent than when I wrote the Academy of Stardom series.

So, I just wrote what I saw, and somehow, those dance scenes became words on paper. They became the feelings that Pen, Xeno, Dax, Zayn and York had trouble expressing. Dance became the fifth harem member. Those scenes are what (I believe) made this series so special (to me at least).

I've always said that this series changed my life, and it's true. I had relative success with the series I've written before Academy of Stardom, but this series brought me into the hands of more readers than I ever dared hope for.

I have so much to thank Pen and her Breakers for. So much.

The books that followed, the books that came before, and the characters within them have all played their part in helping me to get to this wonderful point now as an author with readers around the world. Readers who have bought my books, talked about them, shared them with friends and family. Who've sent me messages of thanks, of appreciation. Who've been so incredibly supportive.

When I talk about being grateful for all my readers, when I get emotional about these characters and the others within this universe of twenty-five books, its because I truly *am* grateful.

I spent a lot of my life wanting something more, not that I

wasn't grateful for all I had, I was, I am. But I wanted something just for me. Something I could reflect back on when I'm old and grey, and say, 'you did that, I'm so proud of you.' I wanted to leave my kids a piece of me, something they could treasure long after I'm gone.

These characters, these stories, these books, and all the ones I'm yet to write truly are a piece of me, and to be able to share that with complete strangers is a gift that I'm so very thankful for.

This universe of twenty-five books (listed at the back) has come to a natural end. Is it the end of this world forever? Well, never say never, right? They have kids after all ;)

But for now, I'm so damn excited to move onto a brand new world. One where new characters are calling for my attention. And boy, you're going to love it. I have so much more to give, so many love stories still to tell, and the heirs of Princetown can't wait to meet you.

You'll be hearing more about them in 2024.

For now, I want to say thank you.

Thank you to my readers. To you I owe everything.

Thank you to my street team, and my arc readers who have travelled this journey with me. You're the best.

Thank you to my beta readers, Jennifer, Lisa, Gina, Claire, Janet. Ladies, you have stuck by me for so long, and I appreciate you all so much.

Thank you to Courtney, who has been with me for forever. She isn't just my alpha reader and PA extraordinaire, she is my friend, my confidant, and my sister from another mister ;)

And of course, my biggest most heartfelt thanks have to go

to my family. To James, my hubby, who has walked this rocky path of being an independent author with me, and has drawn me some incredible artwork you've seen in some of my books. To my kids who have endured the moments when I've been working all the hours to get these books written, and understood that mum is doing this for them most of all.

And lastly to Pen, Xeno, Zayn, Dax and York, you have an extra special place in my heart, and I know that even when the words have stopped flowing you'll always be there dancing when I close my eyes.

Much love, and gratitude,

Bea xoxo

ABOUT THE AUTHOR

Bea Paige lives a very secretive life in London... She likes red wine and Haribo sweets (preferably together) and occasionally swings around poles when the mood takes her.

Bea loves to write about love and all the different facets of such a powerful emotion. When she's not writing about love and passion, you'll find her reading about it and ugly crying.

Bea is always writing, and new ideas seem to appear at the most unlikely time, like in the shower or when driving her car.

She has lots more books planned, so be sure to subscribe to her newsletter by following the link on her website.

In addition if you love digitally signed paperbacks be sure to check out her website for special editions.

www.beapaige.co.uk/shop

ALSO BY BEA PAIGE

The Deana-Dhe Duet

#1 Debts and Diamonds

#2 Curses and Cures

Grim & Beast's Duet

1 Tales You Win

#2 Heads You Lose

Their Obsession Duet

#1 The Dancer and The Masks

#2 The Masks and The Dancer

Academy of Stardom

#1 Freestyle

#2 Lyrical

#3 Breakers

#4 Finale

#5 Encore

Finding Their Muse

#1 Steps

#2 Strokes

#3 Strings

#4 Symphony

#5 Finding Their Muse boxset

Academy of Misfits

#1 Delinquent

#2 Reject

#3 Family

The Brothers Freed Series

#1 Avalanche of Desire

#2 Storm of Seduction

#3 Dawn of Love

#4 Brothers Freed Boxset

Contemporary Standalone's

Beyond the Horizon

Short Story

Force of Gravity

(available FREE via my website)

For all up to date book releases please visit

www.beapaige.co.uk

To purchase paperback books:

www.beapaige.co.uk/shop